DREAM OF ATLANTIS

P.A. McAlister

P. A. McAlister Books
Medford, Oregon USA

ISBN: 0985474602
ISBN 13: 9780985474607

Cover Design by P.A. McAlister and Alexander Marchand

This story was originally published under the title name of
Atlantis Rising, by Corbitt Taylore - Copyright 2000

To Mike and Greg - My sons…My friends

Acknowledgements

———

Thank you to all my metaphysical and spiritual teachers; you have helped me to change my life. Jane Roberts/Seth, Dr. Jonathan Parker, Louise Hay, Dick Sutphen, Paramahansa Yogananda, Dr. Wayne Dyer, U.S. Andersen, Shirley MacLaine, singer/songwriter/musician Sting, and so many others whose books and/or recordings that have been a part of my life, and have helped me along the way.

And, a very special thanks to Gary Renard, Dr. Helen Schucman, Bill Thetford, and of course, J.

Thank you to my son Mike, who always believed in me and constantly encouraged me to "go for it." Giddyup, right back at ya!

A special thank you to singer/songwriter/musician, Donovan Leitch, who started it all for me in 1968, with his song, 'Atlantis.'

This beautiful piece was written to me by my husband shortly after we had met in December 2004. I love you, Doug…

Our Journey

Separated by lifetimes…and the span of a continent
like a beautiful dance through a movement of music
our journey began

Soul contracts made too far back to remember…
bring us together today

What might appear to be random luck in the eyes of others is really
destiny by design…but we are not just mere pawns in a cosmic
chess game, for we have done our work…choosing freely to grow
and learn through our
experiences so we can be together now

At last we are united…a gift herein, so it is in this lifetime that our
journey
begins
Feeling blessed from above we can walk
Side by side
Hand in hand
Heart to heart
Two individuals with
One mission
One Love

DOUG MCALISTER
COPYRIGHT © 2004

Prologue

———

Atlantis – 10,000 BC

"You must not bring Hollina back! You know as well as I one *cannot* impose their will over another." Jenielle held her hand tightly around Sylor's wrist. Her fingers pressed deep into the turquoise material of the robe he wore. Her other hand touched the sacred medallion that hung at his chest. "You are a High Priest. You know it is against the laws."

Sylor's grip tightened around the crystal he held in his hand; the crystal that would bring his beloved Hollina back to him. "I will bring her back. She belongs with me!"

"Then why did she choose death? Why did she choose to end her own life by way of the transition chamber?"

Sylor looked toward the ocean and watched a sea gull perched on a rock. A sudden gust blew his long golden locks away from his face, exposing his chiseled features. He closed his eyes and took a breath. He knew he could have stopped Hollina. He knew she had wanted him to stop her, but his pride would not allow it. Not until it was too late.

"Hollina erred. Her mind will change upon her return."

"You selfish fool. The woman you summon will not be Hollina. You cannot reach your hand into the future and bring back the same woman. She will be different."

"Yes, she will be different, a different face, a different name. Only her soul is the same. Her soul is my soul, fused in spirit, only to be separated by two embodiments. One day, when you find the other half of yourself, you will understand."

"It may not work. She may not be able to return."

"I know that is your wish. I *know* your true feelings toward your sister, and you should be ashamed. Hollina will return. Do you not remember she mastered teleportation? I recall you made every effort to deter her from that ability. Because you were not at her level, you proceeded to hold her back. And you will agree one has no control over Hollina."

"Yes, one does not. Not even you." Jenielle smirked and released her hold on his wrist. She looked into Sylor's eyes. The threat that emanated from them did not compel her to look away.

She moved in front of him and placed her hands on his shoulders. She kept her eyes locked with his, while her hands leisurely wandered up the sides of his neck. She moved in closer, and brushed herself against him. He swiftly removed her hands, dropping the crystal, and pushed her away. He felt she purposely fell to the ground and feigned injury. Sylor tried to stir up compassion for Hollina's sister. That's what Hollina would have wanted, but Jenielle's drama left him cold. "I am losing patience. I know what it is you desire, and you will *not* have it. Not now, not ever! I belong to Hollina. Go now and begin preparing for Hollina's return."

"She may not desire to return. She may not even know who you are. Or she may, and wish she did not, remembering the pain you have inflicted upon her, remembering what you have become," Jenielle said sharply, as she picked herself up while eyeing the crystal still lying in the sand.

"Do not!" Sylor reached down for the crystal. "Once this crystal is in her possession she will remember our love, and she will speak of this."

"Ha! You may not like what she speaks of."

"Long ago when our soul split in two, Hollina and I made a promise to always find each other if either of us were to become lost. It is the promise all twin souls make to each other. By becoming lost we must work through many experiences, and move toward becoming one soul with no embodiment to limit us. We must come together to blend, to merge, and be joined in unity with our one source. I will always keep my promise to her, as she would to me."

"You speak of promise, you speak of love. But inside you hold much anger, and little forgiveness. It is not up to you to bring her back. She left for a reason, you know this! You must wait for a future incarnation to reunite. Until then, I can take her place."

"*No one* will take her place! And I will *not* wait! She knows where she belongs. When she returns she will stay by my side, and live by my word."

"You are losing your knowledge of the laws. What you do is wrong, and it will have repercussions. Hollina was correct regarding the ideas of the north. Their controlling ways have influenced you. You are not the same. You are a fool!"

"And are *you* not a fool? Are *your* desires not wrong? You, too, are forgetting the laws. Your sister loved you, but what you desire for yourself..."

Anxiety colored Jenielle's face. "You will not reveal this upon her return?"

"For Hollina's sake, I am grateful your intentions were shielded from her. No, I will not reveal your desire. Go now and prepare."

Jenielle moved closer to him, keeping her eye on the hand that held the crystal. He held onto it tightly, knowing it was his lifeline to Hollina. "Do not fight me! My mind, my heart, and the crystal will bring her back. My eye sees it clearly, and my will is strong. Her feelings will surface, and the connection will be made. Her desire will be most powerful. Nothing will hold her back."

Jenielle slowly circled him keeping eye contact. One side of Sylor's mouth curled up slightly. She stopped, and again eyed the crystal. She mimicked his expression, and then quickly proceeded up the hill to the temple. Sylor watched her. He felt pity for her, but not as much as he knew he should.

He turned to the ocean, and for a moment watched the lone sea gull still sitting upon the rock. He closed his eyes and envisioned himself holding Hollina in his arms again. "This time she will not leave me," he whispered into the wind. He walked toward the water and stood where there was a distinct line between the wet and dry earth. He moved a few steps forward. Water rushed through his sandals, though he paid no notice. He gazed up at the orange orb suspended perfectly in the blue that matched his eyes.

He majestically held the dome shaped crystal up to it. The crystal that had once brought joy now brought heartache. It was the crystal he had given Hollina when they were children. It was one half of a crystal ball that contained the essence of his love, his heart, his entire being. She had left it behind when she chose to end her life. Tucked away in his room at the temple was the other half, the one Hollina had given him which contained her essence. It was the only thing he had left of her. His eyes watered, the core of his pain clearly etched in his face. He would now give himself to her again.

He brought the crystal to his chest, and affirmed in the deepest part of his soul that it would bring her back. It must! He believed what we hold in our mind and heart, with clear intent, must come to pass if it is written. Everything fit! He took hold of the gold medallion he wore with pride. Was he still worthy of this precious gift?

He leaned back and eyed the horizon. "Come back to me Hollina!" he screamed as he thrust the crystal high into the air, for it to plunge deep within the ocean where another of nature's miracles would take over. Playing its part, the dolphin grasped the crystal in its snout, and vanished into the hole in Time.

But afterward there occurred violent earthquakes and floods, and in a single day and night of rain all your warlike men in a body sunk into the earth, and the island of Atlantis in like manner disappeared, and was sunk beneath the sea.

(Plato's Dialogues)

Faith consists in believing when it is beyond the power of reason to believe. It is not enough that a thing be possible for it to be believed.

(Voltaire)

Chapter 1

————

Cape Cod – Present Day

Again, she could see only the back of him. The long turquoise robe belted with a fine gold tie, the blonde shoulder-length hair, and his tall slim stature. She kept screaming at him, "Turn around, turn to me!"

She could feel his arrogance, his ego in full bloom, as she eyed him up and down, all six feet of him. Again she made her demand. She longed to see his face, the face that roused the womanly flame inside her.

As he was about to turn and grace her with his magnificence, she abruptly awoke. "Damn it! Not again!" Lisa Burke half opened one eye and checked the time; 7:23 a.m. She let out a deep breath and moaned. Four hours sleep was not enough. She turned over on her stomach, hugged the pillow, and began thinking about the recurring dream she'd been having.

It started about a month before, ever since she asked Dave, her husband of twenty two years, to leave. The dream always left her with an ache in her heart. She could see the robed one clearly in her mind. She wanted so much to stroke his sunlit hair. There was something about the strands of shimmering silky light that beckoned her touch.

Tears filled her eyes as she recalled standing behind him feeling his highly charged aura. A faint scent of vanilla permeated the air around him, making her breath deeper. She wanted to inhale his breath with him, so to take his essence into herself.

The robe he wore seemed to naturally suit him, and would place him at another time in the past. Whoever he was, she knew she loved him deeply. But how could a dream, something beyond reality, bring up such intense emotion? How could she be in love with someone she had never seen…someone that wasn't even real? Yet, a voice inside whispered to her that he was *very* real.

Her petite body jerked when the phone began to ring. She wondered why the answering machine wasn't picking up, and then remembered it hadn't been working…like her life. As she reached for the phone her hand brushed against the quartz crystal she had found on the beach the day after Dave left. She shivered, remembering what had happened when she first held it.

She had barely uttered hello when a deafening voice sang, "It's time to wake up! It's time to wake up!" The voice sounded familiar to her but, still being in the alpha state, Lisa's left brain failed her.

"Who is this?" Still singing, the voice quoted Emerson, "It is one of the blessings of old friends that you can afford to be stupid with them."

"Karen! It is so good to hear from you," Lisa said, half lying. Guilt befell her as she hadn't been in touch with her childhood friend for almost two years. Actually, she was sort of avoiding her.

"Oh sure it is," Karen said snidely. "I haven't heard from you since your last book came out. Don't you ever answer your phone? And why haven't you returned my calls? I've left at least a dozen messages in the last three months."

"I know, I know. I'm sorry." Lisa rubbed her eyes and let out a sigh. She felt she didn't need this first thing in the morning, especially with so little sleep, *and before coffee*! But, in a way she was glad Karen caught her. It *had* been too long.

"So what's wrong?" Karen asked.

"What do you mean?" Lisa dreaded the thought of spilling her guts.

"You haven't changed a bit," Karen said sarcastically. "Still clamming up when you have a problem. But thinking back on it I don't believe you've ever had a *real* problem in your life anyway."

Lisa held the phone an arms length away for a few seconds, and wondered what was up with Karen's attitude. She longed for a cup of coffee.

"Well, what's going on Lisa?" Karen sounded very impatient.

Lisa rubbed her forehead. "Oh, I don't know…just stuff. I've had writers block for months, and I hate saying that, it sounds so stupid. My parents finally moved to Florida after driving me crazy for over a year debating whether or not they should go." She hesitated, and blinked back the tears. "Then I had to put my dog to sleep, and now, well, Dave and I recently separated. So I guess it's…"

"If things are that bad, I'll be right over."

"What?" Forgetting about the dream, Lisa jumped out of bed and scrambled for her clothes. She threw on the jeans she had worn the day before, took a deep breath, zipped them up, and then shook her head in disgust when it hurt to button them. She never had a weight problem in her life, but recently had gained nine pounds. She figured it was probably from eating too much pizza and ice cream. She managed to untangle her purple sweatshirt, and quickly pulled it over her head as she ran to the bathroom. She threw her half brushed, golden mane up into a ponytail, and splashed cold water on her face.

Downstairs, she picked up some books and magazines that had been lying around for days, and threw them in a corner. She ran a finger across the glass coffee table and grimaced as she rubbed the dust particles between her fingers, then watched them drop to the cream colored carpet.

In the kitchen, she scooped up the dozen or so M&M's left in the candy dish, and shoved them in her mouth wondering why there were still some left. The dishwasher quickly disposed of the dishes that had been sitting in the sink from the day before. She had just finished filling the coffee pot with water when she heard the knock at the side door. Her stomach knotted up.

She didn't like this one bit. She had always been so together, decisive, and strong. She had always been the rock, listening to all of Karen's problems when they were growing up, and helping her as much as she could. Now it was *she* that was falling apart, and hated the idea of having a witness.

The knock came again, and quickly, another. "Gees, no patience," she mumbled. She could partly see Karen through the glass door; something was *very* different. She took a deep breath to get her bearings, and then opened the door. "Karen?" Lisa stood frozen to the spot, not believing her own eyes.

"Yes, it is I." Karen stepped in passed Lisa. Lisa laughed as Karen began prancing and twirling just like a model would for a photo shoot. Karen's body was adorned by a pair of tight jeans, and a light peach, waist-length sweater. Her once long, mousey brown hair was now shoulder-length, with a light touch of bangs, and some reddish highlights. Her glasses were gone; *so was her humped nose*. Her blue eyes couldn't have looked more beautiful, Lisa thought.

"My God Karen, what did you do?"

"I found a new way of life, and lost seventy-five pounds."

"You look absolutely beautiful," Lisa said as she wiped a tear and hugged her best friend, truly happy to see her. "I hope you're staying in town for awhile."

"Oh I'll be staying for a long while. I've moved back. I'm staying at my mother's."

"That's great!" Lisa said, feeling somewhat apprehensive. She knew she could be pretty intuitive at times, and she was feeling Karen's return was going to create a whole new chapter in their lives, especially her own. They moved to the kitchen table, while waiting for the coffee. Lisa noticed Karen had a bandage on her left pinkie finger. That brought to mind how they had first met.

They were both eight years old, it was summer, and Karen's family had just moved from Rhode Island to Cape Cod. Karen had watched Lisa walk by every day to go to the little variety store at the end of the block. Too shy to speak, Karen came up with another strategy. She showed up one day on Lisa's doorstep with a beautiful gray kitten in tow. Lose a kitten, make a friend. Lisa had felt honored until she found out there were four more that needed homes. Karen was no dummy.

Two weeks later and heartbroken, Lisa had to say goodbye to 'Charcoal' because her older brother Kevin was allergic. In those two weeks Lisa and Karen had become inseparable. With an innate knowing that this was for life, they pricked their fingers and became blood sisters.

"So you and Dave split," Karen said dryly. "Where is he now?"

Of course she would want to know about Dave, Lisa thought. "Let's wait until the coffee's ready, and then we can walk down to the beach and talk. The weather's been so nice."

"Umm, okay, but do you have any juice? I don't drink coffee anymore."

"What?" Karen related to her that she was into health and wellness. Lisa was stunned. Here she was planning for them to drown her sorrows that evening in beer and pizza. She could not believe she had lost her partner in junk food crime.

No more would they be downing burgers and Twinkies. No more endless cups of coffee and beer binges. Now it was herbal tea and carrot juice, raw veggies and nuts. *Nuts?* That's how she felt listening to Karen, believing some alien must be inhabiting her now slim body. Suddenly, she longed for the old days. As she walked over to the fridge and pulled out the carton of creamer, she informed Karen there was no juice or herbal tea, but would she settle for some bottled water?

Karen took a sip of her water, and sat back. "You will never guess who I saw yesterday."

"Who?" Lisa shrugged.

"Jimmy Rogers. The one I asked to the junior prom. Remember him?"

Lisa leaned back against the counter, and frowned. She remembered being crazy about Jimmy Rogers for months and had planned to ask him to the prom herself, only Karen had beaten her to it.

"Yeah, I remember him. He was a nice boy."

"Well that boy turned into a 'nice' man. He said to say hi. Didn't you have a crush on him or something?" Karen smirked.

"Yes, I did," Lisa said, as she pulled a mug out of the cabinet thinking about the issue. *Karen had known full well she did.* She hadn't stayed angry at her for very long though. She couldn't. She had felt sorry for her because she had such low self-esteem, and no other friends, especially boyfriends. In fact, she was so surprised that a very shy Karen had gotten up the nerve to even ask a boy out.

The prom issue was nothing anyway compared to what had happened several years later, Lisa thought. It was the big secret Lisa wasn't supposed to ever know about; even now. Karen still had no idea she knew. It should have destroyed their friendship, but Lisa believed in forgiveness, and she loved Karen like a sister. Besides, that was over twenty-two years ago. They were young, and people do change, Lisa affirmed, with a funny feeling in her stomach.

They took their drinks, and proceeded in silence down to the beach. For the first time in her life Lisa felt uneasy around Karen. As they walked down a narrow path, Lisa was a few steps behind her. This gave her a chance to really eye Karen's slim figure. She really was happy for her, but Karen's attitude towards her had changed. Lisa didn't like the negative vibes she was picking up. But then, maybe it her imagination, like Karen used to tell her when she had a feeling Karen could be mad at her.

Karen took in a deep breath, "Breathe in that Cape Cod air. It's a far cry from L.A."

"Speaking of L.A., what made you decide to move back after all these years?"

"Well, I've left nursing."

"Somehow that does not surprise me. I remember how your father pushed you into that. So what are your plans?"

"Well," she teased with a big smile, "I'm going to do something I've always wanted to do. I'm going to open up a bookstore."

"That's great! I remember you used to talk about that in high school."

"Well it's not just any bookstore. It's a New Age, metaphysical type bookstore. There will be inspirational books, mind power books, self help, alternative medicine, meditation, reincarnation..."

"Reincarnation," Lisa interrupted. "I bought several books on that about a year ago, after I saw a past-life regression on TV. It's something I've thought a lot about over the last few years. First, because it has always held my interest, and second, I thought it would be great to use in a novel one day.

But, I also thought that Dave and I had been together in another life, or lives. Remember we used to talk about all that stuff when we were kids? I used to say I had been a princess in a past life, which made you mad for some reason, and you'd say you had been Cleopatra. The whole concept has always made sense to me. Anyway, why did you decide on that type of bookstore?"

"I was going through a bad time. I was still angry about my divorce. Then I was going from man to man looking for something, peace of mind, maybe. And, even though dad was dead I was still harboring a lot of anger towards him. I really needed to work on forgiving him. I finally got my butt into therapy and from there joined a meditation group. I learned a lot about loving and forgiving myself, as well as forgiving others. I'm still working on all that."

"From what I've read in those books, everyone needs to work on all that. To forgive is to heal. Aunt Bella used to say that forgiveness changes everything…if not for the other person, then at least for yourself." Lisa took a sip of the lukewarm coffee, and listened as Karen continued.

"True. Meditation, visualization, therapy, all these things helped me. I feel they can help others too. But, of all the things I've learned I find mind power the most fascinating. A lot of people would deny it, but we create our life by what we think and believe; both on a conscious and unconscious level. Thoughts really are things. They're energy, and what a person continually focuses on, whether they're aware of it or not, can manifest in their reality, good or bad. You can use visualization to help create the life you want."

"It sounds like that whole Law of Attraction thing which I'm not sure about. But, at the moment it sounds great, where do I sign up? Life has really been the pits lately, and I am totally miserable if I can't write." Lisa gulped down the rest of her coffee. They found a spot to sit in the cold sand.

"Never mind the writing. What about Dave? What happened?"

Lisa figured she should get it over with. "Dave had been cheating on me for months. It's funny, I guess in a way it's almost a blessing. We've just existed together for years anyway. He's away on business a lot, and I have my own life. Many times I planned to tell him I wanted a separation, but I didn't know if I would be making a mistake. I'm still not sure. I needed to think things out so I asked him to leave after this."

"I'm sorry."

Lisa wondered if Karen really was. A few minutes passed. Neither of them spoke. She wondered if she and Dave could still work things out, even though she had spent twenty-two years in a marriage she wasn't happy in, but, just conditioned to it. She blamed herself. She knew she never should have married him in the first place. But, she had made a commitment, and swore she would keep to it, no matter what she felt, or *didn't* feel.

"Do you still love him?" Karen asked.

Lisa started digging a hole in the sand wishing she could shrink and jump into it. "No. But, I do care about him. I always have. I always will."

"So…you are going to get a divorce, right?"

"I don't know…I'm not sure. Dave said it was up to me. Maybe we still can…"

"But what do you *want?*"

Lisa stood up, frustrated, hands waving in the air. "I don't know! I don't know what the hell I want. I feel empty and confused, and I feel like a failure. I mean, I made a commitment, and I let him down by not being what I was supposed to be, whatever the hell that was. I feel so guilty to think about ending it. I feel like I'd be making a mistake, that it would be the wrong decision. And, I can't stand the thought of becoming another statistic. What are my parents going to say? They love Dave."

"Whoa. Wait a minute. I don't believe what I'm hearing. *You,* of all people always knew what you wanted, and always *did* what you wanted; you only followed the crowd if it was something you thought was worth doing. You never gave a damn what others thought, not even your parents, who unlike mine always respected you for having a mind of your own. This does not sound like you."

"God, I don't even know myself anymore," she whispered with a lump in her throat. Karen put an arm around her. Lisa felt so needy, and she hated it.

"The only joy I have had in my life in the last few years was my dog, and my writing. I feel like part of me is dying," she said starting to choke up.

"It's okay to cry," Karen reassured her.

Lisa did just that, uncontrollably. She then jumped up, ran to the water, flung the coffee mug into the ocean, and cried more. Years of holding back; the hurt, the anger; the dam at last had burst. Karen ran after her. According to Karen, Lisa was releasing, and that it was a process of life.

"That felt so good. It felt so good to really cry, to let it all out. I can't remember the last time I've done that. Usually, if I get that feeling I put on Beethoven's Fifth or Ninth and jump on the treadmill. Then I settle back with Pachelbel's Canon. Music always helps me, but this time..."

"Meditation can help you too. You can use it to relax, to get in touch with yourself, and you can use it for visualization. I have a basic meditation CD you can use. And, okay, don't laugh but sometimes I even use quartz crystals to..."

"Crystals?"

"Uh huh, I plan on selling them at the store. What's the matter? You have a funny look on your face."

"I found one about a month ago. Right over there." She pointed to the right a few feet away, near the shoreline. "It's an odd shape. It looks like, well, it's dome-shaped, and it looks like one half of a crystal ball, like the ball has been cut in two or something." Chuckling, she added, "It makes me wonder what happened to the other half. But, something strange happened with it."

"Strange? What do you mean?"

"When I picked it up, I don't know why, but, I held the crystal to my chest. I closed my eyes, and I could feel the crystal tingling. Then everything was quiet. I didn't hear the ocean anymore, the sea gulls, or the wind chimes. I started to feel weightless and tingly. Then I began to see this light in my mind, and there was this strange humming sound. When I felt like I was starting to move, I quickly opened my eyes, and everything was just as it had been. I almost wish I had kept my eyes closed just to see what would have happened. I put the crystal on my nightstand and haven't touched it since. Oh, and another thing, the crystal has this strange glow about it."

"It sounds like you were about to have an out-of-body experience."

"Wonderful," Lisa said sarcastically. "Out-of-*mind* experience would be more like it, I think."

"What do you mean? That's fantastic! I should be so lucky," Karen said, pouting. "Some people try for years to have one, and you started to have one spontaneously. That figures."

"What do you mean, that figures?" Lisa asked defensively upon hearing Karen's almost sarcastic tone of voice.

Karen ignored the question. "Why don't you come by the house tomorrow and I'll give you the meditation CD?"

Later, as they walked back to the house, Lisa joked about throwing the mug into the water, and how ridiculous she must have looked. She recalled how, as a child, she would throw things when she got angry. Then, she realized that it was Dave's mug she had thrown. It was the one she had bought him when they were on their honeymoon in Niagara Falls. She mentioned this to Karen, who said nothing until they walked into the kitchen.

"I take it you don't normally drink out of that mug, right?"

Lisa opened the cabinet and pulled out a mug with pink roses on it. "This is my favorite one. I use it every day. Why?"

"Why did you use Dave's today?"

Lisa poured herself some coffee. "I don't know. We were talking and I probably wasn't paying attention and grabbed the first one. Why?"

"Well, this may sound silly but...it's very symbolic don't you think?"

Lisa shrugged, and shook her head. "I guess I'm a little slow here. What do you mean?"

"Well, symbolism in a coffee mug. Think about it."

She did. Karen's words cut right through her. At that moment Lisa knew her marriage was over. There would be no more trying to decide what to do. It was time to end it, and start a new life. *That* was a scary thought… exciting, too. But after all this was over, what *did* she want?

"Don't forget to come by tomorrow for the CD," Karen said on her way out later that morning. "Once you get used to the session, try meditating with a crystal. Crystals are amplifiers of energy. You can use one to visualize. Oh, let me see the one you found."

Lisa rushed upstairs to get it from her nightstand. As she was coming back down she stopped suddenly. She had a flash of the man in the dream she'd been having. Feelings of sadness and longing came over her. She may never know who he was. Frustrated, she had to remind herself it was only a dream. "Here it is." She held it in her outstretched hand. Karen's eyes widened, and she took a step back.

"What's the matter?"

"I don't know. The shape, like you said, a half of a crystal ball. I could swear I've seen something like it before. But, for the life of me I can't imagine where. And it doesn't glow, Lisa," she snickered.

"Can't you see it? It's subtle, but it's visible."

"Have another cup of coffee, Lisa."

Later that afternoon, Lisa took a walk on the deserted beach. She smiled radiantly. She hadn't felt this good in months. She enjoyed the beautiful and unusually warm April day. She felt a new freedom bursting forth inside herself. Life would be different now, she just knew it. She felt in heaven standing by the ocean, and loved feeling the moist, salty air against her face. She began thinking about Karen, and suddenly all those wonderful feelings dissipated. She couldn't shake the funny feeling she had about Karen's return.

She walked over to her favorite place on the beach, the rocks on the east side. She climbed up at an angle about twelve feet high into the small cave-like nook. She loved the way it blocked out the wind, and also being high enough to get a good look at the waves rolling in.

She positioned herself comfortably, and took a few deep breaths. As her body became more relaxed she started to focus on what she thought she wanted in her life. All of a sudden a man…a strange looking man, who seemed to come out of nowhere, caught her attention. He was about forty feet away near the water, and was doing a slow jog. He had a full head of gray hair, and a beard to match.

From what she could see, his face looked old and weathered, but he had the body of a young athlete. He was wearing only a pair of running shorts. She thought it was still too cold for that. When he ran, his whole being seemed to flow. His motions were fluid, and like the crystal, he had a subtle glow about him.

"What am I, able to see auras now?" He waved to her. She waved back, dumbfounded. Then he disappeared around the rocks. She quickly made her way down to see where he was heading. There was no sign of him, and there was nowhere else he could have gone that quickly. It would have been no big deal, except there was something familiar about him. He looked like something out of the Bible; Moses, perhaps? No. It was something else.

She was no stranger to witnessing unusual occurrences, although she was always told it was her imagination. She used to think there was something wrong with her. That nagging thought still existed. But, she knew she could not have imagined seeing the ghostly figure in her aunt's attic when she was a child, especially since her aunt used to see it too.

Then there was that other thing. It happened when she was five years old, and had something to do with a woman in a long, flowing white dress with pretty eyes. As hard as she tried she could not remember. But the feeling of it, though not a bad feeling, still haunted her.

Chapter 2

———

As Lisa drove to Karen's house the next morning all she could think about was the turquoise robed prince. The dream had come again and, of course, as he was about to turn and face her, she had awoken; 5:38 a.m. She couldn't get back to sleep, because she couldn't get him out of her mind. She wanted so much to see his face. She wanted so much to wrap her arms around him.

The ache in her heart was getting stronger. This was crazy, she told herself as she searched the pocket in her jacket for a tissue. She wiped her eyes, and wondered why she was angry in the dream. And why did he give off this emanation of superiority? Who the hell was *he?* Now she found herself getting angry, and didn't know why.

There were so many emotions going on inside her that she had never felt before. She hadn't thought much about other men. Well maybe a little in the last six months or so, since she hadn't been able to write. As long as she could write she didn't need a man. She suddenly realized that the writing had just been a mask, that there had been an empty place inside her for so long, and it had taken so called writers block for her to become aware of it.

Lisa turned on the radio, and then turned it off. The last thing she wanted to hear was a love song. She began thinking about reincarnation, and tried to reject the notion that he was someone she knew from a past life. "Okay Lisa, get real. It's only a dream," she mumbled, as she turned off the ignition of the green Corvette that nearly matched her eyes.

Karen poured her a cup of herbal tea. Lisa took a sip, "Yuk! This is terrible. How can you drink this? Isn't there any coffee?"

The phone rang. Lisa noticed Karen didn't seem to want to answer it. When she did, it was in another room. Lisa wondered who was on the other end. Karen talked in a whispered tone, and then shouted, telling the other party that she was hanging up.

"So when are you going to go for a divorce?" Karen snapped as she walked back into the kitchen. "You are going to get a divorce right?"

Lisa bit the inside of her mouth, and under her breath counted to ten. She looked directly at Karen for a few seconds, and wondered where this was all coming from. "As I told you, Dave is leaving the option of divorce up to me. But, after yesterday's mug incident, I know it's time to end it. So yes, I'm going to divorce Dave." Lisa let out a long breath, and rested her face in her hands. She rubbed her eyes and yawned, "I am not used to being up this early."

"Jesus, Lisa, it's almost 8:30. I've been up since 6 a.m. I've showered, made breakfast, straightened up, and took Mum to work."

Lisa reached over and patted Karen on the back. The excess weight may have been gone, she thought, but her efficiency and organization were still very much intact.

"Isn't there any coffee?" Lisa pushed the cup of tea away.

"You need to change your diet. And you shouldn't drink coffee, that stuff will kill you."

"I'll take my chances." Lisa rolled her eyes, and almost wished Karen was only here for a visit. She hated all this childish bickering.

Karen located some instant coffee in back of the cabinet. A few minutes later Lisa contently took a sip then asked, "What kind of woman goes out with a married man?"

Karen nearly spit out the sip of tea she had just taken. "Maybe she didn't know he was married," she said quickly.

"Yeah, she did, Dave told me."

"I know you said you didn't love him, but it still must hurt."

Lisa pulled a napkin out of the holder and began twisting it. "Yeah, it does, but, not because he was with another woman. It's the lie. No matter how you feel about someone, nobody wants to be lied to."

"True," Karen said, lowering her eyes.

Lisa almost choked on those last words she herself had said. She felt her whole marriage had been a lie. She figured that the saying was true; what goes around comes around, otherwise known as karma.

Lisa threw the twisted napkin on the table. "Do you believe in soul mates?"

"You mean in the romantic sense?"

"What else is there?"

"Well, maybe you and I are soul mates, or you and your parents, or your brother. You and Dave could be, too. It's not all about romance, but usually people do see it in the romantic sense. It can be a very strong connection with another of which you may have had many past lives."

"Oh, okay, I think I get that, but what *about* in the romantic sense," Lisa asked.

"Well, there is what's referred to as twin souls or twin flames, as well. From what I've learned, in spirit the soul is actually one unit, and before it started to incarnate, the soul had to split in two, the masculine and the feminine. Everyone has a twin soul. Supposedly, our twin soul is our true love, and there is no love on earth like it."

"That sounds so beautiful," Lisa said, relishing the thought.

"If that's what you're looking for, forget it. It is very rare for twin souls to incarnate together. From what I've read they may start out together in one life, but then go their own ways for many lifetimes, to gain experience and soul-growth separately. They may come together at the end of a cycle of lifetimes. It's rare to meet your twin."

"Okay, but what if my twin soul *is* alive and here somewhere?"

"That's very doubtful. If it happens that you are here at the same time, he could very well be on the other side of the world, as an eight year old, or an eighty year old."

"Wonderful," Lisa said, and frowned.

She began thinking about the dream, and drifted off into a little fantasy of the robed one being her true love, face unseen. She felt he had a powerful presence. And she knew she had to stop this before she really got herself hooked on a dream phantom.

"Just the thought of being with someone, making love with someone where you feel so connected on every level…a spiritual connection as well as everything else, something so deep…" Lisa placed her hand to her heart.

"You didn't have anything like that with Dave?" Karen interrupted.

"No," she hesitated, "I didn't."

"Come on, not even in the beginning? Dave practically worshiped you. You must have had that feeling, at least for a while anyway."

Lisa's eyes filled up. She was sorry she had brought up the subject. All of sudden she felt like guilt was trying to make her confess, and she didn't want to open the can of worms. But she did.

"I never had that with Dave…I don't…because I don't think I ever really loved him. I loved him in my own way like I do now, but not in the way…I didn't feel what I knew you were supposed to feel." Lisa lowered her head. "I never should have married him."

Karen abruptly got up from the table and slammed her tea cup into the sink. "Then why did you marry him? *Why?* How could you? I was the one…"

Karen stopped herself mid sentence, and Lisa knew why. Lisa also knew why Karen was angry. It all came back to what had happened one night over twenty-two years ago, and everything that

evolved from it. Lisa thought about telling Karen that she knew everything, but upon second thought, she knew it wasn't the right time.

All these years she had held in what she had just admitted about
her husband, and she wasn't sure she felt any better spilling it. She
had always sensed that Dave knew.

Karen relaxed and sat down again. "Why did you do it? Why did
you marry him?"

"I really did care for him, Karen, and I didn't want to lose him."

"Lose him…to whom, to what? He loved you. I remember, I…
never mind. It was a long time ago. We were kids. What did we
know? We all do foolish things we end up regretting but seemed
right at the time."

Lisa knew what had happened all those years before would come
out one day, and she would tell Karen she already knew everything.
Lisa had given her word to Dave to keep it a secret. If only Dave had
not given her an ultimatum, their lives may have all been different.
But then again, she had made her choices. No one forced her to do
anything. And, Lisa believed there is an underlying cause behind all
things, that everything happens for a reason, whether we understand
it, or like it, or not.

Karen dropped the subject much to Lisa's relief. She then pulled
out the meditation CD, and handed it to Lisa. "The session starts
out with a countdown to relax your body. Then there will be about
twenty minutes of silence where you can do visualization, or affir-
mations, or do nothing and see what comes to you. It takes about
thirty minutes."

"It sounds easy enough." Lisa let out a yawn.

"If you are going to use it for visualization to manifest something in your life, then you have to figure out what you really want.
And I'm not talking about manifesting a new stove or new furniture,
not that you can't do those things, but I'm talking about something
meaningful.

So you might have to think long and hard about this, and whatever it is, desire it with all your heart. That's important. Heartfelt desire is emotion, which is energy that can help manifest what you truly want. And then believe what you desire will come to you. Of course it should be of a positive nature. Never visualize for something bad to happen to someone, not that you would, but you'll only create bad karma. You know, what goes around comes around."

"I'm well aware of the phrase."

Karen continued, "Whatever it is you want, see it in your mind. See yourself having it. Use all your emotion as if you really did have it. Try to do this everyday if you can."

"Hmm, I'm not sure I know what I really want. I will have to think about that. Maybe I'll meditate with the crystal I found too," Lisa said eagerly.

"No! The crystal must be left untouched!"

Startled, Lisa sat up straight. A shiver ran though her. The voice she had just heard did not sound like Karen's at all. For that moment it was as if Karen was someone else.

"Why? You said…"

Karen seemed to also be caught off guard. "I…I honestly don't know why. I don't even know why I said that. I think there is something about it. I can't explain it, and I didn't mean to sound so dramatic. But don't use it. Just don't use it."

Lisa said nothing and picked up a deck of tarot cards that had been sitting on the table. She starting shuffling them not really knowing what she was doing. One flew out of the deck and onto the floor. She picked it up and looked at it, then quickly threw it on the table. "Karen, it says *Death*!"

"Oh, the Death card," Karen smirked. "I wish you could see the look on your face. The Death card represents what you're going through right now. It doesn't mean physical death. It means the death of old ways, an old way of life, old ideas, how about the death of your marriage? And didn't you say you felt like a part of you was dying?"

"Yeah, and the ending of my marriage does feel like a death."

"That's right. Look forward to the birth of a new life. The card means change, transformation. Shuffle the deck and pick one card."

Lisa reluctantly obeyed and picked a card called The Magician.

"Great card!" The Magician creates. *You* can create. You can create the life you truly desire."

Karen checked her watch. "I have an appointment to look at some rental space. It's not exactly what I had in mind from what the realtor described, but I figured I might as well check it out. I also have another appointment later this afternoon. Want to come with me now? We can go to lunch after."

"Sure, as long as you don't attack me when I order a burger and fries," Lisa chuckled.

As Karen drove Lisa picked up a book that was lying on the back seat. It was a book on crystals. She thumbed through it and stopped when she caught a word that evoked many emotions. "Atlantis! I haven't thought about Atlantis in years."

Karen laughed, "I remember how you freaked out when you heard that song called Atlantis, when we were kids. I think we were babies when that song came out."

"Yeah, apparently, my oldest cousin had brought it by and left it. Years later Kevin pulled it out and played it a lot. It was by a singer named Donovan. I had never heard of Atlantis until that song. But the weird part was that I knew what he was talk- ing about. I knew." Lisa let out a sigh. "I knew, and I wanted to be there. I felt the sadness, the longing. I felt such a loss. It was as if Atlantis was buried in my psyche...as if there was a part of me that knew Atlantis, and I wanted to be there so bad. Imagine wanting to be in a place that supposedly never existed. That's crazy huh?"

"That was when you thought you had been a princess in a past life. Priestess would have been more like it. But, somehow I could not imagine you being a priestess."

"Gee, thanks a lot." Lisa began reading some of the contents. "God, Karen, it says here that crystals were used to generate power similar to electricity. It also says that certain ones could be used for thought amplification. The knowledge of this way to create was held sacred, and kept secret from those who would not realize the power, and could use it destructively."

Lisa's stomach started to feel funny, and she continued on. "Apparently, the knowledge and use of this crystal energy was abused by those in power, and eventually led to the downfall and final destruction of a once peaceful and harmonious paradise.

This is true! I know this! I don't know how, but I do. Atlantis did exist. I feel it. I know it. It's the same feeling I had when we were kids. I lived a lifetime in Atlantis. I'm sure of it."

"A lot of us did, Lisa. I'm sure I did too. It's said that the United States is the new Atlantis, and you know about history repeating itself."

Early that evening Lisa decided to give the CD a try. She was able to relax quickly and easily. She had come to a point where she was nearing sleep when an image started to form in her mind. She became excited when she saw a man in a white robe, with a gold tie around his waist. Expecting to see the one in her dream, she was shocked when she saw what looked to be the face of the man on the beach. Mr. Moses, she decided to call him.

She forced herself to keep focused on him. A deep love and caring emanated from this man, and she found she wanted to stay in his presence. She was about to ask him his name when she jumped up with her heart beating wildly.

Someone was knocking at the backdoor downstairs. It was Dave, and he wanted to take more clothes. He and Lisa talked. He agreed it was time to end their marriage. She and Dave would part as friends. She wouldn't have had it any other way. She did not want anything left undone. Believing in reincarnation, she knew if they parted as enemies or left the situation unresolved, they would have to work it out in a future lifetime. This much she had learned from the books she had read, and knew it felt right. She knew that all conflict must be resolved, and healed by forgiveness. She once read, 'never die hating someone…you will be sure to meet them again in the future.'

After Dave left, Lisa hesitantly opened the door to the bedroom closet. It was a big walk-in closet, and now Dave's side was empty. Lisa's heart nearly stopped. Everything was gone…every shoe, every dress shirt, tie, suit, baseball mitt, coin collection, hat collection…twenty-two years. She didn't see it as more room for her clothes, but as emptiness inside herself.

She pulled out a green, sequin dress, and a couple of other cocktail dresses. She had worn these to company parties. They were parties that she loathed with all the gossip and phoniness. She left the dresses out to give to Goodwill. She looked in Dave's dresser… nothing but more emptiness. It finally hit her that it really was over.

She dropped down on the bed and cried, thinking and feeling that she was so alone. Suddenly she felt a calmness wash over her, and in her minds eye saw Mr. Moses. She distinctly heard the words, 'One is never alone.'

The next morning Lisa rolled over to press the snooze button when the alarm went off at 8:00 a.m. She had set it early to break herself out of the habit of sleeping late. She was sorry she had. The room was dark and dreary. The gloomy clouds hung above her bed through the two skylights, as the rain knocked at the glass. She dozed off, but a clap of thunder reawakened her. She pulled the blankets up to her neck, feeling disappointed she didn't have the dream. *The mystery man in the turquoise robe*, she thought…*her dream lover*. "Oh, yeah right!"

Lisa pulled herself out of bed, shivering, and threw on her pink, fleece robe. She could hear the wind picking up as she turned up the thermostat, and shook her head, "Crazy New England weather."

As she made coffee she thought of Karen and felt guilty, and then berated herself for feeling that way. She was not about to give up her morning cup of joe. The steam from the brew warmed her as she stood in front of the glass sliders in the kitchen. She sipped her coffee and watched the rain pound the deck.

Entranced, she stared into the tiny puddles of liquid wishing her life was as clear to her as the raindrops. She had gone to bed the night before questioning what she really wanted in her life. She focused on one particular beaded mass of water, and she knew. And she had known all along.

For months she had been visualizing it…unintentionally. She knew she wanted nothing more than to write a best seller, and to find the love of her life…no small task. It had always been there in the back of her mind, something she would only be semi-conscious of. Sometimes she would daydream and imagine this, but never realized what she was actually doing.

But she wondered if it was really possible to create a reality you might desire, or was it already destined anyway. Are we just tapping or tuning into something that was already going to come to pass, which makes us just think we're creating it? Maybe there was a script already written. *Maybe there was even more than one.* She had read that all time existed at once, and that everything has already happened, and we're just living it out linearly.

She continued gazing into the tiny puddles, and envisioned the turquoise robed one in her mind. Her desire for him was overwhelming. It was so much more than physical. She still didn't know what he looked like, but her heart and her soul wanted this man. "This is crazy," she said aloud.

A chill came over her. She looked out into the distance near the shore. "What the hell?" It was pouring out and someone was running on the beach. She picked up the binoculars to see if she was hallucinating. She was not! It was him again, Mr. Moses, clad only in a pair of running shorts.

As far away as he was, he seemed to be looking right at her into the binoculars. The hair on her arms stood straight up. At that same time, the phone starting ringing, and she nearly jumped out of her skin. She quickly caught the binoculars before they came crashing down on the floor.

Karen had called to invite Lisa over for breakfast. She accepted, though she figured breakfast would consist of chamomile tea and rice cakes. Surprise! Freshly brewed coffee, and steaming blueberry muffins. "Gee, I almost stopped at a drive-thru," said Lisa.

"Sorry about the coffee thing yesterday. Sometimes I get carried away with wanting people to change the way they eat. I wasn't in a good mood anyway."

"What's wrong? Anything I can do?" Lisa asked, feeling like they were kids again.

"It's not something I care to discuss, at least right now. I have to deal with it myself. But thanks anyway."

Lisa thought that Karen sure did change. Now, who was the one clamming up when there was a problem?

Lisa sank her teeth into the hot buttered muffin. "How did that other appointment go yesterday afternoon?"

Karen smiled enthusiastically. "The place was much too small. But, on the drive home there was roadwork on Elm Street, so I had to take a detour down Lansing Avenue, and there it was. It's the place I have been looking for. It's exactly what I've been picturing! I have an appointment at 12:30. Will you come with me? We can go for lunch after. I'm buying."

"Sure. You know, I have a real good feeling about this. I bet this will be the one."

"I hope so. I'm dying to get this all going."

Karen went from joy to disappointment all in a matter of minutes upon arriving at the property. There had been a misunderstanding. The small building was not for rent, but for sale. Though she had some money saved, there was no way she could purchase the building, and the owner would not settle for renting it out.

"I can't believe this. It was perfect. Perfect!" Karen roared as she tore a garlic roll in half at the restaurant. Lisa took a bite of a fried clam, and nodded in agreement.

"Well, I'll just have to keep visualizing," Karen said confidently. "Something else will come along, something just like it, or something better. But I still say that place was perfect," she growled.

"Well, so much for my gut feeling. Usually when I get a feeling that strong it pans out. Who knows? Speaking of visualizing, you said that I should know what I want. I've known it all along, but didn't know it," she said humorously. "I've always wanted to write a bestseller, and I know that sounds silly, because what writer doesn't? But I never thought I could, so I never hoped for it. All my novels are so ordinary to me. This time I want to do something so different, really different, and I still want to write Romance, but I have no ideas yet. Then," she hesitated, "I want to find my twin soul."

"Lisa, I told you…"

"Yeah, I know what you told me, but I don't completely buy that. Maybe I'll visualize him into existence. But I feel I need to do the book first anyway. Maybe I should start picturing myself on Good Morning America, being introduced as the best selling novelist, Lisa Burke," she laughed.

"Yes, that is what you should be doing."

"I've been visualizing all my life. From the time I was little I knew I wanted to be a writer, and always saw that in my mind. I did the same thing with my Corvette, and the beach house. It always came natural for me, but I'm sure it must for everyone. I always looked at it as daydreaming."

Karen started to laugh. "That reminds me of something. Remember when our fifth grade teacher, Mrs. Davis, would come and tap you on the shoulder? I think her exact words were, 'Miss Burke, are you with us, or are you daydreaming again? Please keep your feet on the ground where they belong'."

Lisa placed her hand over her mouth trying to subdue her own laughter. "I never knew what she meant. I would look down at my feet and become very confused. I was probably dreaming up characters for my stories when she'd ask that."

"Oh yes, your weekly stories that you read to the class every Friday. I remember some of them being very good, and others put the class to sleep. Then you'd make some foolish looking drawing to go with the story."

"I suppose I was trying to be an artist as well as a writer." Lisa smiled, feeling somewhat proud.

Karen continued, "And there was that same character you would put in every story; the little blond boy with the sad blue eyes. The kids would want to know why he was in all the stories when he really had nothing to do with them. You used to say because he was good. I don't remember what his name was, and you had him growing up as we were growing up. But you never wrote him into your novels." Karen paused, "What's wrong? You look as white as a ghost. Are you all right?"

Karen's voice sounded so far away, but Lisa had heard every word that was said. Her stomach turned, and she could feel the blood draining from her face. Lisa held her breath. Karen had said the right word; ghost…a ghost from childhood's past.

"I didn't put him in my novels because he wasn't good anymore." A pained feeling came over her. "I haven't thought about Jeff since high school. God, I blocked him out because he wasn't good anymore."

"Okay, now you're making him sound like he was real."

"I know this sounds crazy, but somehow he was real to me. He did seem to have a life of his own. Writer's characters can take on a life of their own, but he was different. He was *too* real, and he had been with me since I was very young."

Karen leaned forward with a very baffled expression on her face. "What do you mean, been with you?"

Somewhat embarrassed, Lisa said, "From what I remember I was about four or five when I started making up stories. Jeff was the very first character I had created in my mind. As I got older I used to fantasize about Jeff being my boyfriend. There was something about him. Maybe it was those sad blue eyes. He was everything I had ever wanted. I loved him," Lisa cringed upon saying that.

"Sounds like you had one hell of a fantasy life," Karen snickered.

"In high school I was still writing about him. Then it seemed like I couldn't come up with anything new for him. It was around that same time I think, Dave had come into the picture. But, it was as if Jeff was turning on me, rebelling, and I took it personally. It hurt. In my mind I put him aside…blocked him out…until today."

Karen slowly shook her head from side to side. "I don't know what to say."

"Writers can have weird imaginations at times," Lisa said trying to redeem herself. "Think I'm ready for a straitjacket or what?"

"Einstein did say that imagination was greater than knowledge. Didn't you have a drawing of that character, Jeff, on the wall by your bed? I think it was there when I had first met you. From what I remember the drawing was very life-like, almost as if an artist had drawn it. I know you were not…"

Lisa stood up abruptly. "I need to go to the ladies room."

She quickly locked the stall and sat down. She held her stomach and took deep breaths. It was all coming back to her. She was finally remembering the incident, the one that haunted her. It was the one that happened when she was five years old. She had never told anyone about it.

One day up in her bedroom she had decided to draw a picture of Jeff. She had seen him so clearly in her mind. She had her drawing pad sitting up on a small easel, and her pencil. She tried and tried, and just couldn't do it. She finally got so upset and frustrated that she threw the pad and herself down on the floor and cried.

After she had her cry, she looked up and saw the room was filled with light. Out of this light a woman stepped forward. She thought that the woman would be very nice, and was not afraid of her. The woman wore a flowing white gown, and her hair was worn up in a Victorian style. Lisa saw that she had the most beautiful blue eyes, and wished her own were blue.

The woman pointed to the pad that was still lying on the floor. Lisa picked it up and placed it back on the easel. The woman moved in back of her, and placed her hand over Lisa's hand. Together they drew Jeff just as Lisa had seen him in her mind. They turned the drawing over and wrote something on the back, but even now Lisa could not remember what it was they wrote. After that, the woman smiled at her angelically and literally disappeared.

Lisa came back to her seat and told Karen what she had just remembered. "I know I have that drawing somewhere. I'm sure I didn't throw it out. Most likely it's in the big walk-in closet in the upstairs hall. It would probably take me forever to find it, that closet is stuffed, and it would most likely be way in the back. I'll have to look for it soon."

"But wouldn't you have found it when you moved?"

"No, my parents had helped us move when we bought the beach house. There were some boxes of childhood mementos and things they brought over that were left at their house after I got married. I just told them to put the boxes in the closet. I had never been interested in going through them, and never did."

Karen checked her watch. "We've got to go. I've got to pick up Mum."

It was just as well. Lisa figured the next thing that would be coming out of her mouth was that she was in love with some faceless guy in her dream, and that she kept seeing this Moses like character. Karen probably thought she was crazy as it is. Lisa was starting to wonder about that herself.

Later that night Lisa decided to try the CD again. Her eyes became riveted to the crystal on her nightstand. She picked it up, tempted to meditate with it, but put it down remembering what Karen had said. She lay on the bed and turned on the CD player. After about a half a minute, she shut the player off and sat up. She picked up the crystal again.

She wondered what would be the worst that could happen. She didn't know what Karen was concerned with. What would be the harm in having an out of body experience? She felt she could use some adventure in her life. The last time she felt that way she had tried skydiving, and loved it. She had risked her life, then. This could hardly be worse.

Lisa instinctively placed the crystal between her breasts. She wondered about that, but something told her it was right. The woman's voice on the CD was soothing, and she relaxed immediately. She reached the point just before falling asleep.

She felt a fluttering in her heart, and she began to shake. She thought an earthquake was happening and jumped up, or thought she did. Everything was spinning around, and she found herself surrounded by millions of tiny points of light.

An electrical sound invaded her head and a sound as if someone was crinkling cellophane. She was horrified and elated at the same time. She could not open her eyes. She felt like her body was breaking apart into tiny pieces. It didn't hurt, but felt weird. The electrical sound turned into a low gentle hum. As suddenly as it began, it stopped.

Lisa opened her eyes expecting to see the night sky through the skylights above her, but found herself standing in a tube-like device that looked to be made entirely of diamonds. Her vision was hazy, but she could see the colors of a rainbow reflecting off her body. A white light pulsated above her head. "Am I dead?" she asked weakly.

A door about thirty inches wide slid open. Her vision still wasn't clear, but she could see the outline of a woman standing before her.

"We have expected your arrival," the woman said in an acidulous tone. Before Lisa could speak, the woman shoved a gold chalice at her. "Drink," the woman coldly demanded while Lisa stood dumbfounded. "Drink now!"

Lisa slowly took the chalice, brought it to her nose, and sniffed the non-odorous liquid.

"You must drink now. There is no time for foolishness."

Hesitantly, she drank the small amount of what tasted like water, and almost immediately, her vision returned to normal. Startled, she held her breath as she looked into the face of a woman who looked almost identical to Karen, except she had a Cleopatra-style hairdo with eyes matching her very dark brown hair. The woman wore a long sleeved pastel blue gown, with a thick silver colored belt.

Lisa thought this was a joke. Yes, she was dead, and this was the spirit guide from hell!

"We have expected you."

"Who…me?" Lisa felt giddy, and proceeded to take a step out.

"Stay where you are. You must stay in the capsule. You are not ready."

"Ready for what?" she giggled.

"Your physical body is not ready for our rate of vibration. Your vibration is very dense. We are of a higher vibration here. It will take much time for you to adjust to the higher level."

"What?" Lisa asked, feeling like she was in the middle of a sci-fi movie, only no one had clued her in on the plot.

"You must return to your level now before there is damage. Think of your level." Lisa had to refrain from laughing. She felt like she had drunk one too many shots of Tequila.

"I don't know what you mean. I…" The woman slammed the door shut. Lisa figured that the woman meant she should think of her home. "Oh God, I'm not wearing my ruby slippers!"

Chapter 3

———

"**W***hat the hell just happened?*" Lisa looked up through the skylights at a sliver of a moon. She felt like her head was both expanding and contracting, and her stomach started to churn. She sat up slowly feeling like her head was not attached to her body. She hung on to everything she could as she inched her way to the bathroom. "Why did I eat all those clams?" she said as she walked slowly back to her bed feeling like she was suffering from a bad hangover.

Lisa rested her head on the pillow, and began trying to put everything into some sort of perspective. Was it a dream? Maybe. An out-of-body experience? A definite possibility. Could it have been a near death experience? After all, the ill-natured woman did tell her she was not ready, and to go back. Did the crystal do this?

Where *was* the crystal? She thrust about looking for it, and found it in the middle of the bed. She held it in her palm and examined it. What was this odd shaped piece of quartz all about? She wondered if it was something magical as she gazed at the faint glow around it.

Lisa was about to place the crystal back on the nightstand, when she had a vision. She looked at her hand, but it was a child's hand, and it was outstretched with palm up waiting for something to be given.

The next thing she saw was another hand over her own. The hand was large with long fingers. Deep wrinkles and creases were embedded in the skin. She felt something between the two hands. As the large hand slowly pulled away, her small hand was left holding the crystal as the vision faded. "So what the hell was *that* about?" She placed the crystal down and rubbed her forehead, wanting so much for the throbbing to stop.

Lisa reached over into the drawer of her nightstand, and pulled out a notebook. Karen had told her to start keeping a journal of her meditative experiences. She felt so weak, and could barely write. She leaned over to put the journal away, and her stomach started to churn again. Maybe she had some kind of food poisoning! She had eaten a whole plate of fried clams for lunch, and they could have been bad. Could this have made her hallucinate?

She thought about calling Karen, and then declined figuring she would scold her for meditating with the crystal. Lisa picked up the phone anyway deciding she didn't need Karen's approval for anything she did. Karen's mother told her she wasn't home, and wouldn't be home until tomorrow, and could offer no other information.

"I told you not to meditate with that crystal!"

"Karen, will you keep your voice down?" Lisa retorted, as they were eating lunch at Bob's Place two days later.

"It *could* have been food poisoning. You should have had the salad anyway. If it wasn't an out-of-body-experience, then you must have fallen asleep and it was only a dream."

"It sure as hell didn't feel like a dream. But then…you're probably right…what else could it have been? But whatever it was, I know the crystal triggered it. I didn't think so at first, but after having that vision with the crystal being placed in my hand…"

"You're *not* going to meditate with it again, right?"

"Are you kidding? Of course I am! I have to know what this is all about. I have to know."

"What is it they say…curiosity killed the cat?"

"Speaking of curiosity, where were you the night before last when I tried calling you about this?"

"I stayed with a friend," Karen said with a downward gaze.

"Anyone I…oh, look who just walked in."

Karen looked over then quickly looked away. With trembling hands she picked up her water glass, and took a large swallow.

Dave came over to them. A man and woman followed. Dave introduced his new business partner along with the man's wife. They made some small talk then the hostess came to seat them on the other side of the room.

"Karen, what's the matter? You seem nervous."

"Nothing's the matter. My stomach feels a little queasy, that's all."

"Must be that salad you're eating," Lisa quipped. She then looked over at her soon to be ex. "Dave didn't seem all that surprised you were back in town. I knew they looked familiar, now I think I remember where I've seen them before."

"Who?" Karen repeatedly tapped her fork against her salad bowl.

"Dave's new partner, Steve. I met him and his wife I don't know, five, six years ago. It was at a party. Of course, then, he worked for another company. She was very pregnant and a week over due and he was a nervous wreck. He would not leave her side."

"I'm ordering a glass of wine," Karen said as she impatiently waved down the server.

Lisa looked at her inquisitively, seeing the pissed off look on her face.

"You know, I think Dave gets more handsome as he gets older. I have to admit I miss him. I wish we could have…"

"You wouldn't be thinking of getting back with him, would you?"

"No. It's over." Lisa put her spoon down, and sat back. "What's going on? You've seemed awfully anxious about my getting a divorce. I would have expected you to suggest counseling or something when I first told you. Instead you…"

"Yes, you're right, and I probably would have." Karen paused, "There's something I should tell you. I suppose it's time. It's just that she said it was essential that you were out of your relationship before you knew, so you wouldn't end it because of what I'm about to tell you."

"Karen, what the *hell* are you talking about?"

"Several months before I left California I went to a psychic. She was someone who is very good, and celebrities pay big bucks to have a reading with her. She told me some things about my life, and since I was already planning to move back here I asked about you."

"Oh, I hope this is good." Lisa pulled her seat closer, and took a sip of wine.

"I'll try to tell you exactly what she said, because it's kind of strange. She started by saying you were very creative and that the books you've written were practice for a greater book."

Lisa's heart nearly leapt out of her chest. "Does that mean…"

Karen waved her hand. "Let me finish. She said you had a mission in this lifetime, and that you must get out of your current relationship. But you had to be ready to get out of it. She said there would be a new relationship coming into your life, someone from the past. She didn't know when or how you would meet. She did say by the time I moved back here you would have already been getting clues."

Lisa started thinking how strange things have been lately.

"She also said that in a previous life there was a lot of hurt, and the two of you must work things out in order to fulfill your mission, because this mission is something you must do together. She kept saying, 'The future changes the past which changes the future.'"

"What the hell does that mean?"

"I don't know. But she said you should keep an open mind, and that you already know anything is possible."

Lisa sat back stunned, and irritated. "Why didn't you tell me this before? Not that I understand any of it."

"It wasn't meant for you to know before. You had to have split with Dave on your own, and not because there was someone else coming into your life."

"Did she say anything else?" Lisa asked curtly.

"Yes. She said there would be confusion at some point, and mistakes, but they would only seem like mistakes. Her exact words were, 'Some mistakes are life's music.'"

"Some mistakes are life's music? Did she also tell you that some things are beyond understanding, like the mysteries of life? Who is this woman to say things that are going to happen in my life…things that I can't even understand! I don't like this!"

"Calm down. I'm just telling you what she told me. No psychic is one hundred percent accurate anyway. These are only probabilities. The energy of it can change as we change. There is free will. And remember, we create our own reality by what we believe on a subconscious level, as well as a conscious level."

"Well, I'm still not so sure about this 'create your own reality' stuff. I think maybe we come into this life with some sort of destined plan…like a script that's already been written. Creating reality vs. destiny…who knows maybe they both fit together!

Maybe we come into a life with more than one destined plan, like parallel lives or something. And like you said the energy changes as we change, and as we change maybe we unknowingly merge into a parallel lifetime, with a slightly different script or destiny. I don't know…sometimes I think so much depends on how we react to the things that happen to us." Lisa took a deep breath and let it out slowly. "Was there anything else she said?"

"That was about it, but she was serious. She even had *me* spooked. I felt it was time to tell you."

Lisa went home feeling flustered, but with a spark of hope about her future. Mistakes…confusion? She could live with that if a new novel would be the result, and a new love. But a mission…what was that about? Funny how the two things she wanted most in her life is what this woman touched upon. Then again, she considered maybe Karen was making it all up.

Lisa was tired and went up to bed early that night. She crawled under the pink, satin comforter. She felt like the crystal was calling her. With twinges in her stomach she picked it up, and then realized the dream had started the same time she had found the crystal.

"Let me try you again." She shut the light, and turned on the CD player. She knew one thing; if nothing happened, she would be very disappointed.

Again, it all happened; the shaking, the sounds, and the light. Then it stopped. The door slid open and the same woman stood before her. Lisa could see her clearly, but she felt dizzy, and yet at the same time her head felt so heavy.

"You may step out if you are able," the woman said with a frosty tone, and not looking happy at all.

Lisa tried to lift her leg, but it was as if she had forgotten how to move. She practically had to tell each muscle what to do. She managed to get one foot out. The woman took her hand. Lisa felt a shock shoot up her arm. The woman guided her to a nearby room, and had her sit up on a table that wasn't much larger than a doctor's table. She was handed a gold chalice to drink from. The heavy feeling in her head cleared up. She was told to lie back on the table and close her eyes.

The woman stood in back and placed her hands on Lisa's head, saying nothing. After a moment she did the same with her feet. Lisa just wanted to go to sleep. She was then told to open her eyes. She found the woman staring right into her face.

"You look nearly the same as she."

"The same as whom?" Lisa started to shake.

"You will know soon."

Lisa stood up and noticed the table she had been lying on. She ran her hand along the outer edge of it. It was made of a white, pearly substance. In the middle were circular panels of quartz.

She focused on her surroundings. The room was completely round, and about twenty-five feet in diameter. The domed ceiling was made of quartz, and was about twenty feet high. Like the table, the floor consisted of circular quartz panels, only larger.

The walls were made of marble, with a line of gold four inches wide that ran along the wall half way up. She moved away from the table and turned to follow this line until she came to a symbol. She thought her heart would stop as she held her breath. She kept trying to grab something at her chest over and over, but not knowing why.

She stopped and stood still for a moment focusing on the symbol. Somehow she knew this symbol. No, it couldn't be, she thought. It was impossible. *Impossible!* Lisa felt overwhelmed with déjà vu. She stared back at the woman who looked so much like Karen, closed her eyes and took a deep breath. She was afraid to ask... afraid to know, but she had to. "Where am I?"

"Do you not know?"

Lisa searched the woman's eyes, as tears formed in her own, "*Where?*"

The woman grinned as she slowly walked around the table never taking her almond shaped dark eyes off of Lisa.

"*Tell me!*" Lisa pleaded, hating being toyed with like this.

"Atlantis," the woman casually said.

Lisa moved back against the table. Tears streamed down her face. "No, this can't be. *This just can't be.*" She wiped her face with her hands. "I feel like I've come back home. I'm home, my real home. How..."

"No! Our real home is within the source. You must go back to your time frame now."

"Why?" Lisa asked, almost hysterically with tears flowing again.

"You cannot stay just yet. It will take time. Your body must adjust to this vibration slowly. You will know when to return. Though it is my opinion you should *never* return again...it is my thought that you will. You are as stubborn as she, and possibly more stubborn than he."

"Who?"

"Then the day will come when you will have to make a decision."

"A decision? What are you talking about?"

The woman took Lisa by the wrist pulling her. "You must go."

As they entered the room that held the capsule, Lisa stopped. Her mouth dropped and her eyes widened. "Oh God, that's incredible."

The capsule was embedded in a huge quartz pyramid forty feet high, with the apex going right through the center of the domed ceiling. She stood rooted to the spot, not being able to take her eyes off the awesome structure. The woman now grabbed hold of Lisa's upper arm and quickly walked her to the capsule.

"Wait!" Lisa said, as the woman started to close the door. "Do I know you? Have we met before?"

The woman stared coldly saying nothing.

"What's your name? Lisa asked gently.

The woman put her head down, and said softly, "Jenielle."

"That's beautiful." Lisa noted a hint of vulnerability about the woman, but Jenielle slammed the door shut before Lisa could say another word.

Lisa slowly moved from the bed with the intent of heading to the bathroom. The next thing she knew she was on the floor. She wasn't out for more than a couple of minutes, and made it to the bathroom just in time.

She poured herself a glass of club soda to help settle her stomach. She went back to bed with her journal, and wrote everything down. "This has to be nothing more than a dream."

Then why did it feel so real? And why was she sick again? Who was this Jenielle? What was that symbol, and why was she grabbing at her chest? *Atlantis?*

As she questioned all of this, a feeling of longing came over her as tears filled her eyes. It could be dreams she pondered, or out-of-body-experiences, or even past life memories coming into her conscious awareness. Whatever it was, she knew she wanted more. Atlantis was a part of her, and very much alive inside her.

Lisa felt like she had some kind of flu so she slept a lot over the next several days. During this time she called Karen to see if there was any progress with the hunt for rental space. Karen said there was nothing new, and that she didn't have time to talk. Lisa swore she heard a man's voice in the background. She had no plans to tell Karen she had meditated with the crystal again. She also didn't tell her how sick she was feeling.

Several nights later when Lisa was getting ready for bed, she noted how much better she was feeling, and nervously thought about embarking on another adventure. She felt she could do this on her own without the help of the guided meditation. She took a few deep breaths with the crystal lying on her chest. It all happened more quickly this time.

Jenielle stood before her dressed in an aqua, Grecian style gown. "Are you stabilized?"

Lisa wanted to laugh, but contained herself. "Yes, I guess I'm stabilized."

Jenielle guided her out of the capsule. She felt a little lightheaded and stopped while Jenielle supported her. Lisa noticed Jenielle kept looking her up and down.

"Most strange," Jenielle finally said as she ran her hand down the side of Lisa's jeans. She then touched the material of her own dress, and again touched Lisa's jeans. "Most strange."

"Why am I here? I don't understand any of this. What's…."

"Have you not discovered your gift of the crystal?"

"The crystal…you know about that?" Lisa's eyes widened.

"Yes. There are two halves. They fit together to make a whole."

"I have a crystal. And if I have a half, then where is the other?"

"You have many questions. They will be answered in time."

"But why am I here, in Atlantis?"

"You should not be, and *he* should be damned!" Jenielle said raising her voice.

"I don't understand. Is this a dream?"

"It may be wise for you to believe that."

"Are you upset that I'm here? And *who* should be damned?"

"Sylor!"

"Who is Sylor, and again, why am I here?" Lisa was becoming upset, and tried to move passed Jenielle to go somewhere, but didn't know where.

"Do not!" Jenielle held her back. "You do *not* understand. My advice to you is to go back from where you come, and never return, or even think of Atlantis again."

"Please, I need to know what's happening here. I'm in Atlantis and I believe I've lived here before. I have a strong feeling we knew each other. And why shouldn't I come back here. I know I loved Atlantis."

"Yes, you are correct. You were here, and you did love Atlantis, which is one of the reasons you left."

"I left…why, where did I go?"

"What is your time frame in the future, how many years between us?"

"I think, well, from what I've learned, there is possibly twelve thousand years between us, maybe more."

"You are twelve thousand years into the future. And how is Atlantis? Is she flourishing?" Jenielle raised her brow.

Lisa looked at her sadly. But by the look on Jenielle's face, Lisa suspected she already knew. "You know, don't you?"

"Say it!" Jenielle demanded. "What do the records reveal?"

Lisa hesitated for a few seconds, not wanting to believe it herself. "Jenielle, where I come from, Atlantis *does not* exist, and supposedly there is no real evidence it ever did. Atlantis is only seen as a myth, or a legend. But there are many who believe it did exist, and that one day proof will be discovered."

Jenielle turned and walked a few feet away looking downwards. When she turned back tears were evident. "Is it not enough we are headed for a fall...*but to never have existed at all?* Yes, your proof will be found, and your records will be rewritten. What was the cause of our demise?"

Lisa tried to hold back her tears. She swallowed the lump in her throat. "I'm so sorry to have to tell you any of this, but from what I've read, the continent of Atlantis broke up, and then sank from earthquakes brought on by the misuse of the crystal energy. The whole continent was destroyed."

Jenielle said nothing for about a minute or so. She kept staring down at the floor, and then finally raised her head. "You and the others were correct. He would not believe you. He would not hear your truth. He is caught up in his selfishness."

"Who...who are you talking about?" Lisa was starting to feel weak, and looked around for a place to sit. Her body was starting to shake.

"Sylor," Jenielle said in disgust.

"Who is Sylor?" Lisa was becoming visibly ill. Jenielle guided her back inside the capsule.

"You have stayed too long, you must go back."

"*Who* is Sylor?" Lisa demanded to know, as she stepped inside the capsule.

With no expression, Jenielle coldly said, "He was your husband."

Lisa opened her eyes and was nearly blinded from the sun streaming through the skylights above her bed. She sat up and noticed her stomach didn't feel too bad, but she did have a headache.

So Sylor was her husband. But who was *she*? And what the hell was going on anyway? Then it occurred to her that the man in her dream, the turquoise robed one, *was Sylor*. The man she desired with all her heart and soul had been her husband.

This acknowledgement took her breath away. Tears trickled down her cheeks as she placed her hand over her heart. She knew she loved this man like no other. She remembered how angry she was in the dream. What kind of man was he? Jenielle obviously didn't like him. And, how could she herself have been married to him if he wasn't benevolent in character? Was any of this real? *Was she losing her mind?*

She wanted so much to believe that somehow she really was in Atlantis, but how could it be possible? She looked around the bedroom. She looked at the pink curtains, and the floral wall covering. She noticed the shelf that held the Barbie doll, and the teddy bear she had since she was a child. She glanced down to the side of her dresser at the gallon jug of nickels she had been hoarding. These things were there as they had been for years. These things were solid reality. How could she have been anywhere else?

Lisa felt she could easily let herself buy in to all of this. She was told she had left Atlantis. Why did she leave? But more importantly, why was she going back there now? She had so many questions, and she was determined that they would all be answered.

In a weakened state she made her way downstairs, and managed to get the coffee going. She did have some mild nausea and poured herself some club soda. Even though her head ached, she felt mentally restless.

While Lisa waited for the coffee she tried to make herself comfortable on the sofa. Her hands shook as she reached for the television remote. She skimmed through all the channels. Boring! She picked up one of her favorite magazines lying on the coffee table. She impatiently thumbed through it, and then threw it on the floor. Boring!

What could top what she had been experiencing; except more of the same? She thought of Sylor. She would have to go back soon. She had to meet him. She had to see him for herself. The longing inside her was too much. Though she still felt weak, and knew it was probably too soon, she would try going back again early that night.

"You did not heed my advice," Jenielle commented, as Lisa slowly stepped out of the capsule. "I am not surprised. Hollina could be headstrong at times."

Lisa ignored what Jenielle had said. "I want to see Sylor."

"Why would you want to see a man that hurt you with disrespect? A man who did not…would not believe your truth."

"He was my husband."

"He is not now your husband." You are not the full embodiment of Hollina. She is only an aspect of you now.

"Hollina?"

"Hollina is a part of you that once lived."

"I'm Hollina reincarnated?"

"You are many. Hollina is the strongest aspect at this time, and with good reason."

"What reason?"

"Sylor planned it this way, but he will pay for his misdeed. Everyone pays for their misdeeds, whether they are in thought or in action."

Lisa walked a few feet away from the capsule. She felt a little lightheaded, but she knew she would be all right. She turned around and gasped. A living, breathing lion had come into the room. Lisa glared at Jenielle, who seemed unconcerned. As it slowly approached, Lisa began to relax, and all fear vanished, though she didn't know why.

The lion stood by Lisa's side and let out a roar. Lisa raised her eyebrows at Jenielle waiting for some kind of explanation.

"I have summoned him. He will walk by your side. He will help your energy to balance and adjust. He will also act as your protector."

"Why would I need protection?"

"One day you may. You need not concern yourself at this moment in time."

"What was Hollina like?"

"Very much like yourself. It is most strange. I did not believe she would be this strong in you. And you have talked of our demise, as did she."

"I don't under…" Lisa jumped. The lion had let out a roar.

"It is time. You must go."

"Why? I feel fine"

"The animals sense the energy better than we do," Jenielle commented. "It was not always that way. At one time we could sense it just as well. Some are still able, but they are few. You were one."

"But I want to see Sylor." Lisa looked around. She felt so desperate. She thought she would never see him. "Please, I…"

"There is no time. Though, you will be able to stay longer with each visit. Then you will have to make a decision."

"A decision?"

"There will come a time when your being will not be able to sustain itself at both vibrational levels. When you are fully adjusted and are capable of sustaining yourself here, you will have to choose whether to live your life here, or stay in your own reality of time. You will be unable to continue to do both. Once your choice has been made, you cannot *ever* go back to the other. You must weigh your decision carefully. Go now."

It was only a little after 10:00 p.m., which made Lisa wonder about the whole concept of time. She felt like she couldn't hold on to the pen as she repeatedly dropped it while writing in her journal. So she was the incarnation of someone named Hollina, and Sylor was the man to whom she had been married. This much she knew, but not much more.

She still didn't know why she was going back to Atlantis, *if* she was there at all. What about this Jenielle person, who reminded her so much of Karen?

"Wait a minute," Lisa said out loud. If she was the reincarnation of Hollina, then could Karen be Jenielle? "Yes, of course," she whispered, as the feeling seemed to hit her right in the solar plexus. With the way both Karen and Jenielle were acting towards her, they had to be cut from the same mold. She chuckled, but really didn't find it all that funny.

Lisa awakened almost twelve hours later, with a mild headache and, to her surprise no nausea. She made coffee and walked down to the beach. It was the first week of May. The sun felt warm on her face, and the breeze was invigorating. She looked out at the ocean and remembered that it covered three quarters of the earth, and somewhere down under all that ocean lay Atlantis…maybe. Damn! Why were there still doubts? Her head told her one thing, her heart another.

As she gazed out at the water she was overwhelmed with feelings of gratitude, and happily acknowledged everything she had in her life. She thought that if we do create our life by what we think and believe, then more people need to know and understand this concept.

Instead of focusing and believing in war and hate, if we chose forgiveness, peace and love, then maybe we would have world peace. It was really all in our mind, and we had a choice. She felt like a Pollyanna thinking that, but sometimes the truth can be quite simple, and supposedly she already knew anything is possible.

She thought about Karen. She felt that despite the fact Karen had this new life, she really wasn't all that happy. Lisa also sensed there was something secretive going on with her.

She started thinking about the small building that Karen knew was so perfect. She was right…it *was* perfect. In a trance, Lisa watched the waves coming in. Then it hit her. "Why didn't I think of this before?" She pulled out her cell phone to call Karen.

"The building on Lansing Avenue," Lisa said, "I don't know why I didn't think of it before, but I could help you out with purchasing the building. Hell, I could even buy the building. Yeah! I'll buy it!"

"Are you nuts?"

"Absolutely! Come on, it will work, I know it."

After much discussion and convincing, Karen agreed. "Okay, okay, let me call the realtor and get back to you."

Karen called back later that day. It was evident she had been crying. "You're not going to believe this. Someone put a binder on it yesterday. They really want the place. I'll just have to keep working on it. Thanks anyway, it was a great gesture."

Lisa hung up the phone feeling like a heel, even though it wasn't her fault. But she still felt it was the perfect place.

It would be a couple of more days before Lisa would take another 'trip' to Atlantis. She wanted to regain all her strength. The dreams of Sylor had stopped, since the Atlantis thing began. She had only one goal in mind this time, and that was to meet Sylor.

She nervously thought of the decision she would have to make. She did not like the sound of that. To have to make a choice of whether or not to stay in a place that supposedly never existed… how absurd!

What if Atlantis *is* a myth? What if it *was* only something in Plato's imagination? Was this all in *her* imagination? Had she watched too many reruns of *The Twilight Zone?* She felt Rod Serling had nothing on her!

"Will I meet Sylor this time?" Lisa anxiously crossed her fingers waiting for Jenielle to answer. Jenielle said nothing, but motioned for Lisa to follow her. The lion clung to Lisa's side. She eagerly stroked the animal, feeling an attachment to him. "Jenielle, I want to…"

"Yes, you made your demand known at our last encounter."

"Well?" No answer. Lisa felt like throwing something at her. What was with this woman's attitude?

Lisa was requested to lie on the table. Jenielle swept her hands over Lisa, and revealed she was cleaning her aura. After ten minutes Lisa was given the chalice to drink from.

"Jenielle, if I was Hollina, well, obviously we knew each other, but how? What was our relationship to each other?"

"We were sisters."

"Oh." Lisa's eyes widened, she could hardly believe it. She thought about Karen and how they had become blood sisters when they were children. Somehow, Jenielle didn't seem like a sister.

Jenielle brought Lisa to another room known as the bathing room. It was larger and had a small pool in the center of it. The room had a domed ceiling, which was made of quartz. Lisa noted how beautiful the rays of the sun had shone through, creating a brilliant cascade of colors that reflected off the pool of water. Two woman wearing tan colored gowns arrived with toiletries, and large pieces of cloth which Lisa assumed would be towels. The woman began removing their gowns.

"Remove your clothing," Jenielle said lifelessly to Lisa.

"What?"

"You must remove your clothing," she repeated with a tone of impatience.

Lisa looked around feeling uneasy. A woman she hardly knew, two women she didn't know, plus a lion, and she was suppose to take her clothes off?

"Why do you hesitate?"

"I'm not used to taking my clothes off in front of others."

"Are you not foolish? I have not heard of such a thing. Remove your clothing now."

Lisa winced. Obviously, in Atlantis they had no problem with nudity…unlike us, she thought. She began removing her clothes, slowly, piece by piece, feeling humiliated. She kept telling herself she really didn't have to do this, but she *was* curious. And if this is what it took to finally meet Sylor, well…

She stood totally naked, using her hands and arms to cover strategic places. "This better be a dream," she mumbled.

"I do not understand this foolishness."

"Jenielle, where I come from nudity is seen as something wrong, something dirty. If we don't cover our bodies, we are talked about, and not too kindly."

"Is this the direction we are taking as humans?" Sadness showed as Jenielle shook her head. "Then with all that is happening, I should not be surprised."

The two women stepped forward smiling warmly, took Lisa by the arms, and then gently led her into the pool. Jenielle left the room. Though Lisa still felt self conscious, she did relax a bit in the pinkish colored water, until the women began to bathe her. She stiffened up, leaving a baffled expression on the women's faces. It finally occurred to her that this was the norm, and forced herself to let them bathe her. The women smiled thoughtfully, but never spoke.

Lisa was guided out of the pool, and the women dried her off. They rubbed oil over her body that smelled like roses, which reminded her of the rose oil she sometimes used in her bath.

Jenielle returned carrying a pale pink, long sleeved gown for Lisa to wear. The neckline was cut low, and had gold trim. The gown had an empire waist, and tied in the back. Lisa felt it was a tad tight, but not uncomfortable. Her hair was brushed up in a ponytail and tucked under with ornate pins with flecks of gold.

One of the women slipped a long chain holding a gold medallion, over her head. The medallion itself measured about two inches around and hung down between her breasts. Lisa held her breath upon seeing it. She clutched the pendant in her palm when she realized it was the same symbol she had seen on the wall. Lisa felt Jenielle must have sensed her forthcoming question.

"It is the symbol of Atlantis. This medallion is worn *only* by the priests, and priestesses of Atlantis."

"Hollina was a priestess?" Lisa chuckled inside upon thinking how Karen would hate *this*. The two women bowed to her, and smiled. Jenielle turned away and said nothing.

Jenielle then motioned for Lisa to follow. The lion accompanied them. They walked down a long hall, which had pillars of marble, and walls made of blue lapis with gold etched into them. Statues were set into some of the walls, and light poured through quartz ceilings. Lisa looked down, and to her amazement saw that the floors looked to be made of opal.

Jenielle said nothing, but Lisa knew where she was being taken. Butterflies danced in her stomach as they stood outside of a large gold door. Jenielle stepped in front of her, opened the door, and then stepped back.

"You may proceed inside," Jenielle said in a soft tone, as she looked downward.

The butterflies in Lisa's stomach were now doing the twist, and her hands had become sweaty. She felt like she had waited forever for this moment. She inhaled as if going underwater, and took one step inside the room. She let the breath out, taking another, and took two more steps in passed the open door.

She quietly gasped. There, about twenty feet away he stood, but with his back towards her. She turned and looked for Jenielle. Only the lion remained. Lisa stood fixed, holding her breath, as she waited for him to turn and speak. Silence reigned. Anger began to well up in her. He *knew* she was there. Lisa could feel the false pride in him, as well as in herself.

She eyed him up and down, all six feet of him. It was just like in the dream… the long turquoise robe, and the blonde hair which brushed his shoulders. She wasn't sure which emotion she was feeling most; anger, fear, or excitement. The tension was mounting and her shoulders tightened. The stillness had become intolerable.

"Turn around, turn to me," she called. He remained motionless. She figured if she was smart she would turn around and walk out. *But no, she was in love*. Again she swallowed her pride. Her neck was beginning to hurt. "Turn around, turn to me," she bellowed.

He didn't budge. She had come back to be treated like this? Maybe Jenielle was right. How could he humiliate her like this? She clenched her fist as she bit the inside of her mouth.

"Damn you, Sylor!" She walked swiftly to him, and stood about five feet behind him. "Turn around, turn to me. *Look at me!*" she demanded.

Slowly, very slowly, he turned. Lisa's breath became shallow as she stood shaking, with her pulse racing. Then it happened. She took one look into his sky-blue eyes, gulped, and stood completely still. Her chest ached, and her heart wanted to engulf him. The urge to move into him, to meld with him was overwhelming.

"Oh God," she whispered as she looked into a face she felt God had sculpted with His own hands…a perfect masterpiece.

She felt beams of light streaming forth from inside herself. Her aura was expanding and enveloping them both. She knew he had to have felt the love that was radiating from her. He had to have felt the love that was exuding from every pore of her body. She could feel the same coming from him. She immersed herself in his light, going into the very core of his being, where she was exposed to the depth of love that his ego unsuccessfully tried to keep hidden from her.

Then she felt his light beginning to contract. Though she was becoming mush inside, she knew she had to stand strong. There was an intensity about him that shook her. With that feeling she forced herself to look away, and moved her gaze downward. She saw he was wearing the same medallion as she.

The strength of his gaze drew her eyes to his again. His features hardened as he examined her face. One corner of his mouth curled up. Part of her wanted to smack the smugness off his princely face. The other part wanted to wrap herself around him. After what seemed to an eternity, his face softened and his mouth dropped some. The sternness washed away, and was replaced by an expression of longing.

"Hollina," he whispered as he moved closer to her, "it is really you." He lightly touched her face with one hand.

His touch made her tremble, and every hair on her body stood on end. She didn't say a word. She just wanted to drink in the feeling. She held her breath, afraid to break the connection. It took all she could to hold herself together.

His eyes began to well up unmasking his vulnerability. He took her face in both hands. His touch relayed to her the words he could not yet speak. It didn't matter. She could feel his every emotion as if they were one being.

"I have you back," he whispered. "You have come back to me."

She saw him smile for the first time. It was a sad smile that would stay impressed in her mind.

He pulled her to himself, and inhaled her scent. He gently embraced her, and caressed the back of her neck. She detected a faint scent of vanilla coming from him, and at the same time she could feel the heat emanating from his body…the body she was longing for.

She gazed up at his tear-covered face. Abruptly, he let her go and turned away. She knew he didn't want her to see him like that. She knew he did not want her to have that kind of power over him. The lion let out a roar warning Lisa she had to go.

"Sylor," she said, taking his hand. "Where I am from, my name is Lisa, not Hollina."

"It matters not. You are still Hollina. You carry her within you."

He smiled softly as she stroked his face, his hair, and touched his mouth. She declined to do the thing she had wanted to do since the moment she saw his face; meet his lips with hers.

"You will return," he said confidently.

"How can I not?"

They said nothing more. She walked to the door where the lion waited, and turned back. Sylor's face was expressionless, even hinting of coldness. And then again, he turned away from her. She knew she had hurt him somehow, and now he was guarded. He had so much pride, she thought…too much.

Chapter 4

———

L isa opened her eyes and gazed at the stars that hung above her. She turned over on her side, and brought the comforter up to her neck. "Oh God, I don't want to be here."

Atlantis was where she wanted to be, where she belonged, with her beloved. She recalled what had taken place the first time they had looked into each other's eyes. He was everything to her. She wiped her eyes knowing she had found her twin soul.

The next morning, Lisa took a cup of coffee and headed down to the beach. She was too tired and depressed to walk to the east side and didn't wander very far. She found a spot to sit in the sand. She began questioning what was happening. She knew she couldn't keep it to herself much longer, and decided she would tell Karen soon.

But what would she tell her? That somehow she was meeting her twin soul in Atlantis, a place that supposedly never existed, and eventually she would have to make the choice of whether or not to stay there?

While growing up Lisa had always felt different from the other kids. This feeling hadn't changed much as an adult. Sometimes when she looked at her reflection, she felt like she was on the wrong side of the mirror. "A psychologist could have a field day with me," she whispered.

As difficult as it was, she wanted to put Sylor and the whole Atlantis thing out of her mind for the moment and relax. Before she was able to, she saw someone running up the beach coming her way.

The person was yelling gibberish, and ran as if they were trying to break a record, or a leg. She realized it was Karen. "Oh God, something's wrong." Lisa ran to meet her.

Karen practically tackled her, and they both fell in the sand. "You've got it, you've got it!"

"Got what?" Lisa scowled, as she stood up and brushed the sand off herself. "Christ Karen, I thought someone died."

"The building!" Karen caught her breath. "You've got the building! The other party backed out. It's yours if you still want it. You still want to do this, right?"

"Yeah. Yeah, I do. This is great!"

"All right!" Karen threw her arms around Lisa, then kicked off her shoes, and raced into the water up to her knees. She began laughing and yelling, "Life is great!"

Lisa ran down to meet her. Karen grabbed her hands and they danced around in a circle giggling like two children, until they both fell into the water.

"I'm freezing," Karen yelled.

"Me too, let's go back to the house." Lisa retrieved her coffee mug from the sand.

As they were running to the house Lisa came to a dead stop. "There he is again."

Karen looked around, puzzled. "Who?"

"Mr. Moses," Lisa mumbled under her breath.

"Who? I don't see anyone."

"Never mind."

"That's your problem," Karen said as she pointed to the coffee mug, "that crap you're drinking."

"Sorry Karen, but carrot juice just doesn't do it for me."

Lisa hadn't gone back to Atlantis since meeting Sylor. It had been over a week and he hadn't left her thoughts. She felt like she was walking a fine line between fantasy and reality. It was just this state of mind that kept her from going back just yet.

A few days later, she and Karen went out for dinner. Lisa couldn't contain herself any longer and told Karen everything. But oddly, she refrained from telling Karen that she was the incarnation of Jenielle.

"You must think I'm crazy." Lisa took a sip of wine and let out a sigh, feeling some relief of being able to bare her soul.

"I think you could be getting vivid past life memories, or it's out-of-body experiences. And that man you've seen, the one on the beach, he could very well be a spirit guide. We all have them. Sometimes they make their presence known at certain times in our lives."

"But it all feels so real in Atlantis, and Sylor...I mean it's like I'm experiencing it as myself, not as an observer."

"Then maybe it *is* all just dreams," Karen said impatiently. "I don't know what to tell you."

"No, no, I know it's not dreams. And what's so hard is that...I don't want to be here anymore." Lisa put her head down. "I want to be there...with him."

"Now you're scaring me," Karen said, rubbing her forehead. "Look, not that long ago we were talking about Atlantis, and twin souls. We were...look, Lisa you are *not* actually going back to Atlantis. It's all in your mind."

"You think I'm losing it, don't you?"

"I really don't know *what* to think. This sounds so...its makes for great fiction but..."

"Yeah, it does make for..." Lisa placed her hand to her stomach hoping to calm the queasiness she was suddenly experiencing. Fiction? She hadn't considered that. Was her mind somehow creating all of this for a new book? No, that could not be. *Sylor was real.* He *had* to be.

"Look... again; I don't know what to tell you. No, maybe I do. Get rid of that damn crystal!"

"No!" Lisa raised her voice, "Absolutely not! That crystal is my connection to Atlantis." Her voice softened, "And to him."

Lisa didn't want to think anymore about reality versus fantasy. She missed Sylor long enough and decided to go back that night.

"Where is Sylor?" Lisa anxiously stepped out of the capsule. "I want to see him."

"Sylor is not available," Jenielle said. "He is with the other scientists in the ambiterrium."

"What's that?"

"Do you not remember?"

Jenielle's tone of sarcasm angered Lisa. "If I did…" she silently started counting to ten. "No, I don't remember."

"The ambiterrium is where Sylor and his fellow scientists work."

"Sylor is a priest *and* a scientist?" I know he is a priest, I saw the medallion."

"Sylor is becoming less of a priest as he is moving away from the ways of spirit. He holds the highest position as head scientist. He is well respected, and knows it. This has made him big inside his head. He is but a fool."

"When can I see him?"

"He will be back shortly. Come, you will be bathed while you wait."

They, along with the lion, proceeded to the bathing room. The same two women came forward. Lisa removed her clothes, this time without hesitation. Jenielle nodded with approval and left the room.

Lisa had just finished dressing when Jenielle re-entered the room with a chalice. Lisa drank from it. "I should have asked this before, but what is this that I've been drinking?"

"It is made from the flowers. It helps to clear our aura, the energy field around each of us, so that illness may not set in. Sylor has not yet returned. We must wait."

"Jenielle, you said I…I mean Hollina was your sister. Are you older or younger?

"I came before Hollina."

"I know who you are in my reality. You reincarnated as my friend Karen. We've always been like sisters. This is incredible."

"Incredible, yes." Jenielle raised a brow. "What of Sylor? Is he too in your reality?"

"No, at least not that I know of."

Jenielle quickly turned away. "The woman who I am in your time frame, is she with a husband?"

"No. She was once, but it didn't work out."

"How did you feel for this man that was her husband?"

"I never knew him. She lived in another part of the country at the time, and they weren't together very long."

"And there is no Sylor in your time frame. This you are sure of?"

"If Sylor is in my reality…my time frame, then I haven't met him. I would know Sylor. I would know him anywhere."

"Let us cease discussion of Sylor."

"What did I do here as Hollina. What was my work?"

"You were a healer. Many came to you. You knew the power of the mind and what it could do."

"Why did I leave here?"

"You ask big questions." Jenielle walked a few feet away, and paused. She turned back with a somber look. "You were one of the few left who were prophetic. Two times in the distant past there were earthquakes. This was long before you and I. These earthquakes destroyed parts of our land. Atlantis was much larger than it is now. In a vision you and six others saw the destruction that would end us. It may soon be upon us. You…Hollina, vowed never to witness this."

"So…what happened, and what about Sylor?"

"You could not bear to be a part of the death of the land you loved so much. You wished to make Egypt your new home with the many others, and then bring the knowledge of our culture to other areas of the planet."

"So Sylor and I went to Egypt?"

"No. No, you did not go to Egypt. Sylor would not hear of it. He too knows the power of the mind and what your beliefs can create. He refused to believe you or the others. The bigness in his head was beyond your vision. He is a brilliant scientist. There are none like him. But the others who work with him are not so brilliant. And they are dangerous."

"What do you mean?"

"In the vision, you saw these very scientists. They fool with the crystals, and have found a way to grow them, but it is not the same. These crystals have no heart, unlike the crystals we have unearthed. These scientists have evil within. Their desire is to gain enough power to control the entire planet, and they intend to use the crystals to do this. There are certain experiments that…"

"But what about *Sylor?* Is this what he wants too?"

"He does not. He will not give his word to experiment in this way. The experiments are written in code and are…"

A woman in a tan gown entered the room and nodded her head to Jenielle, and then left. "Sylor has returned. I will take you to him, but there is little time."

Lisa made a mental note to continue this conversation. She wanted to know more about the experiments, and how she came to leave Atlantis.

As they made their way down the hall, Lisa felt her heart beginning to beat faster in anticipation. Sylor opened the door as they approached. He and Jenielle exchanged glances. Lisa felt the tension and wondered what the problem was between them, but it would have to wait. Sylor was the only thing she wanted to focus on at the moment.

Sylor and Lisa stood facing each other. There was a moment of silence as they took in each other's essence. She shivered as he made the first move, taking her face in his hands. "I long for the day when you will again be my wife."

Lisa couldn't move. She couldn't speak. The thought of being with him...there were no words. She slowly moved her hands through his hair. Gradually they made their way to his face, and to his mouth. She ran her fingers along his upper lip. It was all she could do to keep her dignity.

He then cloaked her with his embrace. Lisa took in his scent and couldn't take it anymore. She wrapped her arms around his neck, and pressed her lips on his. He quickly accepted the invitation, and reciprocated deeply with all abandonment.

A passion swept over her, as she had never known before. Aching for more, she pressed herself against him, and felt his readiness beneath his robe.

He pushed her back, straining to breathe. "No! We cannot! We cannot give ourselves to each other at this time. It would be detrimental to your being. It is too soon."

"Then when?" The lion let out a roar. "When can we be together?" Lisa didn't like hearing the desperation in her own voice.

"You must go."

"But Sylor I..."

"You must go *now*."

"Sylor, I don't want to leave you."

He took her in his arms and tenderly kissed her mouth. "Be not concerned. We will have our time. Two embodiments connected by one soul, one heart, cannot forever be separated. We will be together, and our love will be all that it was meant to be. I promise you." He slowly backed away. "Go now."

Lisa walked back to the bathing room to change. Jenielle was nowhere to be found. The lion alone walked Lisa back to the capsule.

Two days later, and against her better judgment, Lisa found herself on Karen's doorstep. She still felt somewhat dazed from her recent excursion to Atlantis, and her heart ached more than ever.

Just as Lisa walked in the door, the phone began to ring. Karen looked hesitant to answer, but picked up before the answering machine did. Lisa could hear a man's voice on the other end. Karen told him she couldn't talk, and quickly hung up.

"Lisa, what's the matter? You look lost."

With tear filled eyes, Lisa looked down at the floor. "Karen, I don't belong here. I know how crazy this all sounds but…"

"Oh, please, not this Atlantis stuff again."

Lisa sat down and rested her head in her hands. "My life has turned upside down. I don't know what's real anymore. Now that I have met Sylor, I know he is my twin soul, and I *cannot* imagine my life without him." She stood up, and started pacing the floor.

"I don't think I want to hear any of this." Karen let out a breath of annoyance.

"Two embodiments connected by one soul, one heart, cannot forever be separated," Lisa said as she wiped her tears.

"What?"

"Sylor said those words to me. Karen, you said it could be dreams, or past life memories. Well, what about time travel? Maybe I'm going back in time to a life I actually once lived, a life I am so emotionally connected to, and it's important that I…"

"Lisa, listen to yourself! Stop it! None of this is *real*. Sylor is not real, just like Jeff was not real!"

Lisa almost hated her for saying that. Karen either didn't see the incensed look on Lisa's face, or chose to ignore it, as she continued her admonishment.

"Lisa, did you ever think that this is nothing more than your writer's imagination? Think about it. How long have you been trying to come up with something new? You even said yourself you wanted to write something different. Well, how different can this get?"

"How can you say something like that? How can you insult me like…*you know me*. Damn it! I can't believe you…"

"Look, I'm sorry. I didn't mean to...Lisa, maybe you should..."

"Maybe I should what?" Lisa quickly challenged.

"Well...maybe you should see someone. I'm sorry."

"You mean like a therapist...so maybe I should seek professional help?" Lisa shook her head. "You were the one person I thought would understand these things, metaphysics, reincarnation, dreams. But you..."

"Maybe the breakup with Dave hit you harder than you realize."

"Oh, I'm out of here." Lisa thought for sure she broke the door on her way out.

"Proof...I need proof," she kept repeating on the drive home. Yes, proof. Proof she really was in Atlantis. Proof that everything she was experiencing was real. *Proof she wasn't going crazy*.

Why couldn't she just trust what her heart was telling her? Instead, she kept falling into the left brained, show me, 'if I can't see it then it doesn't exist society.' A very limited and close-minded way of thinking, she felt. But she had to face it; these things just do not happen in this society, *or* in reality. No one time travels back to Atlantis; no one time travels. She would have to bring something back from Atlantis, even if it was just to prove it to herself.

Chapter 5

––––––

"Jenielle, last time I was here you said something about experiments written in code," Lisa said as they walked to the bathing room.

"Yes, the experiments are recorded in the journals, but they are coded. The information contained within them could prove dangerous if they were to fall into the wrong hands. Only Sylor knows the codes. He wrote them himself, and will allow no one access to them, which is his right."

"So, what about these experiments?"

"There are certain experiments, experiments that must be done with right use of mind, and purity of heart. The energy is neutral. What is manifested depends on how one directs and applies the energy. If used in a positive mind fashion then they could benefit the entire planet. If one has intentions otherwise, the same experiments could bring about disastrous results."

Lisa shivered. Somehow she knew what Jenielle had just said was absolutely true.

"The scientists press Sylor for this information, but he will not comply. You and the others feared one day Sylor would be overruled, and his fellow scientists would seize his journals. It would take much time, but the codes could one day be deciphered. That day may soon be upon us."

Knowing this is very likely what would happen, Lisa thought Sylor should burn the journals. But, even if he did, Sylor would still retain the information. What would the scientists do to get it from him? The hair on her arms stood on end with that thought. She knew his life would be in danger, and that he should leave Atlantis.

"In his bigness," Jenielle continued, "Sylor believes his word is law and no one will overrule him. There is still time. He still has the power to stop this, to send the scientists away, but he will not believe. But now, you are from the future, and you know what has taken place. You must convince Sylor to put an end to this before it is out of his hands. It is up to you now. This may be our last chance. You must convince him!"

"*Me? I* must convince him?" Why was this suddenly *her* responsibility? "If he didn't believe me then, why would he now?"

"You have seen. You have confirmed this. You say there is no Atlantis. You are proof!"

"I'm proof! Oh God, I'm proof that Atlantis doesn't exist?"

"Yes!"

"Oh God, this can't be. This is nuts. I was hoping I'd be able to take something back with me today to my reality, to convince myself Atlantis *did* exist, and that what I'm experiencing is real. I need to know that I am not going crazy. And now I'm here as proof to you that Atlantis does *not* exist?"

Lisa felt like the figure in Evard Munch's painting, 'The Scream.' It took her several minutes to get her bearings. Then a thought occurred to her that maybe *none* of this was real, that maybe life was not real…like Einstein said; it was all just an illusion. Maybe life *is* but a dream…like the song says.

"Jenielle, I don't think Sylor will believe me even now if I tell him. He won't believe me. I can feel it. He'll just think I've come back with more of the same."

"Then we are doomed."

Why did she have to say *that?* Lisa thought. Why was it her responsibility to convince him? And why did she feel so guilty?

"Jenielle, you said that I left here, and wanted to go to Egypt, but I didn't. Where did I go?"

"You could have gone to Egypt. You *should* have gone to Egypt. You see, you would not go without your beloved Sylor," she said snidely, "And he knew this. What he did *not* know," she snickered, "is that you would choose to make transition."

"Transition? Is that what I think it is? I chose to die?"

"You are surprised?"

"But I *chose* to die?"

"Nearly everyone of your standing chooses their time to make transition. It is when they feel their work is done here." Jenielle's narrowed eyes looked coldly into Lisa's. "But some make the mistake of thinking they are done, for reasons only they can speak of. Is this not the way in your future?"

Lisa had drifted off. There was something not right about why Hollina chose to die. She could feel it. It was all wrong.

"What?" Lisa asked. "Oh…no, no, we do make transition or die, but we don't choose to, or want to. We die from disease, accidents, old age. We are a society that is afraid of death."

"Afraid? What foolishness you bring. Why would one be afraid of being free of our embodiments? They serve a purpose as we learn and grow from each lifetime. That is a gift. There is so much more in spirit, until the time comes when we no longer need to live other lives and we awaken and rejoin our Source in the ecstasy of oneness." The lion let out a roar. "There is little time. You must be bathed."

"I have longed for your return," Sylor said, as he opened the door.

Lisa and the lion stepped in, and Lisa noticed the large bed on the other side of the room. It had been there before, of course, but she focused on it this time. She imagined Hollina lying on it with him.

Sylor secured her in his arms and kissed her lightly, then pulled away. "As much as we desire each other, we can not love each other until you make your full adjustment here." He took her hands in his. "Then we can be together again, and forever…in body, and then when we awaken to our source."

Lisa pulled her hands and looked away.

"What is wrong?"

"I don't know if…I don't know if I'm staying here."

"What do you speak of? You will stay!"

"Sylor, I'm not sure how to explain this to you." She couldn't bear to look at him. "When I'm here this is all very real. But when I'm in my reality, your future, it's as if what's transpired here is all a dream, or something else. I'm not sure. All I know is that when I'm in my reality none of *this* is real. In my heart I believe it is real, but I have no proof that it is, and I need that proof. Especially since…"

"What are you speaking of? This *is* real! You are standing here before me. We have touched. Our lips have touched. Why are you with doubt? Why is proof needed?"

"You are not going to like this…" Lisa took a deep breath and worked up the courage to look at him again.

"Tell me!"

"One of the reasons I need proof is because I'm 12,000 or so years into your future, and…and Atlantis does not exist, and supposedly never did. There is no real evidence that it ever existed. Atlantis is seen only as a myth or a legend in my reality. It is…"

"Stop! That is enough! I will hear no more. That is a *lie!*"

"No. No, it's not. Sylor, please listen."

"I will not!" He turned his back and walked a few feet away. "Jenielle has poisoned your mind, has she not?"

"No, no, it's not like that, listen to me."

"I will not," he said, keeping his back turned.

Lisa took a deep breath and bit the inside of her mouth. She ran up to him, grabbed his arm and swung him around to face her. She was surprised by her own strength as was he. One side of his mouth curled up. She remembered that look the first time they had met. God, it turned her on. The magnetism he exuded nearly knocked her over.

"Sylor you are going to listen to me. Where I come from there are people that *do* believe Atlantis did exist. But the story has it that Atlantis was destroyed by their own doing. They blew themselves up, so to speak. They got greedy with power, control, and they used the crystals wrongly. And from what Jenielle tells me this is what could be starting to happen."

"Jenielle knows nothing. She should learn to quiet her voice. And you my true, my one and only love, have not changed. You *still* insist on telling tales."

"Sylor, it's true. Please believe me. Atlantis does not exist in the future. But it doesn't have to be that way. Stop your people, the scientists. There still could be time. Stop them now while you still have control."

"I will continue to have control. They will not work against me. They may have ideas that I feel are unwise, but there is nothing they can do."

"That could be true for now, but it will change. They will insist on their own way. Stop it now! Send these scientists away. Do something with your journals. Burn them."

"I will not! There is much good that will come out of the experiments. Goodness for us, and the entire planet. The energy will be used wisely."

"*You* will use the energy wisely, but they won't. Can't you see? Why won't you listen to me? I have the truth. Once you loved me enough to listen to me, I know you did…I know you did."

Sylor kissed her tears, and then embraced her. "Do not doubt my love for you…ever. You are the other half of my soul. Without you I do not want to live. You left once, and I cannot allow that to happen again. When the time comes you will stay, and there will be no more tales to tell. We will be together."

"You still don't understand. I need proof. I need to take something back with me to my reality. I need to know this is not a dream, or that I am not going crazy…losing my mind. Is there anything I could take back with me? Is it possible?"

Sylor paced, looking down at the floor. Lisa didn't like the taxed look on his face. "It is possible."

"What? What is it?"

"There is something, one thing, but I cannot…will not…allow it."

Sylor walked over to an altar that held a jade box. He lifted the lid off of it, and took something out. He turned and held it up. "Is this not like the one you possess?"

"The other half of the crystal! Yes, it is exactly like mine." She took it and examined it. She noticed the differences in the inclusions. Still, the crystals were basically the same, but she could tell the two apart.

"These crystals as a whole were created from our hearts, and they fit together perfectly. It is only *this* crystal that you could possibly transport, for it is a part of you, a part of us. This crystal holds *your* essence, *your* heart, *your* soul, which is a part of mine. This crystal holds your love for me, and it is what I hold of you. The crystal you possess contains the same of myself."

"Then let me take this."

"Never!"

"Why not?"

"Do you not understand? It is these crystals that are our gift. They will forever bring us together while we are on earth. They are our connection to each other. When you left me, you left behind the crystal that contains my essence. It is that crystal you now possess in your reality. I had both crystals and I needed to unburden myself; I needed to give myself to you again. I needed to bring you back to me. If you take this crystal you will have both, and our connection will be broken. You will not be able to return here to Atlantis, and it may be eons before we are together again."

"Oh, no. No, I don't want that to happen. I couldn't stand the thought of never being able to come back here. No, I couldn't stand the thought of never seeing you again."

The lion roared. Sylor and Lisa stood at the door facing each other. Neither could pull away.

"I could not bear to lose you again." He stroked her face. "When you hold the crystal in your time frame; know that I am with you. Know my love is always with you, Hollina."

Lisa's heart sank when she opened her eyes. "Back to reality." Or was it? She pulled out her journal to record everything. When she finished, she rested her head on the pillow and began to think about everything. Was she setting herself up for a big fall? Every time she went back to Atlantis she felt she might be digging herself in deeper. If in the end none of this turned out to be true, what would she do? Where would she go from here? It scared her to think she might not want to live anymore.

Lisa still didn't have her proof. Why was that so important? She knew what her heart was telling her. Why couldn't she just have enough faith, and trust it?

The next day Lisa was comfortably relaxed listening to Beethoven's Moonlight Sonata. She envisioned herself and Sylor lying together, holding each other, until she was interrupted by someone knocking at the side door. "It has to be Karen," she said annoyed.

It seemed Karen was the only person ever to use the side door. Everyone else used the front or the back. Lisa didn't want to answer. Feeling like a ten-year-old she decided she didn't like Karen at that moment, recalling their last meeting. She still wondered if she had broken the door. "Oh grow up," she told herself, and decided to answer the door.

"Hi," Karen said meekly with an expression of remorse. She was holding a big cardboard box.

"Hi. Come in."

Karen placed the box on the kitchen table. Lisa thought she heard a noise coming from it.

"Open it up," Karen said, smiling.

Lisa looked at her, reluctant to do anything. "What is it?" she asked suspiciously, expecting some kind of 'jack in the box' joke to pop up at her.

"Just open it."

Lisa scowled, and backed away as she opened the box. When nothing popped out she stuck her head in the box to be greeted by a fully grown solid gray cat. She quickly picked it up.

"Oh my God, he's beautiful. Or is it a she?"

"It's a he. I know how much you love cats, and it seems you've never been able to have one, seeing everyone you've ever lived with was allergic."

"Dave didn't like cats. So he told me he was allergic. Where did you find this one?"

"The animal shelter you used to volunteer at. I figured I'd rescue one from death row."

"Don't remind me…that always broke my heart."

"Oh, and you are not going to believe this. I couldn't decide on this cat, or another that looked similar. Then the attendant called this cat by its name. Would you believe he's called Charcoal?"

"You've got to be kidding."

"You do want him, don't you?"

"Of course I do!"

"All right, I'll be right back! I've got all kinds of kitty supplies in the car."

It was rather cool outside, but they took a couple of bottles of wine and sat out on the deck.

"Gee, the first time you gave me a cat you wanted to be my friend," Lisa said with a hint of a smile. "So what about this time?"

"The same...it's sort of a peace offering. I'm sorry about what happened. I should have been more understanding. I shouldn't have said the things I did. I'm really sorry. And by the way, I thought the glass was going to shatter when you slammed the door!"

Lisa burst out laughing, and told Karen she thought she may have done some damage. Even though things seemed better at the moment, she felt she couldn't confide in Karen. But what was the alternative? A therapist was out of the question. She was *not* crazy.

They both watched Charcoal peering through the glass sliders. The cat brought them back to their childhood. They talked about when they played with dolls and how someday they would have lots of children.

"At this point in my life, I don't think I would want to have kids, the way the world is today. Dave never really wanted kids, and I didn't want them bad enough so....I guess you could say my books were my children."

"I would still like to have one, and there's not much time left for that. But after having a miscarriage, and then..." Karen wiped the tear that rolled down her cheek.

"And then...what?" Lisa urged.

Karen turned away, eyeing the ocean view. Then turned back and looked into Lisa's eyes for a few seconds. "And then...nothing. I don't think I was meant to be a mother this time around, that's all."

Karen's hands shook as she picked up her glass, and continued to stare out at the water. Lisa watched her. She felt genuinely sorry for Karen. She noted that Karen covered herself well. She knew Karen had two miscarriages. Not one. Lisa wasn't supposed to know about the first one, which was part of the big secret she wasn't supposed to know *anything* about. Karen had the second a few years later when she was married briefly.

Karen poured herself more wine. "Well, the closing is next week. I hope to be in business about two weeks after that. I am so looking forward to this. I need some fulfillment in my life," she said with a far away look in her eyes.

"God, I remember when we were little; fulfillment was getting the man of your dreams and living happily ever after." Lisa raised her glass.

"The man of your dreams, right, that's nothing but a big, very big, fairy tale. It's the big lie. No, we do *not* get the man of our dreams. Someone else always gets him."

Karen gulped the rest of her wine, and poured herself another glass. "You know, I can't even visualize getting the right man. He's not there. In my mind, he's not there. He's always with someone else. Someone else always gets him."

Lisa flinched, feeling the cynicism in Karen's voice, and then calmly said, "You're seeing someone aren't you?"

"Righto, missy." Karen guzzled the rest of her wine.

Lisa grabbed the wine bottle and poured what was left into her own glass. Karen had drunk enough.

"He's married, isn't he?"

"Right again. But you always are. Actually Lisa, he's separated. And he doesn't want his wife to know..."

"Do I know him?" Lisa asked, holding her breath. She didn't like what she was thinking. After all, they were all grown up now.

"Sort of."

"Sort of? I sort of know him?"

"Last September, Dave came to L.A. on a business trip. Do you remember that?"

"Uh huh," Lisa said, biting the inside of her mouth.

"At that time, I had felt very lonely. Even though I had done therapy, and my life had definitely changed for the better, I was still lonely...lonely for a man. By some so called coincidence, a friend and I were at this little out of the way restaurant. Dave walked in.

With him was another man, Steve, now his new business partner. Steve was a fatal attraction for me. I knew the moment he walked in the door.”

Lisa breathed a sigh of relief. She now realized what was going on that day at the restaurant when Dave came in with Steve and his ‘wife.’

“I didn’t know right away that Steve was married. We saw each other the entire two weeks. He told me he was married the last night he was there. He assured me it was okay, because they were separated, and were going to divorce. He is the reason I moved back here. He couldn’t move out there, because of his daughter. He would never leave her, and I agreed with that. I could understand. All those months he kept calling me, and telling me he loved me, and that we would be together.”

“So what’s going on now? Are you together?”

“Yes and no.” Karen picked up the empty wine bottle. “Do you have another one?”

“No,” Lisa lied, feeling guilty and wanting another glass herself.

“Steve’s wife doesn’t want a divorce anymore, she wants him back. And now he’s not so sure. He doesn’t want her to know he’s been seeing someone.”

“So where does that leave you?”

“I don’t know. He keeps telling me he needs time, and that he doesn’t know what he wants anymore. And I don’t care what his wife wants. She let him walk out the door. She didn’t try to stop him. And now she wants him back. But you know these are the ones you always read about. And they always end up back with their wives. Well, it’s too damn bad. He’s mine now. She shouldn’t have let him go in the first place. You know, I hate this. I can’t believe I’m in a situation like this. It’s so Ann Landers.”

“Does Dave know about this?”

“Yes, but from what Steve said, Dave doesn’t want to know about it.”

"I had a feeling something was going on with you. Why didn't you tell me?"

"I had planned to tell you when I came back. It was very difficult keeping it in. But how could I tell you I was seeing a married man? You had just told me about your situation, and... So just tell me what you think of me and get it over with."

"Karen, in my state of mind right now I am in no position to judge you, or anyone. I guess I believe there are reasons for everything, and that everything goes the way it's supposed to." Lisa paused, and thought that maybe it's all in the script. "Who knows? As much as I hate to say it, at least your problem fits right in with our society, being that it's of an earthly nature and believable."

"Why doesn't Sylor meet me here?" Lisa asked Jenielle as they were on their way from the capsule to the bathing area. Lisa ran her hand playfully through the lion's mane.

"Sylor is above that. It is not his position to greet others when they arrive. Not even you. Everyone is brought to him."

"Is that a rule?"

"His rule."

"Why is he like that?"

"He was not always. He was once a loving, and humble man. He changed when he journeyed up to the north."

"What do you mean?"

"I'm sure it is all impressed into your memory. Maybe you are wise not to remember."

Lisa caught a hint of a smirk on Jenielle's face. "Please tell me about it?"

"Sylor was given an assignment from one of the Elders. For three years, he was to teach a small group of scientists there. The three years passed, he returned, and four of the scientists accompanied him. They had convinced Sylor that they were needed here, and that they also needed Sylor for his expertise."

"And these are the scientists that want control?"

"Yes. The people of the north are very different. They are shut off from spirit, as we here are slowly becoming. They wish to dominate. They believe living in unity is for fools. Sylor truly desires the highest good for our planet, with that he is sincere. But they are using him, and he will not believe. The north's egotistical ways have rubbed off on Sylor, but he will not hear that truth. He foolishly insists that he will never be overruled."

"Sylor wouldn't believe me. I told him Atlantis didn't exist in the future. He wouldn't listen."

"Sylor has held on to *much* anger since you made transition. When you left, he was beyond himself. At first, he repressed his anger and became ill. He would lie about for days clutching your crystal. Later, he made the decision that he would not wait for a new incarnation to be with you. That is when he acted in a manner that is forbidden."

"What did he do?" Lisa sat on a marble bench near the bathing pool, nervously awaiting Jenielle's answer.

"You, Hollina, had left for a reason...whatever reason matters not. It was *your* choice and *your* right, your free will. Sylor used the crystal you left behind to overrule your reason. It is law that one can *not* impose their will over another. He did just that attracting you back here. He was being tested, and he failed. One gifted with great power does not use it selfishly. One does not abuse their gift. Sylor set the crystal free to the ocean, where it would find you."

"What about *my* free will? If I, Hollina, didn't want to be here in Atlantis? I don't understand this because I am here."

"In your reality, did you not have a desire?"

"What do you mean, a desire?"

"If there was not a part of your consciousness that desired this, you would not be here now. Nothing can happen in our lives unless we desire it, even if that desire is hidden from us, tucked away in another part of our consciousness. Even if it is something we think we would not possibly desire, you must remember that it is some-where within your mind. What he desired, you desired. You there-fore attracted each other. Your desires corresponded."

"I think I understand that. I've always believed that everything happens for a reason, whether we understand it or not. And even though I have free will, it is my choice *now* to be here. I can choose to leave here right at this moment, and never come back."

"That is correct. Is that now your choice?"

"No. I need to be here now, for whatever reason. I feel it in my heart." Lisa put her hand over her breasts.

"If you truly feel it in your heart, then it is your soul's choice, your higher source, and that is what you must listen to. You must learn to know the difference. Sylor didn't act from his heart, he acted from his ego. That was his choice. Had he gone within and listened, he may have acted from his heart. Then he would have respected your decision, and let you go."

"But I do believe everything happens for a reason. What if Sylor had done just that and had gone on with his life without Hollina, instead of acting on his ego? I know I wouldn't be here now, so how would we have gotten together again?"

"It would have been taken care of somehow. You would have been brought together. Not now, but in the future. It is law. Sylor did not have sufficient patience to allow it to happen naturally."

"But what if this is how it was supposed to happen?"

"Sylor took it upon himself, which was the wrong use of will. Somehow it will balance out. In some way, we all receive what we have given. That is law. Both of you had created something that need not have been created."

Lisa still didn't quite understand. She still felt it was all part of some kind of script that needed to be lived out for whatever reason.

The women came for Lisa's bath.

After, as Lisa was dressing, she asked Jenielle a question that had popped into her mind. "How did Hollina and Sylor come together here, in Atlantis? What were the circumstances of their meeting? How did…"

"The soul as one unit contains both the masculine and feminine aspects. As one soul, you made the decision to experience life on earth in a human embodiment. You wanted to learn more about being what you were, you wanted to expand and grow as a soul. Earth provides the greatest learning experience at this time. In order to fulfill this plan, you had to split apart into the masculine and feminine form to experience a human existence. This is true for everyone here on Earth. This was Hollina's and Sylor's first Earth experience, the beginning of their incarnating cycle, if there was to be a cycle."

Lisa listened in awe as Jenielle continued.

"They could have experienced much in one lifetime with the possibility of never having to incarnate again, but they both have brought on much to be balanced and forgiven. Otherwise you, Lisa, as you call yourself, would have no need to be here at all."

"If we split apart into masculine and feminine, and we are all part of the Source, come from the Source, then the Source would have to be masculine *and* feminine, androgynous."

"Yes. To think anything else would be foolishness. But they are only labels as we live here in duality. The Source is *One.*"

"In my society, most see the Source as masculine only. And women are seen as lesser beings, though that is starting to change."

"This had been predicted."

Lisa was impressed with how much knowledge Jenielle had. But she also felt this knowledge was the norm, and it didn't matter how much knowledge one had. What mattered was how it was used, how one lived their life, how one treated their fellow human beings. And she also felt there was so much more to all of this than what Jenielle was telling her. Maybe things Jenielle didn't even know of, herself.

"Jenielle, tell me about Sylor and Hollina's first meeting, when they saw each other for the first time." Lisa took a deep breath, feeling her heart flutter.

Jenielle stared at her coldly. "I should not have to give you detail. Hollina lives within you. The memory lives also. You should be able to think on it and know."

"Maybe so, but it's not easy to recall. It is very difficult to remember when we are just two or three year's old, in the present life, let alone past-life memories."

"The future is much worse than has been predicted if what you are telling me is true." Jenielle looked disgusted.

"Oh, it's true. I really wish I could remember what my life was like here. I wish I could remember everything."

"If you really mean that, there is a way..."

Jenielle stopped suddenly. By the look on Jenielle's face, Lisa thought that maybe Jenielle revealed a side of herself; again a vulnerability that she really didn't want Lisa to know was there.

"Yes, I really mean that. If there is a way to remember my life here, then I want to know."

"Come with me."

Chapter 6

———

L isa and Jenielle entered another round room with a whitish glow, reminding Lisa of the glow around her crystal. The walls contained little compartments, like cubby holes with hieroglyphics above each one. Each compartment held a small crystal disk one eighth inch thick, and the size of a quarter.

Jenielle removed a disk from one of the compartments, and held it up. She also pointed out the compartment that held Sylor's disk, as well as her own. "Your life as Hollina is contained within this crystal. You may experience Hollina in both the mental and emotional realm. Everything is within the akashic records, and is transferred through the crystal disk."

Lisa jumped up on the solid quartz table, and lay back nervously. What was she getting herself into *now?*

Jenielle placed a copper band on Lisa's head. It had a small opening in the middle at her forehead in which Jenielle dropped the crystal. Lisa had a tough time getting comfortable on the hard table.

"When you relax you will feel much comfort."

"What can I expect?"

"I will ask you to close your eyes and use your mind to relax. As you do, I will cleanse your energy field."

"And then what?"

"You may experience only events of significance. But it is best that you experience sequentially, starting when you first met Sylor as a child."

"Will I be able to remember everything?"

"Yes. But you must keep in your mind that you will feel everything that Hollina felt, and at times it may not be pleasant. Your identity will be apart from hers, so there may be a conflict of feelings. Close your eyes now and I will help you adjust."

Lisa could feel Jenielle's hands running through her aura. She actually started to feel quite comfortable on the hard table as she felt herself becoming light and floating, and then settling into an altered state of consciousness. It seemed as if she was traveling through a tiny pipeline.

She had a strange sensation, and suddenly became aware that she was in a child's body. She didn't like feeling little at first, but she did like the feeling of lightness. The child's body felt almost weightless, as if she could walk on air. Lisa was amazed and couldn't believe what she was experiencing. This child, little Hollina, was five years old, and so full of love, joy, and innocence. It was a feeling of elation to be within this child's body that she could hardly contain herself.

The scariest feeling was when she tried to make Hollina walk and couldn't. She had no control in any way over her body, mind, or emotions. She was there to experience, and to learn.

"Hollina! Hollina!" A little girl looking to be about eight or nine years old came running down the beach, and was very excited.

Hollina ran to her, dropping the shell she had picked up. "Yes Jenielle?" she said, giggling.

"He is here. Sylor. He is here." Jenielle pointed up the hill.

Lisa could feel an inner light, a beautiful radiance come through Hollina, as she saw the little boy with long blonde locks coming toward her. He was a beautiful child, so full of love. Lisa and Hollina's feelings were very much in synch. They both felt the deepest love one could for another.

Hollina and Sylor stood mesmerized by each other. Hollina knew exactly who he was and what he was to her. Her joyous laughter engaged Sylor, who took her by the hand, and together they started to run down the beach. Hollina stopped and turned, expecting Jenielle to be with them. All she could see was the saddened look on Jenielle's face from a distance.

From that moment on, Hollina knew their relationship would change. The sister she loved so much would grow distant, and there would be no reason for it. Hollina's love for her sister would never change.

Sylor and Hollina laughed and played near the water. Lisa felt like she could stay in that little body forever. She had never felt such happiness. They soon heard a voice call. A bearded man in a white robe sat on a rock beckoning them to sit before him.

"Dreedon!" Lisa heard coming out of Hollina. They ran to him as if their father had come back from a trip, and had a present waiting. In a way that was true.

Lisa could hardly believe it when she got close enough to see his face. It was the man she called Mr. Moses. She wanted to cry, feeling more at home in Atlantis than ever.

Dreedon spoke, and both Lisa and Hollina didn't like what he was saying. This would be the first, and last time Hollina and Sylor would see each other until they were adults. Sylor's father was a scientist whose work would take him to another part of the planet, and his family would accompany him.

This made Hollina and Sylor very sad. Lisa could feel Hollina's tears. Hollina turned to Sylor, only to see his tears. Dreedon lovingly touched both their faces, and as if by magic the tears disappeared, and in his hand he held a crystal ball.

"My One, do not be sad. Look forward to the joy of your reunion, *and* the joy of when you awaken to your true self when all is done in the flesh. For there can only be joy in the end," he said softly. "Your tears are contained within the crystal. This crystal I hold symbolizes you, Hollina, and you Sylor, as whole. It is the *One* that you are, the *One* that is your true being contained within the Source. With this, you have agreed to the tests that will come before you. Life without each other may be known, and with this, a promise was made to always search for the other."

"Remember," Dreedon continued on, with Lisa noting the firmness now in his voice, "with your love you must release each other to find each other. And always trust your heart."

Hollina and Sylor sat mesmerized by this powerful, but gentle loving man. Dreedon then took the crystal, and with a twisting motion, split the ball in two. He placed one half in their tiny hands. Lisa remembered the vision she'd had. It was exactly the same.

"My One, now place the crystals to your hearts."

Hollina and Sylor did as Dreedon asked, and the crystals disappeared. The two children giggled as Dreedon's loving eyes embraced them. Lisa felt like he was the grandfather you loved so much, and with whom felt so safe.

Dreedon placed his hands over their chests, and the crystals reappeared. Again he placed a crystal in each of their hands.

"The crystals carry the essence of your being, which is love. Not only your love for each other but for all others. Love is the strongest force in the universe. Always face your enemies with love, especially if that enemy is yourself. Always see yourselves and others as whole, perfect and innocent, because that is what you truly are. The Source knows nothing else. Remember, compassion, understanding, and most of all love and forgiveness. Forgiveness may change the course of your life. Now give yourselves to each other."

Hollina and Sylor exchanged crystals, giving to each other a part of themselves. They hugged and held each other. Though it would be many years before they would come together again, they released each other with love, trusting completely in their reunion one day.

With witnessing this, Lisa realized the adult was as much a part of little Hollina as was the child. To have and to hold. Neither rings nor paper could make these two more truly married.

Dreedon placed his hands on his lap and leaned forward. "Also, remember, your life is a dream you have created. Your true reality, your true home, is within the Source, and one day you will awaken to this, and find you never left the Source at all. Forgiveness is the key. Take care of your gift my One. It will forever bring you together. I will watch over you always, but your will is your own. My love is with you, eternally."

Lisa watched as the elder faded from their sight. The love she felt for him was just as deep as her love for Sylor, only different.

"Return! You must return now!" Lisa felt herself being shaken and the band being removed from her head. She felt groggy and thirsty. She sat up when Jenielle gave her a chalice from which to drink. She took several deep breaths, and turned to Jenielle.

"That was incredible! I wasn't just an observer...I *was* Hollina! I felt everything she did; the laughter, the sadness, and like you said I still had my own identity. I actually experienced a part of Hollina's past, a real part of her life. And then Sylor, oh, and Dreedon...I can do this again?"

"If you wish. You have witnessed enough for now and must go back."

"But what about Sylor? I have to tell him, I have to..."

"There is no time. You have stayed far too long."

Sensing someone had entered the room, Lisa turned.

"I had received word of your presence." Sylor took her in his arms. "I have missed you terribly. My heart yearns."

"I know," Lisa whispered, "I know. Sylor I..."

"Enough!" Jenielle said vilely as the lion roared.

Sylor cupped Lisa's face; his lips lingered on hers, and apparently a little too long. The lion roared again. Sylor quickly released her, and then left the room never looking back.

Lisa had quite a headache when she opened her eyes. She closed them, and then drifted off to sleep for just a few minutes. Her body felt so heavy and tired. She also felt like she could not contain herself. She wrote in her journal, but it wasn't enough. She had to tell someone. What would Karen think *now?* She decided that she didn't care what Karen would think, and picked up the phone.

"Karen, it's me. I…"

"Hang on," Karen said weakly, and then blew her nose.

"Do you have a cold?" Silence. "Karen, are you okay? Have you been crying?" Silence. "Karen?"

"It's Steve. I saw his car at his wife's house last night. He didn't call and I thought he was working late. I went by the office, and then the apartment. I told myself not to do it, but…it was already 10:30, and I hate this situation."

"Did you have plans to be together last night?"

"No. But if we don't he will usually call."

Lisa didn't know what to say. "Well, maybe he was visiting his daughter." How lame, she thought.

"At 10:30 PM? Come on."

"Were the lights on?" Lisa crossed her fingers.

"Yes. Yes, they were. Oh, what the hell does that matter? He was there. I think I'm angrier with myself for doing something as stupid as checking up on him."

"Karen, you're human. You haven't talked to him today?"

"No, he's at a meeting out of town. You know, I don't need this right now. The store's opening in three days and I still have so much to do."

"I told you I would help you until everything was done."

"You've done so much already.

"Karen, I'll help you in any way I can with whatever needs to be done."

So much for telling Karen about her experience in Atlantis. Lisa was somewhat relieved that she had *not* spoken of it.

The opening of "The Crystal Pyramid" was a great success. Lisa couldn't believe the number of people that were on some kind of spiritual path, and involved in New Age pursuits. Everything was discussed, from astrology to quantum physics to alternative medicine. And of course the day would not have been complete without some reference to Atlantis.

Lisa was bursting at the seams, biting her tongue, almost feeling like the expert on Atlantis. But then a man, a doctor, casually made a remark that if only the Atlanteans with all their knowledge would have visualized peace instead of preparing for the worst, then maybe they would have stood a chance.

With that remark, Lisa felt an intense sense of guilt sweep over her, and almost felt sick. Why did she feel so guilty? Could she, as Hollina, have played a part somehow contributing to the destruction of Atlantis? Were both she and Sylor a part of it?

Karen locked the door and placed the "closed" sign in the window. "Well, if every day goes like today I'll be able to have an early retirement,"

Lisa gave Karen a hug. "Congratulations on a very fun, *and* profitable first day."

Karen nodded her head with tears in her eyes. "Steve never showed, but he never promised me he would. At least I know why he was at the house that night. Although, I wish it hadn't been because of his daughter getting hurt. I'm just glad she's okay, stitches and all. We do have plans this weekend, but he is going to have to make a decision soon because I can't take much more of this."

The next morning, Lisa took her lounge chair and walked down to the beach which was deserted, except for the sea gulls. It was a dull day, cloudy with a hint of a sprinkle on the way. She didn't care. She had the need to be by the ocean.

As she relaxed, she realized how drained she felt all the time. There was something peculiar about the way her body felt. She thought it may be something to do with adjusting to the higher vibrational rate of Atlantis.

She dozed off for a while, but then was awakened by a thunderous sound, and the ground shaking. She could not believe what she was seeing. A giant pyramid had risen out of the water, and the top of the pyramid, the apex, was glowing with an almost blinding white light. She saw many beings, both male and female dressed in white robes.

They all stood in front of the pyramid side by side in a large circle. The circle opened, and all eyes were on Lisa. She knew they were waiting for her. Startled, and feeling like she couldn't breathe, her eyes flew open, and she sat straight up. Everything was just as it had been.

"What the hell was *that?*" She sat back, relaxed, and began thinking about how she had always wanted to go to Egypt. From what she had read, the Egyptians had the Atlantean knowledge. She had also read that the knowledge was written and also embedded in quartz crystals, and buried somewhere in the great pyramid. When humanity was ready for this knowledge, it would be found and revealed.

After a couple of days, Lisa began feeling her energy come back some. As she lay on her bed to go back to Atlantis, Charcoal jumped up and lay beside her head. He had become her constant companion, just like the lion had. He was even following her to the beach at times.

Only the lion greeted her as she exited from the capsule. As she walked to the bathing room, she heard voices arguing. As she got closer, she knew it was Sylor and Jenielle.

Lisa recalled a quote by George Bernard Shaw that Karen had recently repeated, 'Silence is the most perfect expression of scorn.' Nothing could have been truer when Lisa entered the room and Sylor laid his eyes upon her. He walked in circles around her, looking her up and down. He finally made eye contact, holding her gaze for a few seconds, and then again eyed her up and down. He then looked directly into her eyes, seeming astonished, yet saying nothing.

He backed away and pointed. "What...what is *this* that clothes you?"

Lisa badly wanted to laugh, but held back after seeing the incensed look on his face. She looked down at her white tee shirt and jeans, trying hard to keep a straight face.

"And what is this that amuses you?" His expression was more serious than ever. Lisa glanced over at Jenielle hoping that they could humorously share this little episode. Lisa came to the conclusion that Jenielle had no sense of humor.

"Bring her to me when she is dressed appropriately." Sylor stomped out of the room, nearly knocking over Jenielle.

"Sylor, Sylor come back!" Lisa started to go after him, but Jenielle stopped her. "What's the matter, what's his problem? And what were you two arguing about?"

"Sylor is impatient with the slowness of your adjustment here. It is the way it must be. Of this he knows well. He wants to fool with the flower mixtures to hasten the process. This has become the very attitude of our scientists. They wish to interfere with natural law, believing they can better life. In many ways they can, but it can be taken too far. You can not go against law without repercussions. We may all be doomed in the end."

"No. In the end there will be joy. There cannot be sadness or doom without joy, in the end."

"What philosophy do you speak of?" Jenielle asked heavily.

"Dreedon said something like that." Lisa wanted to tell her to lighten up. The seriousness was getting to her.

"Dreedon may be very wise, but even the elders can be too optimistic at times."

How dare she? Lisa thought. How arrogant to think she knew better than the elders. Lisa took a deep breath and let it go. "I have seen Dreedon in my reality, but I didn't know who he was."

"Dreedon has come to you?"

"Yes. I have seen him running along the shore."

Jenielle looked down at the floor with a peculiar look on her face, and then looked back at Lisa. "He is a foolish one."

Lisa laughed inside, wondering how Jenielle must have pictured Dreedon running on the shore…in a robe?

"Come, you must prepare for Sylor."

Again, he looked her over, up and down. She searched his cold blue eyes for validation. She was relieved when he smiled approvingly, but hated to think she could be putty in his hands.

Their bodies met like two magnets. He held her face in his hands and slowly kissed every inch of it. Lisa savored every bit. He made his way to her neck, brushing his mouth lightly. Lisa took his hand, and slowly walked him to the bed.

She knew they couldn't make love, and accepted it. She wanted to lay with him, to hold him, be close to him. As they lay facing each other, she could feel energy building between their chests, their hearts. She placed her hand over his heart. He did the same to her. She took deep breaths, swearing she could feel his energy coming into her. It nearly took her breath away, and she had to stop.

He stroked her cheek and tenderly kissed her mouth as she shivered all over. Knowing she couldn't have him, she almost wanted him to stop. But then again, she couldn't get enough of him, and moved closer feeling as much of his body against hers as she could.

Even if they had made love, it wouldn't have been enough. It wasn't just his body; it was his very *being* she craved. She wanted to be with him, in him, through him, joined with him as one soul. This was the heartache that wouldn't go away.

He wiped the tear that edged down her face. "I know of your suffering. I, too, suffer. One day soon our bodies will be joined, as will one day our soul."

Lisa moved off the bed, and walked over to the altar. She opened the jade box and picked up the crystal. She held it to her chest. It gave her great comfort knowing Sylor had a part of her in the crystal. Yet, it was the only thing that could prove she was in Atlantis. Lisa didn't want to bring up the subject of the destruction, or the fact she still needed proof. She didn't want to argue with him. She only wanted to love him.

She took hold of the medallion he wore, and then touched her own as well. She knew of the great power that is given with the wearing of this symbol, and given with that power is even greater responsibility.

The lion roared, and to Lisa's surprise Sylor walked her back to the bathing room. She faced him and stroked his hair.

"I love you."

"Yes. You are my love. It is my vow to you there can never be another...ever!" Warmth shone through his eyes reassuring her.

Sylor left. Lisa changed back into her tee shirt and jeans, and then started to laugh remembering the look on his face. She removed the gold medallion, and started to tear up. She wanted so much to know all the details of her life as Hollina, but this would take time. And what if she didn't like what she learns?

"How could I doubt any of this?" Lisa asked herself, as she finished writing in her journal. But it never failed. Each time she opened her eyes and saw her room, every doubt came right back. She had to talk about this. She had to tell someone. She would go pay a visit to The Crystal Pyramid.

"Lisa, I don't want to hear anymore. Please don't do this."

"Karen, you said it was very doubtful that I would meet my twin soul in this life. I'm not so sure about that, but if what you say is true, then maybe this is why I'm going back to Atlantis now. Maybe that's the only way he and I can be together."

Karen looked down at the floor shaking her head, saying nothing.

"And remember that psychic you told me about? She said I already knew that anything was possible. Maybe this is what she was talking about. And what of that mission? What if it's...?"

"Chagall said, 'All our interior world is reality, and perhaps more so than our apparent world'. Don't you understand? I believe that what is happening is true. But it's all happening in your mind.

You are not physically going back to Atlantis. In mind maybe, in body, no. Lisa, you are writing a book and you don't even know it."

Lisa did not want to hear that. Here, she had found the love of her life, in a place that wasn't supposed to exist. Then there was Jeff, who was so real to her it scared her. And the beautiful lady that helped her draw Jeff, and then of course Mr. Moses. Is this what all fiction writers go through, imaginations that cross a line that shouldn't be crossed?

"Lisa, you need to stop talking like this. Think about your Aunt Bella. Your family said she was deranged. She used to talk to a spirit in the attic."

"Aunt Bella was a kind and generous woman who wrote beautiful poetry and short stories. She wouldn't have hurt anyone or anything. She didn't like gossip, and had not just a 'live and let live' attitude, but a "forgive and let live" attitude. She kept to herself unless she was doing some kind of volunteer work. It was because of her I got involved at the animal shelter."

"I know, but, come on; she used to say that the spirit in the attic gave her advice and helped her write those things. It was all in her head. Lisa, she wasn't all there."

Lisa picked up a book that was lying near the cash register, and began skimming through it. "And you go to psychics, fool around with tarot cards, and work with crystals. You've also said that we all have a spirit guide. Gee, some would say that *you* aren't all there!"

Before Karen could respond, Lisa went on. "Aunt Bella loved people, loved nature, loved life, and truly enjoyed doing for others. She never judged anyone, and believed in giving others a second chance. She was one of the most educated and intelligent women of her age. As far as I'm concerned it was a privilege and an honor to have been a part of her life. Can you imagine how she must have felt knowing her own family thought she should be put away? God Karen, there should be more people in the world like her!"

"I'm sorry, Lisa, you're right. I…"

"And I, too, saw the spirit in the attic one time. It was an old Native American woman, but I learned very quickly to shut my mouth about it. Bella's been gone ten years, and I wish to God she was here now. It's seems that you can be mean, cynical and untrusting, and that's perfectly acceptable. But if someone is kind, caring, and loving, and happens to see things beyond the normal perception, then they're a candidate for the nut house."

As Karen began to speak, the phone rang. Lisa continued skimming through the book, while Karen took the call. The word 'faith' caught her attention, and she turned back to that page. 'Faith consists in believing when it is beyond the power of reason to believe. It is not enough that a thing be possible for it to be believed,' said the philosopher Voltaire.

Aunt Bella's experiences seemed much more 'normal' than what she was going through. Bella never claimed to be going back in time, or to another land or dimension. Everything that she talked about was in the present. If Lisa's family thought Bella was deranged... Faith. 'Faith consists in believing when it is beyond the power of reason to believe.' She would have to keep telling herself that.

Lisa jumped when Karen slammed the phone on the counter, and then kicked a chair. "Gee, I thought I was the only one that did those things." Lisa chuckled.

"I can't believe he did it again…two nights in a row. We had plans last night and tonight. Paperwork he says…right. I told him the other night that if he doesn't file for divorce soon, it's over. He's been distant ever since. His wife desperately wants him back. His daughter wants her daddy to read her a bedtime story every night…if I had any class I'd bow out of this gracefully. I love him, but I won't wait forever."

Feeling bad for Karen, Lisa said, "Look, its Saturday. Why don't we go out for dinner tonight, and get our minds off everything?"

"Sure. Why not? Here we are, two decent looking women that could give some twenty-year old a run for her money. It's Saturday, and the only dates we've got are with each other. What's wrong with this picture?"

"Want to go to Quints? I'm in the mood for lasagna."

"I'm not sure. Steve loves that place. I don't know. I really don't need any reminders. They do have the best salad bar though, and... all right."

"I'll pick you up at 7:00," Lisa said, and decided she would forget about the conversation they were having just before the phone call.

On the drive home, Lisa thought about what Karen had said. Saturday night and their only dates were with each other. Putting the Atlantis issue aside, Lisa began thinking about what it would be like to date again, now being in her forties. The thought of all the formality, the phoniness, the nervousness, the nausea…she wouldn't even know how to act! Was it worth it? Of course!

Suddenly, Lisa felt like dressing up and wearing makeup. Something she hadn't done in a long time. Her heart sank thinking that the only man she would ever want to date was not of this world. But what if he was here in her reality? Would she find him through an online dating service?

"Whoa, you look great," Karen commented on Lisa's short black skirt and red silk sleeveless top. "I'm changing out of these jeans. Hey, maybe we can hit a nightclub later."

"A nightclub?" Lisa got a twinge in her stomach. She wasn't ready for a nightclub. She didn't *do* nightclubs. She just wanted dinner! Maybe Karen was kidding. What if she wasn't? Oh hell, it was only one night. *What a night!*

Chapter 7

———

"As always, this place is packed. I can't believe we got a table as soon as we did," Lisa said as they were being seated.

"I need a drink. Want to split a carafe?"

"I'd love to, but I'm driving."

"We should have made a night of this, and rented a limo. It's no fun drinking alone. And I'm in the mood to get lit. I want to party tonight."

"That dress looks fantastic on you," Lisa commented on Karen's body-hugging black tank dress.

"Thanks. This is the first time I wear it. I was waiting for some special occasion with Steve, but...I was really looking forward to being with Steve tonight. Mum's in Atlantic City and we would have had the place to ourselves. I even bought a bunch of new candles."

"You still like to do the candle thing?"

"Oh yes. Lovemaking is not complete without at least a dozen candles burning, so says my friend Julie."

The server came to take their orders. Lisa ordered lasagna. So did Karen. "I can't believe you ordered that," said Lisa.

"The way I feel tonight, I don't care. I want to eat anything and everything."

Halfway through their meal, a large group of people walked past their table to leave the restaurant. Karen dropped her fork on her plate startling Lisa, who knew by the look on Karen's face that something was wrong.

"What is it? What's the matter?"

"I...I didn't see him before. The people that just walked by were blocking him."

Lisa turned around to see Steve, with his wife and daughter eating, laughing, and looking like they were one happy family. "Oh God, are you all right?"

"I don't know." Karen hands were shaking as she picked up her full wine glass and quickly drank half of it. She wiped her eyes, took a deep breath, and pulled herself together. "It's over! That's it. It's over. I will not live my life like this. I like myself more than this. It looks like they are almost done. Let's get out of here before he sees us."

Lisa motioned to the server, who came and asked if there would be anything else. Lisa asked for the bill, and Karen mumbled something about a shotgun. The server then had a small crisis with the busboy, and a full tray of dirty dishes. There would be a wait before she came back with the bill.

Karen's fear came true. Steve and his family would have to walk by their table to leave. Steve said hello. Lisa said hello and thought Karen's face would break from the forced smile she had put on.

"He looked embarrassed," Lisa said.

"The asshole...he *should* be."

The server came with the bill. Lisa ordered dessert, and Karen a double martini. The server walked away shaking her head.

"Think you'll hear from him?"

"If I don't hear from him, he is going to hear from *me*."

"Maybe he needs more time. Would you want him to rush into anything if he wasn't absolutely sure and then..."

"I've given him too much time already!"

Lisa nodded in agreement. Even though she felt bad, she couldn't wait to get home. Karen sat back, and put her face in her hands.

"When am I ever going to learn? He's not the first married man I've been with, you know. In L.A. you would not believe...I always seem to want a man that belongs to someone else. Men that are available…I'm not…oh, let's get out of here. Let's go to that new club on Maplewood Avenue."

"I would rather go home," Lisa said, knowing full well that would *not* happen, because just like when they were kids, she felt sorry for Karen.

"Oh, come on. We'll have fun. Meet men, dance, and party! We can do shots. Come on."

"*You* can do shots. I have to drive, remember? And you've already had enough to drink."

Off they went against Lisa's better judgment, feeling like she was at the mercy of Karen's misery.

"Damn! Whose idea was this? Karen? It's mostly college kids here. It doesn't look like there's anyone over twenty-five."

"What?" Karen was snapping her fingers and moving to the beat of the music. "I'm getting a drink." Karen led the way to the bar.

"Did you hear what that guy said? He said we didn't look bad for *old* babes." Lisa put her hand on her hip. "He has a lot to learn."

"Rum and coke for me," Karen handed Lisa a drink, "and this is for you."

"What the hell's this?"

"Club soda with lime…so sorry you can't drink."

"Wonderful. If ever I needed a double shot of something…I guess I'm supposed to experience the full effect of this night. This reminds me too much of when Dave and I were first married. We used to go clubbing sometimes. I wasn't too fond of it then. And now it seems so much louder!"

Lisa thought it was a blessing when they found a table near the ladies room. At least she could duck in now and then. Wrong! The first time she tried, girls came in droves, and some with big hair. Wasn't that out of style?

While Karen 'danced' in her chair, Lisa studied the map of Cape Cod on her cocktail napkin. She had a feeling she was being watched, and resisted the feeling to look up. Suddenly, having no conscious control over her actions, she found herself staring into a pair of baby blues.

The two men were standing about eight feet away. They looked a little older than the rest of the crowd, but not by much. She felt a twinge in her stomach. 'Baby blue' reminded her of Sylor…just a little. She turned away quickly hoping they didn't think the eye contact was an invitation. Too late, and Karen had caught it, too.

"Hey guys, want to join us?" Karen shouted over the music.

Lisa noticed baby blue couldn't take his eyes off Karen, but seemed to want to converse with *her*.

"Hi. I'm Scott, and this is Russ."

Lisa hesitantly motioned for them to sit. Scott ordered a drink for them. Did that mean they were committed? After some small talk and a little drink, Russ whisked Karen off to the dance floor.

Lisa felt attracted to Scott, but not in a physical way. Sure, he was good-looking, very good-looking. She loved the piece of hair that kept falling into his eyes, and the way his muscular body filled out his t-shirt, but something else made her attracted to him.

"So, what are you doing here? Your friend seems to be having a good time. I'm not so sure about you."

"Actually, Karen's going through a bad time, and needed a night out."

"And I'll bet you bucks it's to do with a relationship."

Lisa looked back at him with a warm-hearted suspicion, and smiled. "And how would you know that?"

"I know the signs. I went through it about eight months ago. My lady broke it off, and I went partying… got wasted. Not something I was inclined to do." Scott held up his bottle of spring water. "This is the strongest elixir I normally partake of. She's going to hate herself in the morning."

Lisa laughed. "Yeah, the morning after always puts a different perspective on things."

"Would you like to dance?" he asked benevolently.

"Yeah, I would." Lisa was starting to relax. Her intuition told her Scott was a very nice person.

Fifteen minutes later, Lisa staggered back to the table feeling like she had just done a high impact aerobic workout. She gulped down the rest of her soda. "I've got to get back on the treadmill," she said trying to catch her breath. "You, I must say, look remarkably intact. What's your secret?"

"I run."

"You don't even look like you've broken a sweat. Do you run any marathons?"

"A few local road races, but I'm not much into that. I just like to run. I love the freedom, the fresh air. Running makes me feel connected with life...with Mother Nature. I can't put my finger on it, but running brings me to another plane of existence, like maybe there's some kind of spirituality going on, I don't know..." He shrugged. "It just makes me feel good."

Lisa watched his face closely as he spoke about running. He seemed almost lost in another world just talking about it. She shivered, feeling he was someone that she could relate to.

Karen ran over to the table, took a gulp of her drink, made a silly smile, and ran back to the dance floor. Lisa and Scott looked at each other amused. She watched him watching Karen.

"What type of work do you do, Scott?"

"I manage a health food store in Hyannis."

"What about you? I heard your friend say something about you being a writer. What do you write?"

"Romance novels. But I don't feel like much of a writer these days. I haven't written anything in a long time." Lisa started thinking about her journal. She wasn't about to accept she was writing a book, like Karen insisted she was.

"My sisters read those all the time. They love them."

"Well, I'm thankful for the women who do."

Lisa couldn't help staring at him. "Do you mind if I ask your age?" Lisa cringed, wishing she hadn't asked, but she figured she would never see him again anyway.

"No, I don't mind at all. I'm thirty-one, and don't worry I never ask a lady her age, or even guess for that matter. That got me smacked once. I was about seven years off in the wrong direction. I was only eighteen at the time. What did I know?"

Lisa nodded, and laughed. Karen and Russ came over to the table hand-in-hand, and with a fresh drink in the other. Karen leaned over nearly spilling her drink on Lisa, and yelled in her ear. "Guess what? Russ believes Atlantis really existed."

"Wonderful. What brought that up?" Lisa asked through clenched teeth, wondering what Karen may have told him.

"We were talking about the store and the crystals, and he said he did a paper in college on Atlantis."

"Boy those crazy people really blew a good thing." Russ said.

Lisa could not believe this. Here she was in a nightclub, a place she did not want to be, talking to a couple of guys she has never seen before in her life, and one of them happens to have done a paper on Atlantis!

"You know," Russ continued, "If I believed in reincarnation I would think I'd had a past life there. I've always had a fascination with quartz."

"Well, you'll just have to drop by the store sometime," Karen said, with a Southern accent, and laughing loudly.

Lisa shook her head and rolled her eyes, and then scolded Russ, telling him not to buy Karen any more drinks. Karen stuck her tongue out at Lisa, and dragged Russ back to the dance floor. Lisa felt like she was back in high school.

"I wasn't sure if you wanted to dance," Scott said.

"I think I'll pass. I'm going to be sore tomorrow as it is, and this loud music is giving me a headache." Upon saying that, Lisa realized she couldn't deal with loud noises anymore. It was as if the sound went right through her. "Feel free, if you'd like to ask some-one else."

"No, I'm fine. Russ had mentioned reincarnation; do you happen to believe in that?"

"Do you?" Lisa asked suspiciously.

"I have a friend in Hyannis who's a hypnotherapist. At first he was skeptical, but more and more clients were getting memories they claimed were from other lives. He began studying this and now does past-life regressions. He eventually wants to put it all into a book. You didn't answer my question. Do you believe in past lives?" Scott asked with the sweetest of a smile.

"You didn't answer either, but yes, I do."

"I do, too. I sat in on a couple of sessions and took notes for him...very interesting."

"Have you ever been regressed?" Lisa asked.

"No. I don't know if I'm ready for that yet. I don't want to find out what an ass I've been." He laughed. What about you, have you ever been regressed?"

"Well...no. No, not formally. I've just done some work on my own." Lisa now wanted to drop the subject.

"And I bet you had a life in Atlantis, right?"

"Umm...yeah," she said nervously.

"Was it at the end, with all the earthquakes and everything?"

"Yeah, but apparently I didn't stick around long enough to see it." Lisa's stomach was becoming queasy. She did not want to have this conversation.

"Did you go to another country before it all happened? Egypt? Peru?"

Lisa saw how excited he was talking about it. "No. For some reason I chose death instead. I don't fully understand why, and to be honest it's not something I'm comfortable talking about."

"I'm sorry. I didn't mean to intrude."

"That's okay. Karen's the only person I've told."

"If you ever want to be regressed, this is your man." He took a business card out of his wallet and handed it to her. She thanked him, and put the card in her purse without looking at it.

"I'll have to stop in your friend's store sometime. Are you there often?"

"She just opened recently, but I do go in and help her out some. It's fun."

Karen tripped over her own feet and almost fell, as she and Russ came back to the table.

"I can give you a ride home," Russ said to Karen.

"Oh thanks, but I'll take my chances with the priestess from Atlantis," Karen said, pointing to Lisa.

Both Scott and Russ looked at Lisa oddly. Lisa shrugged feigning ignorance, and tried to control the hand that wanted to go straight for Karen's neck. The slyness on Karen's face quickly vanished when she saw the enraged look on Lisa's.

Karen walked a crooked line to the ladies room, and Russ went to the bar.

"I wasn't too keen on coming here tonight, but Russ wanted to check the place out. I'm glad we did. It was nice meeting the both of you," Scott said.

"Ready to go home missy?" Karen asked, with a British accent.

"Oh, I'm ready."

"Karen, I'll have to come by and check out your shop." Scott looked longingly at her, which didn't escape Lisa's notice.

"Righto," she chirped.

Okay, so it didn't turn out to be the worse night of her life. Except for the priestess stuff, and the fact she had to stop on the way home three times so Karen could throw up, it wasn't all that bad. They had met a couple of seemingly decent guys, that she was sure she would never see again.

Lisa called Karen around noon the next day but the line was busy. Unfortunately, Karen's mother didn't believe in call-waiting and apparently Karen's cell phone was turned off. After a few more tries of both, and getting no where, Lisa headed for the market.

She wondered if Karen had a hangover, as she went through the aisle with the aspirin and antacid. The Sunday morning hangover… she remembered them well and was grateful she had driven.

In the produce section she happily picked up strawberries, green apples, and a couple of grapefruits. As she stood deciding whether or not to get a pineapple too, someone started singing in her ear.

She found it unnerving and quickly turned around. With a huge grin, and holding a bunch of carrots, stood Scott.

"Didn't mean to make you jump. Sorry."

She relaxed, then smiled. "Why…is someone who manages a health food store buying carrots here?"

"Because we ran out of organic carrots yesterday, and sometimes they have them here. Not to mention we are closed on most Sundays. How's your friend doing?"

"I don't know. I couldn't get in touch with her. I might just drop by her house later."

Lisa and Scott shopped a couple of aisles together. Ben & Jerry's for Lisa, and bottled water for Scott. Lisa felt comfortable with him, like he was an old friend. He asked for her number. She hesitated at first, but he did remind her of Sylor. And as much as she hated to think it; Scott seemed nicer.

Karen's car was in the driveway as Lisa pulled up. "*Uh, oh.*" Karen's head and arms were hung over the steering wheel, and as Lisa approached she saw Karen was wearing the same clothes as the night before. *Not a good sign!* Karen jumped when Lisa knocked on the window. Tangled hair, red eyes, streaks of black tears. *What a mess!* Between sobs she managed to get out that she and Steve had broken up for good…maybe.

Lisa helped Karen into the house, put her in a bathrobe, and made her some tea. Lisa now kept herbal tea on hand for Karen. "So, what happened?" Lisa sat with a bowl of strawberries.

"After you brought me home last night, I...I don't even remember making it up to my bed. But I do remember waking up about 5:30 this morning. I got up and threw up, then started to remember everything that happened last night. I couldn't get back to sleep, so I took a ride by Steve's place, and his car wasn't there. But I knew where it would be. And I was right. Steve spent the night with his wife."

"Karen, I am so sorry," Lisa said sincerely. She hated seeing Karen go through this.

"I talked to him for two hours this morning. He told me he wants to break it off for the time being, and you know what that usually means, but he did say he wasn't going back to his wife. He said it was only fair to break it off because he still doesn't know what he wants."

Lisa didn't say anything, but as far as she was concerned the man *did* know what he wanted.

"You know, I was ready to accept that it was over. But then he told me he loved me. Why did he have to say that? Now it makes me believe there is still a chance, that maybe I should hang on. At least if he told me he didn't love me anymore, granted it would hurt, but at least I would know where I stand, and could get on with my life."

"Karen, I know it's easier said than done, but get on with your life anyway." Lisa could have very well given herself the same advice.

"Sure. Life goes on, doesn't it?"

"You'll never guess who I saw at the market."

Karen gazed down at the floor, oblivious to what was just said.

"Karen? I saw Scott at the market."

"Huh? Who?"

"Scott. One of the guys we met last night. Remember?"

"I remember," she snapped.

"He asked about you. I think he likes you."

"Well, I think I hate men, so, lucky him."

Yikes! Lisa thought that perhaps she should give Scott a heads up, just in case he really wanted to pursue Karen.

Karen spent the night at Lisa's, and they talked about all the boys they liked in high school. Karen confessed she secretly had crushes on many of the boys Lisa liked.

Jenielle met Lisa at the capsule, and immediately informed her that Sylor was gone for the day. Lisa was disappointed, but perked up when she was told they would go to the Records room.

"Jenielle, could I ask you something?" Lisa said as she jumped up on the quartz table. Jenielle stared at her.

"Are you in a marriage? Or, is there a man that you love or care about?" Lisa hoped she wasn't invading Jenielle's privacy.

"There is one I desire. He is with another. One day he will see the foolishness in that, and I will have him. I *will* have him." And Karen is still having man problems. Talk about history repeating itself, Lisa thought.

Jenielle, again placed her hands on Lisa's head for a minute, and then did the same with her feet. "You are progressing as you should. Soon you will have to make your decision." Lisa didn't want to hear that. She wanted things to continue just as they had been.

The copper band was placed on her head, and the crystal disk inserted. Lisa began relaxing her body. Different scenes passed by quickly. It stopped, and she found herself walking in a beautiful flower garden. Birds and butterflies were all around. Hollina was eleven years old.

As she walked, she came across a bird on the ground trying to fly. It was hurt. Lisa could feel Hollina's empathy as she carefully picked it up and cupped it in her hands. Other children had gathered to watch.

Hollina used her mind and envisioned a stream of white light coming down through the top of her head and out through her hands.

Lisa realized Hollina was calling on the energy of the Source to heal the bird.

Hollina visualized the bird completely healed. Lisa was amazed as Hollina held no doubt in her mind that this was possible. It was total faith that left no room for doubt. Hollina then silently thanked the Source, for allowing her the privilege of participating as a channel for its tremendous healing power.

The bird chirped and danced in her palms for a few seconds, then flew off. Hollina was delighted. She had just done her first healing on her own, after much training.

Another scene came to her. Hollina was a few years older. A tiger had come to her side. She sensed the animal was very sick. She mentally asked the animal to lie down. Green light emanated from her hands as she moved them over the tiger's body.

Hollina knew it would take more than what she was doing to help heal this animal. She coaxed the tiger up and led him into the temple to one of the rooms. The room had a small round pool, and twenty feet above the pool a large quartz point hung from the domed ceiling.

Hollina guided the tiger into the shallow pool of water, having it lie down with just its head above the water. She then focused on the crystal point, and it lit up with a brilliant white glowing light. With her mind, she intended for the light from the crystal to go where the animal needed healing.

Lisa saw the light coming from the crystal. She could feel Hollina's intense concentration, and became excited as to how using the mind is imperative in healing the body, but she also knew you had to believe it could be done. In her reality people were just becoming aware of how the mind can affect the body, for good or ill. In Atlantis, apparently it was the norm.

Hollina sensed the healing was complete and again, using her mind, turned off the crystal. When she led the animal out of the pool Lisa saw through Hollina's eyes what looked to be a tumor almost the size of a baseball. Lisa didn't want to look at it, but it didn't seem to faze Hollina at all. The animal walked away as if it was never sick at all. Hollina had not been aware of a woman who stood in the background watching the entire process. Lisa thought she was very beautiful, with thick red hair that hung well below her shoulders. Her large, round blue eyes looked familiar to Lisa. The woman nodded, smiled, and then told Hollina she had done well.

"The animal became your companion for the rest of your life here," Jenielle related, after Lisa explained her experience. And the woman was Eldreena. She was a master teacher. Hollina was one of her students. She taught you the power of the mind and what it could do. Hollina didn't know at the time that Eldreena was Sylor's mother."

"Sylor's mother? Is she here now?"

"Eldreena has since made transition."

"But I thought Sylor's family had moved away."

"Eldreena alone would return from time to time. She was a gifted healer and teacher. She was also a gifted sculptress, and created great works of art."

"What happened to the tiger? Where is he?"

"The animal made transition shortly after you. He was heartsick without you. He did not want to be saved."

"Oh God," she whispered with guilt sweeping through her.

With a sharp tone, and as if Jenielle could read Lisa's mind she said, "You did *not* have to make transition." She stared Lisa down for a few seconds then left the room.

Back on the home front Lisa lay in bed depressed. Jenielle's words haunted her. She did *not* have to make transition. Then why did she? Hollina wanted to go to Egypt, but Sylor didn't. He wouldn't believe her about the vision she had had, and God knew he was just as stubborn about it now.

Hollina must have been frustrated, maybe angry and hurt too. Did she make transition to hurt Sylor? Was it revenge? Lisa didn't want to think that. She knew Hollina was not a bad person…far from it. How could she want to get revenge on a man she loved more than life itself? Yet she felt there might be a little twinge of truth in that, and the guilt she was feeling about it all was driving her crazy.

The next morning Lisa took a cup of coffee, and sat out on the deck trying to think everything through, but she couldn't concentrate. She looked out at her surroundings. The view of the ocean from where she sat was incredible. The potted plants and flowers on the deck were colorful, and sweet-smelling. The sound of the wind chimes flowed through her. She sat in a most beautiful setting, yet it seemed dead to her compared to being in Atlantis.

Was she losing her grip on reality? Maybe Karen was right. Maybe she should get professional help. She knew she would have to make that decision soon, of whether or not to stay in Atlantis. If she chose to stay in Atlantis, would she actually disappear from this reality? What if she woke up one day in an institution blubbering about Atlantis? What if the local newspaper did an article on her? Would the headline read 'Local Author Goes Insane?' If she was in her right mind she would do what Karen suggested, and get rid of the crystal. Just forget about all of this, and maybe go back to school, do more volunteer work, or get a regular job and never write again. Her heart nearly stopped on that last thought. To never write again would be the death of her. To stop writing would be to stop living.

No, she would not give up on this. Not on writing, not on Atlantis. The men in white coats may have to come get her, but she was not going without a fight. Besides, she aimed to have her way with Sylor first.

Chapter 8

————

"Jenielle, you said I didn't have to make transition, what did you mean?"

"You thought only of yourself," she said coldly. "You should have gone to Egypt. You see, you were not immune to the negative energy that has been overtaking us. But you were aware of it and could have done something. You had a gift and you wasted it. You let your feelings for Sylor ruin you, and now it is too late."

"You're angry with me."

"The people held you in high esteem. You were much loved. One of your gifts was that you could influence people positively, with compassion, with love. You could help them; teach them to open up to their own higher awareness, the Source."

"Obviously, I couldn't influence Sylor."

"Sylor was your weakness. You had a plan before you allowed Sylor to overtake your thinking."

"What plan?"

"You had taught the power of the mind to others. Some had become adept at it. You and the others had planned to go out to the rest of the planet to work in groups, and teach others how to transmute negative energy to positive energy. This was to be used to focus on peace and unity. Then you would settle in Egypt for a time."

"Why couldn't the others have just gone on without me?"

"You fool. You were the way shower. They felt abandoned and betrayed. They had not yet reached the level of confidence and belief in themselves as they had in you. But that was their lesson, *their* test. They should have had belief in themselves, and in their own inner Source, instead of someone outside of themselves."

"Then I guess I wasn't a very good teacher."

"You *were* a good teacher. There was not enough time."

Lisa let out a deep breath. Depression had overtaken her entire body. She felt like she had the weight of the world as her shoulders cowered in.

"God, I screwed up big time. I feel like such a failure."

"It was not your responsibility alone. Everyone must take responsibility for their actions including what they think, believe, and the words they voice. Everyone must take responsibility. *Everyone!*"

Lisa was grateful Jenielle had said that, but it offered her little comfort. The guilt was more than she could take at the moment.

"I...I can't...do this today. I can't see Sylor, I can't be here. I've got to get out of here." She ran back to the capsule.

Lisa didn't know what was happening to her. She didn't completely understand what had happened between Hollina and Sylor. But she did know that people had counted on her, and she let her relationship with Sylor color everything. No wonder this time around she had married a man with whom she wasn't truly in love.

Now she had met Sylor, her true love, and it was all happening again. He had become the center of her life, her thinking, so much to the point that she was ready to give everything up, even risk her life with the upcoming destruction to be with him. And she still didn't know if any of it was reality!

For the next several days, she did nothing but walk the beach, drink wine, and ponder life's mysteries. She could barely eat, or sleep. Guilt, along with the thought of insanity plagued her. She had never felt so alone. Where was Dreedon?

One day, after drinking too much wine, she decided she was going to end the whole mess she had somehow created for herself. She looked out the window and saw that the weather was exactly how she felt. March in July... murky, raw, wet, and destructive. She popped in Beethoven's Ninth, and set it to the second movement.

She opened another bottle of wine, sat in front of the back sliders and rocked to the music, the bottle in one hand, the crystal in the other. She knew she had to work up the courage. "When the music is over," she kept repeating, "I will end this. I will end this."

Her cue came. This was it. She nervously opened the sliders. Shaking, she walked onto the deck. Bumps rose on her arms and legs, as the drizzle brushed her. Had she been in her right mind she would have put on a sweatshirt and jeans. Had she been in her right mind none of this would be happening, she told herself.

She staggered down to the beach with her bottle. She fell down. Seeing it was too much of an effort to get back up, she decided to sit for a while. She drank, and mindlessly dug a hole in the sand. She put the crystal in, but did not cover it up. When she mustered the strength to stand up, she took the bottle and teetered over to the water.

"It would be so easy," she whispered, and took a swig. "I could do it. I could do it. I could walk right into the great Atlantic." She smiled, and raked a hand through her tangled hair. "And never come out."

She made no effort to wipe the tears that mixed with the steady rain coming down. She wobbled back to where she had been sitting. "I'm not crazy." She rocked back and forth, sitting in the wet sand. "I'm not crazy." Nope, she was totally sane, she told herself. *Everyone* must have a nervous breakdown at least once in their life.

She took another swig. "This is it." She stuck the bottle in the sand, and picked up the crystal. She made her way to the water. She stood, swaying back and forth. Tiny waves of the cold ocean poured over her feet, making them ache. She would now get rid of the menacing piece.

Tears formed again, her lips quivered, and she shook all over. Would she be throwing Sylor away? She had found the kind of love she had dreamt about since she was a child, and now she was about to throw it all away. Why? Because she couldn't handle what she may have had done in Atlantis, because she couldn't handle what she was going through now. Was this the coward's way out?

She stood still and thought for a moment. By throwing away the crystal was she still letting her feelings for Sylor control her? Was she screwing up again, by not being able to go back and face what she had done? What if Sylor is alive in the present, and ready to come back into her life? Was she ready for him yet? No. She knew she still had more to learn, and the only way to learn it was to keep going back to Atlantis. She didn't care. She wanted her sanity back. The crystal had to go.

She sobbed as she raised her arm. As she pulled back ready to release the crystal, a sudden gust of wind pushed her to the ground. A whitish glow appeared above the water, twelve feet in front of her. The glow turned into a form. Dreedon hovered above the water. "My One, there is choice. Is it, in fact, the *crystal* you must rid yourself of?" he asked gently, then faded away.

She lay in the sand, sobbing as the rain poured. Of course it wasn't the crystal she needed to rid herself of. It was all the people she had let down, the plan on which she had not followed through, the self-centeredness, the fact that she had hurt Sylor when she left. It was all the guilt she had suppressed. She lay holding the crystal to her chest, and cried until there was nothing left. Why didn't she go to Egypt? For some reason Sylor's pride had gotten in the way. But she knew he loved her, and may have eventually followed. Why didn't she take that chance?

She didn't know how long she lay there. When she finally stood she felt as if a weight had been lifted. She opened her hand and gazed at the crystal. She held it to her chest, and closed her eyes not believing what she had almost done. She emptied out the rest of the wine, and tossed the bottle in a trash barrel. She quickly made her way back to the house.

She poured herself a hot bath sweetened with rose oil. She laid back and relaxed feeling so much better. She felt as if an inner healing had taken place. She also knew she had to forgive herself for what she did, or didn't do, but then a questioned arose. She had seen and read about past-life regressions, and how people had released guilt and other negative emotions. These people usually go on happily with their lives feeling liberated. Was this Atlantis situation nothing more than an effort to release past life guilt she had carried in her subconscious from that lifetime...releasing the past and getting on with her life? Had this been nothing more than one big past-life regression?

Again, she doubted. She hated herself for this. "No, this is hardly over. There are too many unanswered questions," she murmured. She picked up the crystal she had placed on the edge of the tub. It was time to go back.

Jenielle was nowhere in sight as Lisa and the lion walked to the bathing room. The two women helped her with her bath, and then she made her way to Sylor's room. The door was slightly ajar and she could hear voices arguing. She stepped into the room, unnoticed.

"Hollina is my one and only love. She has come back to me, what does that say to you?" Sylor shouted to Jenielle.

Lisa cleared her throat. Sylor and Jenielle looked at her, stunned. Jenielle grazed Lisa as she fled the room with fire in her eyes.

Lisa and Sylor reached for each other and embraced. She felt at home in his arms. Nothing else mattered besides being in his presence. She felt she could let him have so much control, and that scared her.

"Jenielle reported you will soon make your full adjustment here." Lisa pulled away, and said nothing.

"What is wrong?"

"I don't know what I'm going to do."

"Do you not love me?" He pulled her back.

She thought he sounded like a heartbroken little boy. She took his hand. "With all of my heart and soul, and every breath."

"Then why? Why are you still with doubt?"

"Because I know what's going to happen, and there's nothing I can do about it now. I had my chance. Making transition was a big mistake."

He pulled his hand away and glared at her. He then grabbed both her arms in a fury and shook her. "I will not speak about that day. How could you leave me? How could you do that to me? How could you leave me knowing how much I loved you? You will not leave me again. *I forbid it!*" He continued to shake her.

The lion roared, and came between them, knocking Sylor to the floor. Lisa quickly realized why she was assigned her big friend. In her heart she knew Sylor would never physically hurt her, and she was not afraid of him. She also knew that she had as much power over his emotions as he had over hers.

"Forgive me." He stood up quickly and turned away. "I know not what has come over me." He then turned back, and looked forcefully into her eyes. "Do not leave me again," he said above a whisper.

"Sylor," she said touching his face. "If I don't stay please, please go on to Egypt. You'll be safe there. I don't know how I know, but I do. I'm afraid the other scientists may hurt you. And I would hate to know, that, well...please leave before Atlantis goes down."

"Why? Why do you insist on *speaking* like this? You know what the power of thoughts and words can do!"

"Yes, but it's done. The energy is already in motion. Too many believe in the destruction. Sylor, it has already happened. I don't blame you for not wanting to believe it, though maybe it could all change...there still could be a chance if you ordered the other scientist's to leave now. You have to try, Sylor."

"I will not."

"If only I hadn't made transition. It may not have made a differ-ence as far as the destruction, but it may have made a difference in *our* lives, with you and me. If I had to do it all over again, I..." She started to cry.

"If you had to do it all over again, you never would have released that vision. I blamed you for that, but too many foolishly believe in the words of another. You are not entirely to blame."

"I still had a responsibility here, and walked away from it."

"If you stay in your reality, you will be doing it again."

"But...what of my responsibility to my society, one that has become greedy and power hungry as Atlantis?"

"Where is your heart?" He smiled and stroked her hair.

"My heart is here with you, I can't deny that."

"Jenielle speaks that she has incarnated as your friend, in your reality."

"Yes."

"What of myself? Have we met?"

"No. My friend Karen says you and I will not meet."

"Then you know where you belong."

"No! I *don't* know where I belong! Maybe the only way I can help Atlantis now is to stay in my reality, and do something; I don't know what... if I could just do it over again. Damn it! But then if staying there means never to be with you, I...I think Karen is wrong. I think it's very possible I will meet you in my reality. What if I'm wrong to stay *here?"*

"How could it be wrong to be with the one you love? We belong together. That is why you are here. I am not there, so you are here."

"And that makes sense. But I still don't know if this is real. These things do not happen in my reality. No one believes they can. Where I come from everything is logical. If you can't see it, then it doesn't exist."

"Do your people not know of our Source? From what you speak of, your ways are limited. The Source is limitless."

"That's the way it is, and a part of me believes that way; the part that keeps me doubting any of this. I'll admit for a while I thought I was dematerializing or teleporting, but I know that had to be impossible."

"Impossible?" Sylor said throwing his hands up. "You were adept at it."

"What?"

"You mastered teleportation shortly before you made transition."

"What…what? I can't deal with this, not right now. Where is Jenielle? I want to go back to the Records room."

"Jenielle explained what you were doing. What has been your experience?"

"I experienced the first time we met, as children. Dreedon had given us the crystal, and then you left with your family."

"I remember well." He ran his hand along the jade box sitting on the altar. "I thought about you always. I feared at times you would forget me. I then remembered that no one forgets the other half of themselves."

"The next time was when I used my healing powers. I healed a bird, well it seemed like I healed it, but I just channeled the energy to heal, right?"

"You are surprised? The energy of the Source works through us all if we allow it, and open ourselves up to it, and believe it. When we use the energy of the Source with our mind, we must have only the best and highest intention. If not, we will pay for our misdeeds, if not now, then in the future. No deed, whether in thought or action, good or evil, is unnoticed. Everything must balance out." A somber look came over Sylor's face, and he looked down at the floor. "Though, often, we forget."

The lion roared. There would be no time for the Records.

"You do not need Jenielle to experience the Records. I may assist you next time if you desire."

"I desire." She looked longingly into his eyes, caressed his face, and then left the room.

Two days later, Lisa dropped in at the Crystal Pyramid. To her surprise, she found Karen and Scott in the midst of laughter and having a cup of tea.

"Hey, how are you doing?" Scott asked with a smile as big as life.

"Scott...hi." Lisa felt caught off guard. "What are you doing here?" She felt silly for asking and silently berated herself.

"My day off. I thought I'd come and check this place out. I'm impressed."

"Scott is trying to talk me into having a past-life regression, with his friend."

"Since I'm too chicken." Scott laughed, and looked at Lisa. "Don't worry, I won't ask *you. "*

"Huh?" Karen said, and looked at Lisa.

"The night at the club, I told Scott I thought I had had a lifetime in Atlantis that wasn't very pleasant, and I didn't want to talk about it," Lisa said raising her eyebrows.

"Oh...right." Karen smirked, and shook her head. "As if anyone would believe..." The door opened, and Karen's face dropped. So did Steve's when he saw the three of them staring at him as if he had walked in naked. Lisa grabbed Scott's hand.

"We'll talk to you later Karen," Lisa said, as a confused Scott nearly tripped over his own feet as she dragged him out of the door.

With Scott's hand still in hers, she led the way to the coffee shop several doors down. She ignored his mumblings until they grabbed a seat inside, and ordered a tea and a coffee.

Scott leaned forward. "What was that about?" he said in a calm and patient voice, with just a hint of irritation.

Lisa lost her tongue when a piece of his dark blonde hair fell in front of his face, nearly attacking his right eye. She thought he was incredibly sexy, but she knew he was not for her. He was for someone else. She apologized, and explained.

"So, he's the guy." Scott toyed with a sugar packet that had been lying on the table, while Lisa kept stirring her coffee. "Think they'll get back together?"

"No." She put her spoon down and took a sip. "I'll bet you any money he's gotten back with his wife. I just have a feeling." She noticed that Scott was trying to conceal a smile, as he put the sugar packet back in the holder.

He cleared his throat. "Do you think she would go out with a younger guy?"

"I honestly don't know." She grinned. "Planning to ask her out?"

"I have to admit I am attracted to her."

Lisa smiled. "I know."

"She has such beautiful eyes. I'll have you know I'm an eye man."

"Well, that's refreshing. Are there any more like you at home?"

"Nope, it's just my two sisters."

"Are you going to ask her out?" Lisa insisted on getting an answer.

"It all depends on what happens down there," he said, pointing toward Karen's store.

"If it's officially over I may. My last relationship was with a woman nine years older, and for some reason it bothered her. What difference does the age thing make if you really love someone? As soon as I mentioned marriage she was gone. But it probably wasn't the age thing...more like a money thing. I don't get paid a whole hell of a lot managing an independent health food store."

Lisa saw the pained look on his face. She unconsciously put her hand on his. When she realized what she had done, she didn't pull away. She hated the idea of him being hurt. She suddenly felt close to him, like a sister would with a younger brother.

They walked back to Karen's shop, and they saw through the window that Steve was still there, so they browsed in one of the other shops. Scott picked up a runner's magazine and Lisa a bag of M&M's. Walking back, they saw Steve leaving The Crystal Pyramid.

"I think I'll back out here," Scott said. "If she's upset, she'll probably want to talk to you, and if I'm there, well...I'll get back to her in a couple of days."

"Okay. I think you might be right."

"Oh, and I will be forever grateful if you keep my possible intentions to yourself."

"Forever grateful, huh? I'll remember that." Lisa smiled. "Don't worry, I won't say a word."

Karen was blowing her nose when Lisa walked in, and didn't say anything until after three more blows. Lisa could feel something in the air.

"Do you know what he did?" Karen shouted.

Lisa hoped Karen wasn't really expecting an answer.

"Well do you?" she shouted louder.

Lisa shrugged meekly, but of course, had an idea. Karen picked up a book. Fire was in her eyes. Lisa ducked. She didn't think that Karen actually aimed for her, as the book flew by and knocked over a plant. Scott was spot on.

"That bastard went back to his wife. I hate him! How could he do this to me? He told me he will always care about me, and that I should go on with my life. He said he was sorry. What an *asshole!*"

Karen sat in the back of the store for twenty minutes. While Lisa cleaned up the plant mess, she thought about Karen and Scott as a couple. Maybe it wasn't such a good idea. Scott would probably be good for Karen, but would Karen be good for Scott?

"At least I know now…it's really over," Karen said, as she came out from the back, and wiped her eyes. "What happened to Scott?"

"I told him what was going on. He figured you would want to be alone so we could talk. He didn't want to intrude."

"That was considerate of him. I wouldn't have wanted him to see what you just saw. He seems nice, nice to talk to. And is he good looking, or what?"

"That, he is. And he is nice to talk to. I feel very comfortable around him; like I could tell him anything, and he wouldn't judge me. Maybe we knew him in a past life."

"Maybe. Did he say if he was going to come back anytime soon?"

"Oh, I think he'll be back." She hated keeping this to herself. "By the way, you reminded me of me when you threw that book. It was kind of funny."

"Sorry about all that. It felt so good to get it out of my system. Now it's time to move on."

Lisa was dusting some of the bookshelves when she noticed a book on relationships. If she met Sylor in the present, she wondered how he and Karen would get along, since he and Jenielle do not. She may never know.

She kept dusting, and came to a book on ancient civilizations. Tempted, she picked it up and glanced through it. The word 'dematerialization' grabbed her. She read how in Atlantis a special room was used for dematerialization, and how some were transported from space to serve in Atlantis.

Excited was an understatement when she read that. She wanted to tell Karen, but of course hesitated. What the hell, she was used to Karen's ridicule.

"Lisa please don't say anymore, okay? Maybe you could teleport or dematerialize when you had a life in Atlantis, but not now."

"Why not?"

"Because we….we're conditioned against it. It's not part of our belief system. It just doesn't happen." Karen sighed.

"That's because we've been brainwashed to believe that we're these little peons that have no personal power. We've been taught that some authority figure has the power, or knows more than we do about ourselves. We're told what to do and what to believe, and we go on our merry way believing in someone outside of ourselves. Come on Karen, you know we have power within, or you wouldn't be into visualization. Our power comes from our own mind, our own hearts. Most of us are like robots and puppets; we don't even *question* our beliefs. We need to question."

"You sound like the old Lisa, only more serious…rebel *with* a cause. Look, only the Masters, the Saints, could do what you say you could be doing and…"

"You know I'm not one to quote Jesus or the Bible, but Jesus did extraordinary things, and Jesus did say that what He did we could also do, and greater. I don't think anyone really *gets that*. I don't think there are very many who have thought about what that really means. I think maybe we are all Masters, and we don't know it because we've been taught exactly the opposite."

"That could be true, and we are conditioned or brainwashed to believe certain things. And you're right, we should question, but I can't buy what you're telling me. Teleportation, dematerializing, I'm sorry. I'm being honest Lisa. I can't accept that."

On the drive home, Lisa couldn't get Scott out of her mind. She could not shake the feeling he was to become an important part of her life. She hardly knew him, but she felt he may be open to what she was experiencing. When she got to know him better, and when the time was right, she would tell him.

When Lisa got home, Charcoal ran to her and proudly deposited a dead mouse at her feet.

"Oh, that's real nice," she said as she kicked it on to the grass. Charcoal ran over and sniffed it, then followed Lisa up the back stairs. She thought about how cats torture their prey before they kill it. Not unlike some humans, who could be so cruel to another for the sake of greed and control. With animals it is instinct, but humans? *What's our excuse? Killers and masters we are.*

"Why do you insist on returning? You know what is going to happen?"

Lisa noted Jenielle's foul mood. She ignored her, and thought how ironic it was that she had to deal with Karen's sarcasm in the present as well as twelve thousand years in the past.

Lisa had taken her bath, and as the women were brushing her hair up, Sylor walked into the room. "I have longed for your return." He took her in his arms.

"I will take her to you," Jenielle said sharply.

"And I will assist her with the Records," Sylor said, mimicking Jenielle's tone.

Lisa watched Jenielle's face as Sylor left the room. If Jenielle knew how to flip him off, Lisa was sure she would have.

"What is the problem between the two of you?" Lisa asked, being sick of the tension between them.

"This is knowledge that is not for you to know."

"Then I'll ask Sylor."

"He will not tell you."

Jenielle's smugness irritated Lisa, who was losing her patience. "I know the way to Sylor. I don't need you to escort me."

Sylor met her in the hall, and they walked hand in hand to the Records room. He looked down at Lisa as she lay on the table. She raised her hand to his face. "I want so much to be with you."

Sylor smiled sadly and nodded. He reached over, and kissed her deeply. She felt the hairs on her arms rise, as she became lost in his kiss. His mouth pressed hers harder, and she wrapped her arms around his neck. She wanted his hands all over her, but it was not to be. He suddenly came up for air. He placed his fingers over her lips to shush her, and then placed the headband on her.

She found herself walking in the garden again. The sweet fragrance of roses permeated the air. This would have done wonders for anyone's psyche, but she felt so low in spirit.

Lisa realized she was in Hollina's adult body, which was walking in circles. Sylor was on her mind. The time had come for their reunion. They had not seen each other since they had been given the crystal as children, and there had been a delay. He should have arrived two days earlier, and there had been no word.

Hollina worried that she may never see him again, but then her worry ceased, trusting Dreedon's words that they would reunite. She thought of how wonderful their life together would be. She thought of how they could bring Atlantis back to its original beauty before the preceding earthquakes had destroyed parts of the land. Lisa knew Hollina had no clue yet of the destruction to come.

Lost in reverie she was startled by a voice. "You are even more beautiful than my dreams would allow me to envision."

Her heart leapt, her hands trembled, and her eyes teared up. She stood paralyzed at what her sight was revealing. He stood tall in stature, wearing a royal blue robe. A spark of light emanated from his eyes.

Lisa felt Hollina's feelings of joy, and couldn't wait for them to embrace. Lisa saw a whole different Sylor than she knew. He looked so young and pure. He looked at peace. Yes, at peace.

He moved in closer until he stood directly before her. She looked up into his eyes. He held her face, and wiped her tears with his fingers. "It is my hope these are tears of joy."

"Yes. Oh yes. You are not a dream? You do stand before me? It is your flesh that touches mine?"

"Yes. We no longer need dream of one another."

They wrapped themselves around each other, and kissed. A long, deep kiss; and Lisa reveled in it, allowing herself to feel Hollina's passion, which matched her own.

Lisa heard her name being called, as Sylor removed the head-piece. She felt so happy to see Sylor standing there looking over her, but he looked worried.

"Your eyes flow with tears. Was sadness your experience?"

She sat up, smiling, and put her hand to her heart. "No. No not at all. We were reunited; we had met for the first time as adults. Hollina was so happy...she had been worried and..."

"Yes, you relayed to me your fears. You thought you would never see me again. I had tried to reach you with my thoughts. With my impatience and your anticipation, our communication was blocked. I had become impatient over the delay of my brother, and I could not..."

"You have a brother?"

"Yes. Matua did not incarnate until after my family had left here."

"Did he come back here with you?"

"Yes, though he is not here now. His work takes him to other areas. He returns from time to time. The two of you were very fond of each other. At times, he was more your brother than mine. He was much saddened when you made transition. Sadly, he is much in love with Jenielle, though she has rejected him."

"Why? And why do you and Jenielle argue like you do?"

"I am not at liberty to reveal. I have given my word."

At first, Lisa wanted to drag it out of him. Then she looked into his eyes and realized that as stubborn as he was, he was also a man of honor, and she respected that.

They walked together to the bathing room. "Sylor, after we reu-nited, what was our life like?"

He turned to her, and took her hands in his. "Our life was one of much happiness. At times we worked together, teaching others the ways of mind and spirit, until..." His smile turned to sadness, as he lowered his head.

"Until what?" she asked nervously.

"Until I was called away."

"Called away...up north?"

"Yes. You know? Do not tell me; Jenielle spoke of this? She played a part in my going away."

"What do you mean?"

"There was need of a scientist, a teacher. She spoke on my behalf, and I was elected. I should have been honored, as it was an enviable position. I did not desire to go, not really. I cherished our life together here."

"Did you have to do this, did you have to go?"

"I...I could have fought it, though one does not fight an honor." He turned away. "As I voiced before, it was an enviable position. I was there to teach, but there was much I could learn. My hope was you would ask me to stay. You did not. You did not want to be apart from me, but you would not interfere with what could be my life's direction. It was to be *my* choice."

She noted a tone of resentment in his voice. "Do you feel it was the wrong choice?" She heard him take a deep breath. She waited for his response. He turned, and then looked at her with sternness. She saw the tears in his eyes.

"No!" he said resoundingly, and turned away again.

She knew he was lying, and didn't think she should push it.

"Was this before, or after our marriage or union?"

He turned back to her. "It was years after our union. Neither of us had knowledge of the amount of time I would be away. Never did we foresee it would be three years. We were allowed no communication, not even with our minds. Nothing could distract me from my work. We had to learn not to think of each other."

"That must have been awful," she said with a lump in her throat, almost remembering what it was like.

"In the beginning it was unbearable. I desired to come home. That would have been a dishonor. They tried to distract me...they would send women to me, but I could never..." He looked straight into her eyes and shook his head. "I could never give myself to another in *any* way. This frustrated my superiors. They did not understand how I could not give in to even the most beautiful women. They did not understand how one could love another so deeply. They did not understand love."

"How sad." She stroked his hair and smiled, feeling pangs of jealously at the thought of him being tempted with others. She put her arms around him, and they held each other for a moment.

He abruptly broke her hold, and stared at her. She saw him in a way she had never seen before. The lion got up on all fours, but stayed where he was by the entrance to the bathing area. Sylor's eyes became very small, as he looked through Lisa's soul.

"When I returned, everything had changed. *You* had changed. You spouted tales of our ruin." His voice was getting louder. The lion came over, and stood by Lisa. "You dishonored me by insisting the scientists that returned home with me would induce our doom. You and the others had spread this invention."

"No! Seven of us had seen the same vision, and I gave my consent to reveal this truth. We had to warn everyone. We had to!" Lisa stopped and held her breath. Where did *that* come from? That was not she who spoke those words. She had no conscious knowledge of what she had just said. Hollina had come through loud and clear.

Sylor looked at her suspiciously, and continued his tirade. "Indeed, if this was true...this vision...only fools would spread such a dreadful fate. You are a High Priestess. You know the laws. You know there is power in numbers. You know if enough minds believe, there is the potential to manifest the event whether it is of a positive nature, or a negative one. That vision should have been revealed to *no one!*"

The intensity of his booming voice went right through her. She trembled, hating the fact that she knew he was absolutely right.

"The seven of you should have taken that probable event and quietly worked on transforming it in to the opposite. It is at the point in our time where the masses do not realize the damage of negative thoughts. They have forgotten that thought is energy, which can create for good or ill. Through the energy of fear, they now focus on our doom. Instead of thinking for themselves, they listen to another's words of doom, and believe. They forget that they do it to themselves."

Lisa tried to remain calm despite the hostile energy that was being thrown her way. She began to realize why she had lived a quiet life writing under an assumed name, and rejected giving talks at writers' conferences. She always wanted to hide herself away, and not be known. Though she had always wanted to write something deep and meaningful, she stuck to writing something light and entertaining, because it wouldn't hurt anyone.

"Jenielle said that before I made transition, I had planned to go out to the world to teach others the power of the mind, and to focus on changing the energy."

"Yes. You had become aware of the damage that had been done from the release of that vision. You knew you had fallen into the negative energy. You had insisted that I accompany you. I had my work here that I would not abandon. I would not give into the credibility of that vision. And I will not *now.* I will continue to work for the good of our planet, though the rest continue to focus on doom."

"Sylor, it may still be diverted by sending the scientists away."

"By sending my fellow scientists away I am stating that the vision could come to pass, and I will prove that it will not."

"Sylor, think about what you just said. By trying to prove that the destruction will not happen, you are actually focusing *on* it happening." Lisa jumped as the lion roared. Sylor stared Lisa down for a few seconds, and then left the room without saying good-bye.

Jenielle came in and stood before Lisa, who wondered why Jenielle looked so smug.

"Did Sylor tell you what you wanted to know?"

"What are you talking about?" Lisa let out a sigh not wanting to deal with Jenielle at the moment. Then, she remembered their conversation earlier as to why Jenielle and Sylor argued.

"No. He did not." Lisa was getting tired of Jenielle, and her attitude. "I was your sister, and for some reason you don't like me. Why?"

Jenielle seemed to be caught off-guard. "You...you were the one everyone loved. The people of Atlantis, those in high authority, the animals, and..." She turned away.

Lisa saw Jenielle's vulnerability, and felt for her. "Jenielle, there is someone that loves you. Sylor told me. It is his brother, Matua."

"Yes, I am aware of his feelings. But as I have spoken of before, the one I desire is with another. It is *he* I will be with one day."

Chapter 9

———

"Has Scott been back?" Lisa probed two days later, as she helped Karen rearrange some books.

"No. I was hoping he would be but..."

"Have you heard from Steve?" Lisa wasn't sure if she should even ask.

"No. It's over and, you know, it really is okay. It's almost a relief. Granted, it still hurts, but…now I keep asking myself what the purpose of the relationship was."

"What do you think?"

"When I met him, I had just given my notice at the hospital. I had been scouting around different places to set up shop. I was having a hard time because there are a lot of these types of shops out there. I thought about moving out of L.A., even leaving the state. One day while meditating, it had occurred to me to move back here. That was out of the question as far as I was concerned. There was no way I was coming back here to live."

"Why?" Lisa asked almost feeling insulted.

"There were too many bad memories; childhood, my dad, and other things."

Lisa was sure she knew what those other things were.

"When Steve came into the picture, it was either move back here, or live without him. I suppose life has its way of getting us to be where we're supposed to be, for whatever reason. I never thought I'd say it, but it does feel good to be back."

"Talk about your so called coincidence…amazing. It's like your meeting Steve was to get you back here, seeing you were not about to do it on your own."

"Yeah, all the universe had to do was throw a man at me," Karen said, chuckling. "But *why* was I to move back here?"

With that question asked, Scott walked into the store.

The lion greeted Lisa as she emerged from the capsule. They walked to the bathing room, but it seemed no one was around. A few minutes later, Jenielle came in with a disgusted look on her face. Lisa assumed Jenielle was not exactly thrilled about her being there. What else was new? But Lisa did have a question for her.

"Jenielle, why are you still here? I mean, in Atlantis. I know a lot of the others have left Atlantis."

"My work is here. I belong here. That is all I can speak of."

"Tell me about Sylor's brother, Matua."

"Matua is very handsome, and a caring man. He is in agriculture. He travels the country teaching others how to plant and grow crops."

"Why don't you and Matua…"

The two women entered the room to prepare Lisa's bath. Jenielle quickly left the room, leaving Lisa hanging.

Lisa and the lion walked to Sylor's room. She was somewhat nervous. She wasn't sure how he would react, considering what transpired during their last encounter.

Sylor's greeting toward her could not have been warmer. As they kissed, she wanted nothing more than for him to slowly peel off her clothes and make love to her. She was so afraid she wouldn't be able to get enough of him. After a few minutes, they proceeded to the Records room.

She lay on the table, and again he hovered over her, smiling that sexy smile that took her breath away. She took his face in her hands, and guided him to her mouth. He took her bottom lip into his mouth sucking on it. With a drawn out effort, he kissed his way down her neck.

The hand that he had placed at her waist now made its way up. He climbed up and placed himself on top of her.

This was it. She would finally have him. She began to draw up his robe. He instantly stopped and jumped off of her.

"No! We cannot! We can not yet love with our bodies, not until it is safe to do so, not until you have fully adjusted to this level of vibration."

Lisa sat up, and they held each other. "Sylor, I feel like I am going to lose my mind if we can't be with each other soon."

She hated sounding so needy, but she had never felt this kind of love and passion before, *ever.* She had never wanted a man so much in her life, and she was so afraid it would not happen. She knew this was not the kind of thinking to have if she wanted it to happen.

"Do not be disturbed. I promise you we will be together, joined in body and soul, and you will see that being joined in soul is much greater. When this happens, we connect with our Source which is the greatest love."

She regained her composure, and lay back on the table. He placed the head-piece on her with the disk. It took her longer this time to relax, but she soon drifted off into a light sleep.

Hollina and Sylor walked hand in hand by the ocean. It was the eve of a new moon, and the stars stood out against a velvet sky. This new moon represented the new life they were about to begin. It was the eve of their wedding, and the first time they had been completely alone with each other since their reunion.

Sylor stopped and turned to her. Lisa looked longingly into his eyes through Hollina's eyes. She saw the love, the devotion, and something else. She wasn't sure at first, but realized it was the innocence and purity of spirit that Sylor no longer had. It saddened her how much he must have changed.

A slight breeze blew his locks back, and Hollina reached to stroke his hair. Hollina longed for Sylor, as much as Lisa did. Sylor lightly cupped her face. Lisa felt Hollina shiver. The look in his eyes was to die for. Their lips found their way to each other, and Lisa could feel Hollina's heated response.

"The moon beckons us to touch," he whispered.

"Yes. It is time. It is right. My being is completely open to you."

Lisa, as well as Hollina, wanted to devour him. Lisa could feel the hunger, the craving in Hollina. Yet in every way it was pure. *They* were pure. Not just in body, but in their hearts, in their spirit. Nothing they could do at that moment could be tainted. No two beings could have been more in love.

"My love...my truest love, it will be only you throughout eternity." He cupped her face. "It is only to you, I will ever truly give myself."

"And it is only to you I give my soul, as well as my body," Hollina said softly.

"You are everything that I am. I am everything that you are. We are One."

"One soul," she whispered back.

Sylor reached behind Hollina's neck and untied her gown. He let it slowly drop to her waist, exposing her breasts, as he observed her for the first time. He then let the dress fall to the ground.

Hollina reached behind Sylor, and untied his robe. It quickly dropped to the ground. She ran her fingers along his collarbone, and kissed his hairless chest. Their bodies intertwined, and they inched their way to the cool sand. Lisa could barely contain herself. Through Hollina, she would make love to Sylor.

As their bodies joined, Lisa saw in her mind, a pinkish white glow surrounding them. She felt Hollina's body beginning to tingle as she became immersed in Sylor's love. Lisa came to realize that everything she was feeling had nothing to do with the physical sex act. This was something that went well beyond it. The way it was meant to be, she was sure of.

The tension rose as their bodies danced to the rhythm of the universe. Lisa wasn't sure what was happening. The energy in which they were engulfed seemed to be speeding up, and she felt as if she was going to black out. She then managed to focus only on what Hollina was experiencing.

The pulsating energy peaked, and Lisa felt an implosion. She felt Hollina's heart chakra open as well as Sylor's. Their energies meshed and they became each other; one soul, one heart, one being.

There was a brilliant white light, but in that light they could see all colors...every shade of every color. Their energy vibrated faster until they became that light. They had become each other, and more. They were big, they were small, they were nowhere, yet they were everywhere. They were the tiniest particle of an atom, yet as big as the universe with no ending, no boundaries, total freedom, and immersed in the truest love of all. They had become part of the eternal. It was unreal, yet it was the only thing that could *ever* be real.

Then, something happened. Suddenly they separated from the light, then from each other. The loss was unbearable. They found themselves being drawn back to their bodies, their separateness. Hollina tried to fight it, but it was useless.

Hollina and Sylor lay side by side, wrapped in each others' arms. The remnants of bliss were beginning to fade. Hollina laid so still, holding on as much as she could to the feeling of rapture. Lisa felt Hollina's tears, and watched Sylor's own tears stream down his face.

"Hollina come back, come back." Lisa felt herself being shaken. She hesitantly opened her eyes. She too, wanted to hold on to the bliss. As much as she was happy to see Sylor standing over her, she wanted nothing more than for their separate energies to merge, to mesh, to again feel the joy of which they had become a part. She reached up and embraced him, wanting to hold him forever.

"Hollina, tell me, what is wrong?"

She couldn't speak. She knew there were no words for what she had just experienced. He pulled away, and held her face firmly. "What is it? Tell me."

She saw how worried he looked. "Sylor, it was so beautiful, so beautiful. It was the eve of our wedding. It was the first time we..."

"The first time we touched. The first time our bodies became one." He closed his eyes. The expression on his face reflected the memory. "There is not a more joyous feeling. One day, we may again experience in our earthly embodiments the joy as we had that time."

"You mean it wasn't always like that when we made love?"

"No. What we had experienced that night was rare, being within an embodiment, though always possible. That time was a gift from our Source, and to each other. We were given the gift that night so we would not forget from where we come. That feeling is what we hunger for when we unite with another. It is the deeper yearning to reunite with our Source...to become part of the All."

The lion roared. Lisa clung to Sylor. She had never felt so close to him. Lisa went to the bathing room to change. Then, for the very first time, Sylor walked her back to the capsule.

She had a sinking feeling when she opened her eyes. She lay for awhile, too depressed to get up. Later, when she wrote in her journal, she couldn't stop crying. She kept going over the experience between Sylor and Hollina. To be given something that beautiful never to be experienced again, would be too cruel.

She realized that sex is a spiritual experience as well as a physical one, and is something sacred between two people who are deeply in love. Unfortunately, in her society, sex always seemed to be confined to below the waist. With experiencing an orgasm of the heart she knew she could never again have sex with someone with whom she was not in love.

Hollina and Sylor had brought each other to another place within themselves, a higher place that exists within everyone. Lisa truly felt she had touched God. She longed for Sylor more than ever.

Lisa was taking the groceries out of the car and Charcoal ran to her, getting under her feet. She sighed, put the bags down, picked up Charcoal, held him in her arms, and cried.

It had been a week, and she still hadn't been able to shake the depression. The thought of going back to Atlantis and seeing Sylor, then have to leave him again was too much. She felt like she was in limbo. Going back to Atlantis would make her depressed, as would staying in her own reality. The fact that this could all be the product of an over active imagination didn't help.

The phone began to ring as she walked into the house. She was going to let the machine get it, but suddenly she perked up and decided to answer.

"Hi. How are you doing?" Scott said, on the other end.

Lisa was happy to hear his voice. "Okay," she said, trying to sound upbeat, not wanting him to know that she was *not* okay. "Karen told me the two of you had a great time the other night."

"Is that what she told you? Awesome! She told me she had a good time, but I wasn't sure if she was just saying that. I'd like to ask her out again."

"Ask her. Trust me; she wants to go out with you again."

"Unfortunately, she seemed to want to talk about her relationship with what's his name. I think she just needs to get it out of her system. Maybe I can help her get through it. Maybe I can help her ease the pain," Scott said, with a hint of a chuckle in his voice.

"That would be good," Lisa said, somewhat concerned for Scott. She hoped Karen wasn't intending to use him to get over Steve. "You might be able to help her more than I can."

"Why do you say that? You two have been friends forever, right?"

"Yeah, we have, but it's just that sometimes we rub each other the wrong way."

"Maybe there's bad karma," Scott joked. "But hey, I understand. I also have a bit of a relationship like that with a friend. He can be very stubborn. He's a professor, but he wants to quit teaching. He's sort of a loner, and plans to eventually move here, find a nice place at the beach, and write a book. Hey, maybe you should meet him."

"Yeah, well, maybe, I..."

"The man is forever quoting Mark Twain, especially this one; 'When we remember that we are all mad, the mysteries disappear, and life stands explained,' he just loves that one."

"Mark Twain said that? I like that. Fits right in with my life."

"Oh, and he loves Beethoven too! Karen told me how much you love to listen to Beethoven.

"Yeah, I love Beethoven."

"Well, it is of his opinion that Beethoven's Ninth symphony was the greatest piece of music ever composed."

"I have to agree, especially the last movement, 'Ode to Joy.'"

"His favorite is the one that's fast and intense. I don't know what movement that is."

"That would be the second movement. What's your friend's name?"

"Matt Fields. I don't know how we will get along when he moves here, and we see each other more often. He can be just a bit too serious, but he is a good guy. You know, he's about your age, and I don't remember the last time he's had a date. But then again, he's kind of sworn off women."

"Scott, don't even think about fixing us up. Besides, I'm waiting for my twin soul."

"Your what?"

"Nothing," she said, and then laughed, feeling her face turn red. "And I hate to say this, but I think he would almost be more suited to Karen. She's always quoting someone."

"Then maybe I'll convince Matt to stay in Boston. I do not need any more competition," he said joking, but Lisa picked up on a touch of fear in his voice.

"Scott, you are in a league all by yourself. You're all right."

"Sylor will be away today. You may review Hollina's Records if you desire," Jenielle said, with a slightly hostile tone.

"Oh...Okay." Lisa was deeply disappointed. She wanted nothing more than to wrap herself around him.

Hollina and Sylor stood in the middle of a circle of what Lisa thought to be at least a hundred people. There was soft, harp like music, with chanting in the background, and the air was filled with the scent of roses. They both wore white satin robes that tied at the waist with a thick white belt. Tiny red and white roses garnished Hollina's hair, which was worn down and resting below her shoulders. They were both wearing the symbol of Atlantis.

Lisa couldn't help noticing the smile on Sylor's face that seemed to be set in stone. She then realized it was Hollina's and Sylor's wedding day. Sylor took Hollina by the hand, and together they stepped up to a round marble platform. They carried their crystals.

Suddenly, there was complete silence. A white mist began to encircle the platform, along with a low humming sound. They became engulfed in the mist, which turned into a brilliant golden white light, which surrounded the entire platform. Out of this brilliance stepped Dreedon.

At this point, Lisa found the energy of this light overwhelming, and began focusing to connect to Hollina's feelings. She found it very difficult, and began to feel dazed. Lisa felt like she was going in and out of consciousness. She heard Dreedon speaking, and realized he was conducting the ceremony.

"One single flame, one whole. Born from the One, twin flames emerge. Your destiny has been set into motion according to the order proposed for your own purpose; your choice intended before your division. My One, the laws to you are known. Your will is free, and your choices of mind are many. If you encounter the trials that may come before you with struggle, you must remember to go within to the source, the One."

"My One, within you holds the heart, the soul, and the love, of the other. Take care well of this gift. As you care for yourself, you care for the other. Your love will forever unite you. May your will be done, as you are now joined."

Lisa felt the light begin to intensify as it started to open up to something, but the next thing she knew Jenielle was removing the headpiece.

"Why did you do that? Something was about to happen!" Lisa sat up feeling dizzy, and lay back down. "The light was so intense, the energy, and something..."

"You were thrashing about. I did not know what you were experiencing. I removed it in regards to your safety."

"Sylor and I were being married. Dreedon was performing the ceremony, and this brilliant light was all around us. I couldn't see anyone."

"You were also hidden from the others."

"Why? What do you mean?"

"The marriage of twin flames is the highest marriage rite. No one witnesses the actual ceremony, with every ceremony being different and unique, conforming to the purpose of the twin flames."

"Oh. But within this intense light, well, a part of it was beginning to open up like some sort of vortex, and I saw what looked to be two shadowy figures. I'm sure it was a man and a woman. I felt a sense of urgency and..."

"You must calm yourself." Jenielle handed her a chalice to drink from. The lion moved to Lisa's side, and Lisa sat up again.

"You don't understand. That man and woman ...I couldn't see them, but I knew them, I felt their energy. I felt them as if they were a part of me. I don't under..." Lisa's voice trailed off as she carefully watched Jenielle place the disk back into the cubby hole. As she watched, she suddenly thought of something.

"Jenielle, the disks...if one were to use another's, would you be able to experience that person's life? Say if I used Sylor's, or yours, for instance."

"Yes." Jenielle gave Lisa a cold stare. "Though I do not encourage or recommend so. To invade another's thoughts may bring karmic consequences if there is not sufficient reason or permission."

Lisa wasn't sure why she had asked the question, but she did think it would be a great way to know what was going on inside someone's head.

"So how were your dates last weekend with Scott?" Lisa asked as she poured herself a cup of coffee at The Crystal Pyramid. "By the way, I'm glad you've decided to serve coffee now, as well as herb tea."

"The addicted kept asking for it." Karen poured herself some tea. "It was fun. Scott and I had fun."

Lisa noticed Karen's voice was less than enthusiastic.

"What did you guys do?"

"We spent Saturday in New Bedford, in the Historic District, and Sunday we went up to Boston to the Market Place.

"What's the matter? I thought you liked Scott."

"I do. He's upbeat and funny, caring, sensitive..."

"Oh, it's not the fact that he's younger is it?"

"No. I don't care about that. While we were up in Boston...well. Scott has a friend who lives up that way. We stopped in at his place, and..."

"And what?" Lisa felt anxious.

"Scott's friend, there is, I don't know...I felt very attracted to him."

"Uh oh, Karen, what about Scott?" Lisa found herself feeling protective of Scott, and wasn't sure she wanted to hear anymore.

"I felt turned on by his aloofness. He wouldn't even look at me when he talked, and he has this brooding quality about him, and this arrogance...I couldn't take my eyes off of him. He's almost as good-looking as Scott."

"This might be the guy Scott wanted me to meet. Is his name Matt?"

"Yes, but I don't think he's your type."

"What does he look like?"

"He's about six feet tall, blue eyes," Lisa started to think about Sylor, but then noticed the dreamy look on Karen's face. "Dark blonde hair that's sort of long, and wispy, but not too long. He and Scott could almost pass for brothers. I hope Scott didn't notice how fixated I was on him."

"I told Scott I was waiting for my twin soul when he mentioned my meeting him."

"You didn't," Karen said, rolling her eyes.

"Yeah, I did." Lisa laughed, realizing how silly it sounded as she again began to doubt it all. "But I didn't elaborate. I did tell him that you would probably be more suited to Matt than I would. I don't think he was too happy about that."

"Why do you think *I* would be more suited to Matt?"

"Apparently, he quotes Mark Twain, and he does teach litera-ture." Lisa didn't like the fact that Karen seemed a little too inter-ested. "Are you going to go out with Scott again?"

"Yes, I am. We're going to the Onset Blues Festival on Saturday."

Lisa didn't realize how much she had missed Sylor until he stood before her with his powerful presence, and those mind-blowing blue eyes. She immediately realized the feeling was mutual when he embraced her with an unfathomable kiss.

He pulled away to speak, but she pulled him right back, pressing her mouth hard on his devouring, moist lips. *This is pure hell*, she thought. *Why couldn't we just do it?* She had never craved another human being before.

"It is not every day I am honored with such a greeting. I regret that I was not here for your last visit. I have so longed for your presence."

Lisa let out a sigh feeling the same for Sylor. "Last time I was here we did the Records. It was the day of our union, our marriage..."

She stopped, and thought about the vortex of light and the two shadowy figures of a man and a woman. She got goose bumps all over. Why? What *was* that about?

"It will not be long before we share our life together again."

Lisa touched his mouth and smiled sadly. He seemed to be waiting for a response. She did not want to get him upset again by telling him she might not stay. He then took her hand, and together they walked to the Records room.

He surprised her by gallantly picking her up and placing her on the table. She wrapped her arms around his neck, and his mouth met hers for a long, delicate kiss.

"You will wear down my resistance," he said, as he untangled her arms from his neck. "It is taking all the strength I have to not take you now, and give my full self to you."

"Then do it! I love you, and I want you so much."

His expression turned serious. "You know better."

"No. No, I don't. Why can't we make love now? You're all I've ever wanted. Why?"

"Hollina, nothing would bring me more joy than to love you, all of you. To love you now would have detrimental effects on your wellbeing."

"I don't understand."

"When two people love, their energy fields become meshed... intertwined. It was obvious when you arrived here that you were from a denser, lower-level vibration. Here, our bodies vibrate at a higher level, though at one time it was much higher. Are you not ill when you return to your level?"

"Not as much as I used to be. Sometimes, I feel weird. My head aches and my body will feel bulky or heavy."

"If we loved now you would receive my fluid. The energy contained within could stay with you for days or longer. It is of a much higher vibration than your own. This could cause you much harm. We have no choice but to wait," he said firmly.

As Lisa drifted into an altered state, she found herself in Hollina's body meditating near the ocean with a small group of women. All together, there were seven of them arranged in a circle.

They each carried a crystal disk, similar to the ones in the Records room, but slightly larger. They chanted, and held their disks up to the sun, closed their eyes, and meditated some more. As Hollina meditated, Lisa started to realize what was going on. Sylor had already gone up to the north, and it seemed like he had been gone for quite some time, possibly a couple of years.

Through Hollina's consciousness, Lisa would come to see the most horrifying sight, the sight that would change not only Hollina's life, and the life of everyone living in Atlantis, but a sight that would set the tone for the entire future of planet Earth.

First, Sylor and the small group of scientists that would accompany him home came into view. Lisa felt Hollina's breath nearly being knocked out of her. The dense, negative energy that emanated from these men was pure evil. In this scene, Sylor stood apart from them, but he was still with them. Hollina knew that even though Sylor had been heavily influenced by his stay up in the north, and that this would be manifested in his actions, he would never completely succumb to what the north had tried to program into him. His stubbornness would be an asset in this case.

Hollina and Lisa were also clued in about how these evil ones would try to take control of the entire planet. These men would plant crystals into the brains of the common people, to be controlled from a master crystal. Some would be programmed to be slaves and laborers, others would be programmed to go out to other parts of the world to influence and gain control, even if they had to kill to do it.

Hollina knew Sylor had no clue to any of this, nor would he be a part of such acts. It wasn't in him, and he could not believe that it could be in anyone else. Lisa realized how naive he really was.

The whole process would be a slow-moving one, but a devastating one if it was allowed to go through. This would be a test for all the people of Atlantis. It would be a test of their beliefs, and their faith. Would they look inward and trust in the higher source that resided within, or would they look outside of themselves, and believe in the words and ideas of another without question?

As Jenielle had said, the people of Atlantis were moving away from the ways of spirit. They were forgetting they were part of a higher power of love, goodness, and peace. Everyone would have to change and focus on these things completely if the destruction was to be averted.

The next scene was it. Hollina and Lisa watched earthquake after earthquake consume the land. An angry earth spouted its discharge, while an enraged ocean devoured. The whipping winds added its energy to the fire that engulfed what little beauty was left. Each element competed to outdo the other. Lisa heard the pitiful sounds, the cries, the screams, and felt the mass fear…the *explosion* of fear. She watched the land seemingly flip and break into pieces, falling into the ocean. A few tiny fragments of land remained with no life left.

Lisa wanted out. She couldn't assimilate what she was seeing. She wanted no part of it, and again guilt started to tear at her. She knew, as Hollina, she had become a part of it, and it was all because of that vision, the vision as Sylor said should have been revealed to no one.

Another scene came in. Lisa felt instantly calmed as she watched a beautiful waterfall with a rainbow aura surrounding it. Trees were plush with different fruits, and the fragrance from flowering plants saturated the air. Naked children romped in the water happily splashing about, as others picked their meal from the trees. The elders walked with the commoners. Then Lisa realized there were no commoners. Everyone was equal. Everyone lived in unity. Everyone was at peace with their environment, and with each other, and most of all within themselves.

This was the Atlantis that was supposed to be. This was the vision we were to focus on. It was the love, the beauty, the harmony, the light.

As Lisa tuned in on Hollina's feelings, she felt nothing but the fear of the first vision. Lisa felt like she was suffocating as she tried to control Hollina's mind. She kept telling Hollina to focus on the second vision, but of course it was useless, and she found herself carrying Hollina's fear with her.

She felt the headpiece being pulled off. "What is wrong? You were moving about. I saw how…"

"I've got to get out of here," she screamed, as she pushed Sylor away.

"What is wrong?" Sylor asked again, now very concerned.

"I saw the vision…Hollina's vision of Atlantis being destroyed. It was horrible, it was, oh God, I've got to get out of here." She saw the enraged look on Sylor's face, and she bolted. She heard him start to come after her, but the lion stopped him.

Her eyes flew open and she brought the blanket up to her neck. Her body trembled as she looked around her room noting the skylights, the Barbie doll, her teddy bear, and Charcoal, who was now purring in her ear. She held her breath for a few seconds, and silently thanked a higher power for where she now lay.

Chapter 10

———

It took Lisa more than a week to pull out her journal, and record her last expedition to Atlantis. She began to shake as she recalled the sight that would forever be etched in her memory.

She read over her last entry, the one where Hollina and Sylor were being wed. The scene of the vortex opening up still haunted her. Who was that man and woman she felt so close to? Why was there this sense of urgency? She flung the journal to the floor. How much more of this could she take?

"So how was the festival? And how is Scott?" Lisa asked Karen when they met for lunch.

"The festival was a lot of fun, and Scott is good."

"Are you going to see him again?"

Karen hesitated, "Yes, I am."

"Gee, you don't sound too excited. I thought you liked him."

"I do. I really do. And he's made it clear he likes me…a lot."

"So what's the problem?"

"I'm going to sound like a snob when I say this…but, he doesn't seem to be too ambitious."

Lisa rolled her eyes and sat back. "What?"

"Granted, he manages a health food store. That's fine, but he doesn't seem to want more. I figured he would want to own one someday, but he says he's happy right now doing what he's doing, and he's not concerned with the future. He says he'll know if or when it's time to do something else."

"I think I like his way of thinking. Live for the moment. It sounds like he probably trusts his intuition. I like that too."

"I guess I'm just used to men who want more. I've gone out with lawyers, doctors, even Steve is moving up in the company and hopes to have his own eventually."

"Sure, and these guys all gave you nothing but grief. If Scott's anything, he's sincere. He's also happy with what he does. In fact, the guy seems to be a happy person, period. Maybe you should try a different breed."

"Lisa, he still lives at home with his mother and his younger sister. He's says there's no reason to leave home until he gets married."

"So? He's probably saving a lot of money."

"You don't understand."

"I understand you've found a nice, caring, sensitive guy who really seems to care for you. Give him a chance."

"It's not just that." Karen looked down, and then took a sip of wine. "I can't stop thinking about his friend, Matt."

"Oh, the aloof professor that Scott wanted to fix me up with."

"He's not your type."

"I get the feeling you don't want him to be my type."

"It doesn't matter. Who's to say I'll even see him again? He's probably a jerk anyway."

"Probably," Lisa said tongue in cheek. "But what if you did happen to see him again? What about Scott?" Again, Lisa was feeling protective of him. She did not want to see him hurt.

"Most likely he wouldn't even give me the time of day. I don't think he likes women. I mean, I think he's intimidated, or he's been hurt one too many times."

"Yeah, Scott told me he had sworn off women. Maybe that's good news for us!"

"Sylor is not in the temple. I will assist you with the Records," Jenielle said in her usual wintery tone.

Sylor stood before Hollina, garbed in a royal blue robe with a thick gold belt. He had just returned from the north, and this was their reunion. After three years, Hollina could barely contain herself. She blissfully coiled herself around him as he stood motionless. With no reciprocal gesture, Hollina pulled back and stared into eyes of ice.

"How dare you?" he asked, as if she were the enemy.

"How dare *I*? I know not of what you speak. Sylor, what is wrong?" Lisa knew he had never spoken to Hollina like that before. It felt like he had run a knife through her heart. "Sylor, do you not know to whom you speak? I am your beloved, your wife, Hollina. Do you not know me?" She touched his face. He pushed back her hand, and walked away.

"I do not know you." He turned back and walked directly to her. "My wife would not defame the impeccable reputation of her husband's fellow scientists to bring shame upon them. I know of the tales you tell. How could you conspire to spread such lies…lies about the good men I have brought back, and lies about our lands demise?"

"Sylor, I...but I have seen. With these eyes I have seen. You must believe me. I would not tell untruths. You know me, I am…"

"Silence! I know you, no more."

Hollina proceeded to flee the room. He quickly caught her. He turned her to face him. Lisa felt his solid grip bearing on Hollina's shoulders. He looked into Hollina's tear streaked face. For a second she saw the sorrow in his eyes. He lightened his grip, only to tighten it again when he caught himself yielding to her anguish.

"It is I who do not know you. What has happened? What have they done to you?" she desperately begged to know. "You would not act of your own will. The north's ways are harsh. Love is not something to be shown or felt. They build walls around their hearts. They show no mercy."

"Silence! That is enough!" Sylor raised his hand to strike. Hollina faced him without a flinch, knowing he could never hurt her in that way. He slowly brought his arm down, never taking his eyes off hers. Lisa felt he didn't know what to do with her as he dismissed her. "Leave now. Go to our room."

Hollina searched his eyes for the light that once emanated from them. He would not look at her. She gently stroked his face. "Sylor, my love for you is eternal."

"Return to our room now, Hollina. Go," he said softly.

"Sylor would never strike you." Jenielle said later. "He knows that is not the way. Brutality is not the way of our Source. The way of our Source is love, peace, and unity. No exceptions. We are losing this. It is being forgotten. Sylor's stay in the north changed him. He is not the only one. We have all become hardened to some degree... just some more than others."

"He has never been the same, has he?"

"He has not. He will never love the way he once did. Not you or any other, not even himself. He is dead inside. He can love no one."

"I don't agree. He loves me. He does love me." Lisa shook her head firmly. "No, Jenielle, you are wrong. The love is there, inside him. I know...I have felt it strongly. I have seen it. Like an eternal flame, it can not be extinguished. But it can be covered up...a wall built around his heart, in a sense, so no one can see it, no one can feel it. The wall is built from hurt, guilt, fear, anger, and whatever else. But the flame is still there. The walls need to be knocked down. This is true for everyone. We all have that light inside of us."

"I tell you he can love no one."

"No Jenielle, Sylor may never be the same person, but he will love again like he once did. He will. I can't do it for him, but maybe I can help him."

"You fool, how can you help him? You have done nothing but enrage him thus far."

"I can love him. Love him, and forgive him. That's all I can do. Love him with no conditions. With my loving him, he may be able to love himself again, and that's a start."

"You think big of yourself. You are also committing to an immense task. It will not work, I say. He will remain unchanged."

As Lisa wrote in her journal, she thought about what Jenielle had said about Sylor remaining unchanged, and that he could never really love anyone. There was a part of her that was afraid Jenielle could be right. She knew she would have to think otherwise. Then again, she figured, the only way she could help him was to stay in Atlantis. The scene of the destruction flashed in her mind. The hair on her arms stood straight up. She almost wished this was nothing more than a book she was writing.

Karen and her mother spent a week in South Carolina after the death of an aunt. Karen left Lisa to mind the store. During this week, Scott came to the store one day while taking his lunch break.

"I'm falling in love with her, Leese. But my gut keeps telling me I shouldn't." Lisa wanted to tell Scott to listen to his gut. But her own gut kept telling her not to interfere. "What should I do? Should I tell her how I feel? You must know how she feels about me."

"I know she likes you an awful lot. She enjoys being with you. To tell you the truth Scott, Karen and I don't confide in each other all that much anymore."

"Why? I thought you two were good friends."

"We were much closer when we were kids. There are some things that are going on in my life right now that she doesn't want to know about, or even want to try to understand. I guess in a way I can't blame her, because it is all very bizarre and unbelievable. No one would believe these things could really happen and..."

Oh God, what was she doing! She was ready to spill her guts to someone she didn't even know all that well, yet she knew he would understand. He would.

"What things?"

"I'm sorry, Scott. I can't talk about this. But somehow, I feel you are the very person I could tell."

"You can. Leese, you can tell me anything."

Lisa looked into his eyes and saw the beautiful soul that he was. She could tell him anything. She knew it. She felt it. She saw the radiant light in his eyes. She knew she had found a soul mate. "I know I can," she said with tears in her eyes. "And I will…just not yet."

Lisa's heart sank when Jenielle told her again that Sylor was not in the temple. They proceeded to the Records room.

Lisa felt the vibration of Hollina's booming voice. "I tell you this can not go any further. The experiments must stop! They will soon be approaching a critical turn. It will be beyond your control. This will be done without your knowledge, without your permission. Sylor, you still have influence over the scientists. Do something!"

"Influence? And what of *your* influence? Many are leaving this great land because of *your* influence; the lies *you* have spread."

"Atlantis will be destroyed! Be damned, Sylor! One way or another I will prove it to you. I *will* prove it to you."

"You can not prove it," he snickered.

Lisa felt Hollina's desperation and exasperation. It had been many months since Sylor's return, and he was worse than ever. Hollina's and Sylor's relationship with each other was never the same. The man she loved with all her soul was a stranger to her. She felt she had lost a part of herself, and wasn't sure if she could go on. Lisa felt weakness overtake Hollina's body.

"Sylor, I beg you again. Come with me to Egypt. We can make our life there. There is so much we can teach. We have so much to give. Sylor, I ask you one last time. Let us go to Egypt. Say yes, Sylor. Say yes!"

"As I have voiced before, our life is here. Those who forsake us, betray us."

"Do you not understand? They desire to still live. They do not want to witness this land being destroyed. No, they will not be a witness to it. And neither will I!" Lisa felt all of Hollina's strength come back. She stood upright and rigid. "No! I will not be a witness. This I promise you!"

"What is your meaning?" again he snickered. "What do you promise?"

"I will embark on a new journey."

"You will go nowhere without me. You will not settle in Egypt."

"I can do no more here. And yes, you are correct. I will not settle in Egypt. Your love for me is buried. It is covered with the muck you carry within you from the north. You were once at a high level. Your vibration has become dense. Your light no longer shines. *This tears through my soul!*"

"What do you speak of?"

"I have taken great thought on this. In seven days I will go to the Crystal Cave, enter the chamber, and make transition to spirit."

"You can not leave me. I will not allow it."

"You will not allow it? You have no control over my will." Hollina turned and started to walk away. Sylor forcefully grabbed her arm. He raised his hand to strike her face, but stopped himself. He let his hand faintly brush her cheek. His eyes teared up, and Lisa could see he wanted to say something, but somehow he couldn't, or wouldn't. He rushed out of the room leaving Hollina to hope that he would come to his senses.

"Sylor seems to have softened somewhat since then," Lisa said to Jenielle. "It seems he was almost cruel between the time he came back from the north and the time Hollina made transition."

"Sylor's rage grew when you made transition. He did not believe you would go through with it. When you did, he became lost within himself, and begged the Source to show mercy, and take him. With the antipathy and rage he held within, he was incapable of choosing whether or not to make transition as you did. He wanted nothing more than to be with you again. With your return, his harshness has subsided some. His mind is made up that you will stay. I do not desire to know what he will become if your choice is to stay in your reality."

"Oh God, I don't even want to think about making this choice. I still have no proof as to any of this. In our society, these things just do not happen."

"As I have voiced before, your society is limited," Sylor's voice decreed as he entered the room. He quickly walked over to Lisa, as Jenielle stormed out. "Do not have doubt. This is as true as my love. You will stay here with me, by my side. Jenielle is unerring with what I would become if you left again. You will stay."

"Sylor, I love you more than life. That's why this is all so scary to me. In my reality, I'm a writer. I write stories, and I don't know if somehow I've created you in my mind. I don't know for sure if you are real. Everything in my society tells me you are not, that it's not possible."

"That is all more reason to stay. Many things are possible here."

"Sylor, as much as I love you, I can't make any decision yet. Please understand."

"Understand? I do not."

What *would* Sylor become if she didn't stay in Atlantis? Lisa asked herself several days later when she was minding the store for Karen.

What would he become if she *did* stay in Atlantis? Would she end up living a life being controlled by him? She may have been a priestess then, but she sure as hell didn't feel like one now. Would her love be enough for him to change?

"Somewhere my love..." Scott sang when he walked into the store, expecting to find Karen. "And where is the lady of the manor?"

"She took her mother for tests."

"Oh, right, she told me her mother had been getting chest pains. I met her mother last weekend. Nice lady. She told me I was a nice young man, and I would do well by her daughter. She also asked me to be patient with her. Kind of gives me the creeps, now. I hope she's going to be okay."

"I hope so too. And she's right you know. You are a nice young man." She watched him blush. "And you *will* need patience."

"I'm going to spend the rest of my life with her, Leese. I think I knew that the night I met her at the club. I said to myself, Scott, that's the woman you are going to be with the rest of your life. Then I could hardly bring myself to talk to her. I wanted to give her a rose. She needed a rose. I'm being a silly romantic huh?"

Lisa put her hand to her chest. "Be still my beating heart. God I wish there were more men like you."

"Then I'm not crazy, believing I'm going to be with her for the rest of my life?"

"Crazy? No." That was nothing, Lisa thought.

I take it there is no one special in your life right now, or anyone you have your eye on?

Lisa stared down at the floor. How could she tell him that the man she loved more than life was from *another* life, or, even worse, possibly a figment of her imagination?

"You don't have to tell me. I don't want to intrude on your personal life."

"I'll be honest, Scott. There is someone I love very much. But if I told you about him, you'd never believe me. On one hand, it's something so beautiful, on the other...well, I may be out of my mind. Karen seems to think I am. It's something that is not of this world. It's mystical, it's supernatural or it's...or it's all in my mind, or I'm losing my mind."

Why was she saying this? No one would ever understand. But he would. He would. He interrupted before she could say anymore.

"Leese, you don't have to tell me about losing one's mind. Brace yourself. When I was a kid I used to be able to leave my body at will. You must have heard of out-of-body experiences, or astral projection?

"Yes." Her heart started to beat faster as she eagerly listened.

"I could actually go places, visit people. I was very psychic, too. I knew if someone was going to die soon. I just knew things. It stopped when I was around twelve or thirteen. I still have some psychic ability but it comes and goes, I never know when I'm going to have it. It just happens."

Lisa breathed a sigh of relief, knowing she was not alone. But she still felt that anything he told her was not going to top what she was going through, if she really wasn't insane.

"I didn't have another out of body experience until I was a freshman at the university. That's where I met my buddy, Matt. He was teaching there at the time. Well, anyway, a few of us formed a meditation group and we really didn't know what we were doing. We used a mantra, and I left my body, but it was nothing like the other times when I was a kid. When it was over, I thought maybe I had imagined it all. Everyone told me I did, but until this day I know it was real. And I wasn't smoking any weed, I didn't do that stuff.

I floated out of my body, right through the top of my head. I thought I had died…at first. I was engulfed in blackness. I kept thinking about God. Where was God? I wasn't afraid at all. Then something clicked in my mind. I knew God wasn't just this being we had been brought to believe, he was more. And God wasn't a he. God was all, God was everything!"

"God, Goddess, the All," Lisa added excitedly.

"Yes, but this God force, if you want to call it that, is endless, and we are a part of it. To find and know God we look within, not outside of ourselves. With this experience, I learned that very few really know what God is, and that it's something each one of us have to find ourselves, and it's not what we've been taught. All I know from this experience is this; God is, and nothing else is. Leese, I knew what that really meant."

"Wow, Scott, that's..." Lisa was almost speechless.

"But wait," Scott continued, "with that realization, I started to see these tiny sparks of light. It looked like millions of them. They were coming closer, and they were all around me. They were getting bigger, and finally they all came together, and I became part of it. I became part of this brilliant, beautiful light. I *was* this light! And that's when I realized that only God is real! Nothing else is. Everything else is really just an illusion...just a dream that we all need to wake up from. We are spirit still at home in God; we just don't know it. And what keeps us from knowing what we really are is the ego...all of our little hidden hates, judgments, resentments, and our unwillingness to forgive. This experience lasted only a few seconds, but, Leese, the love I felt...I can't...it was beyond explanation. Words just can't..."

Scott was overcome with emotion. He wiped his eyes and continued. "I became united with this higher power, this love. It was God not as a person or a being, but a feeling. It's like...you don't actually see or hear God. You experience God, because that is what we are, and I did experience this beautiful, loving force. And this force is so close to us. It's right in our face, and we can't figure it out. After that experience, I knew there was nothing to fear, ever. Not death. Not life!"

Lisa grabbed a tissue and sat down. She was overcome with emotion, recalling the experience of Hollina and Sylor making love. It was the same feeling, she thought, one that can not be described, only experienced.

"Do you think I'm a fruitcake, or what?" Scott asked after he settled down. "I don't know why I told you. After that night, I never told anyone again."

Lisa gave Scott one long hug. "Scott, *you* better brace yourself for what I'm about to tell *you*."

Scott let out a deep breath and sat back. "This is incredible. This is one for the books. Sorry, no pun intended."

Lisa started to laugh, and she couldn't stop. Telling Scott was the release she needed.

"Leese, anything *is* possible. You've got to believe that. This is what that psychic was trying to tell you, through Karen."

"I know. I know what the psychic said, and what I'm going through all fits. But there is still so much I don't understand. What exactly is 'the mission?' And 'the future changes the past which changes the future?' I'm still not getting it. And then if I'm to write another book…and if Karen is right, that what I'm doing is writing a book with this whole experience…then that means I won't be staying in Atlantis. That would mean…"

"Do you really want to stay in Atlantis?"

"I want to be with Sylor. I'm totally confused. What's real? What's not? I do feel like I'm losing my mind. Karen says it's unlikely, but sometimes I think he is alive now, here, somewhere in this reality. But then, if he is, why would I have to go back to the past to be with him? I don't get it."

"Maybe he is alive, and you've passed him on the street and not even known it."

"No. That would never happen. I would *know* him. As God as my witness, I would know him."

"Maybe you're not ready to know him. Maybe the two of you are not ready for each other yet."

"What?"

"I don't know…it's just a hunch."

"Scott, if I'm supposed to know that anything is possible, then why do I still feel that I need proof? My left brain tells me it's illogical, impossible. My right brain tells me it's very possible, that this is what it is. So what's the problem? The problem is that I'm still listening to the left brain, because that's what we, as a society, have been programmed to do. I still need proof, damn it!"

"Leese, it's all very simple."

"What? What's simple?" Lisa was starting to feel exhausted.

"Next time you meditate with the crystal, I'll be there with you. I can tell you if you've actually gone anywhere; disappeared, teleported, whatever."

"No!" She shook her head forcefully. "No, no way! I don't know if I'm ready for that. This could prove embarrassing. I don't know if I could stand the thought of somebody watching me go nowhere. Oh God, I don't even know if I really want to know. Scott, I'm losing it. I am. I don't know what to do." He held her as she cried.

"Scott, what if I *did* let you do that? I'm not saying I will, but what if? What if I did 'disappear?' Then I *would* know that it was real, that this is possible, and then...I will have to decide...I will have to make that choice to stay here, or there. I don't know if..."

"Do you know how incredible this would be? You'd go down in history."

"No! No one will ever know about this."

"Leese, you're forgetting something. If you stay there, what happens here? I think you would just disappear from this reality. Then what? No one would ever see you again? How do we explain this? You would have literally disappeared. Who would believe this?"

"Oh God, you're right. That had occurred to me once before. Everything is recorded in my journal...every word, every thought, every feeling. It's all in there. Maybe that's how the book will be written. What if the journal is the book I'm suppose to write? Maybe I am to stay in Atlantis." Lisa raked her hands through her hair. "I...*I can not even believe I am having this conversation.* I'm crazy. I am."

"You're not crazy." Scott held her as she cried.

"Scott, what if I make the wrong choice?" What if I choose Atlantis, and it's wrong? What if I chose to stay here, and it's wrong?"

"Whatever choice you make will be the right one, whatever it is meant to be. Leese, you know there's a bigger picture here, and you're not seeing it yet. Maybe you're not supposed to see it yet."

Chapter 11

Except for the lion, there seemed to be no one in the temple. Lisa walked to the bathing room, and then to Sylor's room. No Jenielle, and no Sylor. She made her way over to the Records room. She sat on the table and thought about the time she and Sylor almost made love.

After a few moments of relishing in her fantasy, she found herself staring at all the disks in the cubby holes. She stood up and slowly walked over to them. She picked out Hollina's disk and inspected it. Still holding it in her hand, she turned to see the head-piece sitting on the table in the corner. She frowned and placed the disk back.

She reached into the compartment next to Hollina's, which held Jenielle's disk. Again, she turned to the head-piece. She didn't like what she was thinking. After all, she had been warned, and it might not even work. She placed the disk back. She slowly moved her hand over to Sylor's crystal disk. She held it for a moment, and then again looked over at the head-piece. Could she do this? Did she have a right? Would it work?

Lisa soon felt herself inside Sylor's body. She felt the dead weight, the solidity, the density. There was even more of a heavy, constricted feeling in his chest area. This was altogether different from the feeling of lightness Hollina's body manifested. As Sylor walked the shore, she felt his anger, his confusion, and his despair. It was nearly intolerable to be within him.

The moon was fading from sight, with the sun beginning to rise. A mild wind blew, and Lisa could hear the faint whistle echoing through the mountains. Sylor walked slowly, stopping for a second or two, with every few steps trying to keep his distance from the one he was following; Hollina.

He watched her stand at the edge of the ocean. He watched the waves pour over her bare feet. The wind picked up more, causing Hollina's sheer, white dress to mold to her frame. He eyed the outline of her flawless body, the one that fit his so perfectly. The one he now ached for.

He continued to watch as she walked toward the mountain which held the Crystal Cave of Transition. He knew what would take place. She would bathe in the pool and cleanse herself under the waterfall. After, she would dress into the white robe and wear the crown. Then she would be guided deep within the cave to the Transition Chamber, and enter her new birth.

He could stop her. He could. He could tell her they would settle in Egypt. He could tell her he was wrong. *Never!* It was *she* who was wrong. Lisa could feel his body become rigid with the hardness of his thoughts. She could feel a dull pain in his chest.

He wanted to call out her name, shout his love for her, and beg her to reconsider. The words remained trapped in his throat. He had his pride. He could not, would not, lower himself. That would mean a loss of respect in the eyes of the other scientists. In the north, husbands did not serve their wives, they battered them into submission. This was something he could never do. It wasn't in him.

Lisa could feel him breaking inside, being ripped apart by his emotions. He did not want his life without her. Lisa could feel wetness around his eyes, yet he still held back so much. His chest was beginning to ache.

He watched Hollina stand at the opening of the cave for a few minutes. Then she moved to sit in the rock that was made like a chair. This chair was for a last contemplation. One sat in this chair to meditate, to be sure that this is what one really desired. There would be no departure once the cave was entered. The opening of the cave would be sealed until transition was made.

As she meditated, she would alter her thinking on this foolish act and stay with him, he thought. *Yes, if she loved me as she has voiced, then she would cease this extreme and unnecessary action.*

He continued to watch her as he stood behind a large rock. He stopped and turned around when a resonating sound began to vibrate through him. Many particles of light danced before him. These particles began to merge into a form, a human form. Sylor now stood face to face with Dreedon.

"My One, why have you so lowered yourself? All you need do is ask for help. None of this has need to materialize. Open your eyes to a new vision. Your power is never lost. You have just forgotten. Use it, and use it wisely."

"Dreedon, she can not love me as she has voiced, or she would be at my command."

"Have you forgotten that no one is at the command of another?"

"She is my wife!"

"She is your wife. She is your soul. You have forgotten that the pain you inflict upon her, you also inflict upon yourself. Go to her at this moment. She waits for you. There is so little time. Go to her now."

"No! I am a man. She will come to me."

"Your will is free. Thy will be done."

Dreedon faded from sight. Lisa felt like strangling Sylor as she yelled at him to go to Hollina. She found his pride and stubbornness appalling.

Hollina was still sitting in the chair when Sylor turned back. He looked away again, to watch the sun rising. He began to ponder Dreedon's words. Could he put his pride aside for the woman who shared his soul? He thought on this for a few moments. His pride began to retreat knowing he would never see his beloved again in this life. The words trapped in his throat were now ready to be released, and he turned to speak. *It was too late.* The opening of the cave had been sealed.

"Noooo! Noooo!" he cried. Sobbing, he fell down on his knees, pounding his fists into the sand. "Noooo...Hollina, noooo!" He slowly stood up, and then gazed at the sky. He knew he could never watch the sun rise again.

Lisa felt the head-piece being removed. The disorientation she felt quickly vanished when she opened her eyes to see Jenielle's look of contempt. It had just occurred to Lisa what she had done. She offered no explanation to Jenielle, and fled the room.

Her head hurt like hell, but she poured herself a glass of wine anyway. She sat at the kitchen table in darkness, except for a single pink tapered candle burning. She wanted to focus on what it was like to be Sylor. She could still feel the heaviness and the tightness, the ego and pride that had its grip on him. She wanted to somehow empathize with him, to come to some understanding of the why of things.

Charcoal jumped up on her lap, turned around a couple of times, found a comfortable position, and fell asleep. He seemed so peaceful. She envied him.

Sylor was anything but at peace. Lisa felt the pain that ripped through his heart when he realized Hollina was gone. This would make him desperate...desperate enough to chance the karma that would incur by bringing Hollina back.

She blew out the candle and cried in the blackness, feeling all of Sylor's pain, anguish, and despair. He truly was a tormented soul.

Over the next couple of days, Lisa thought more about Scott's proposition. It did make sense. This could very well prove the reality of the situation. *But what if nothing happened?* What would she do? *How could she go on?* Karen would love it since she would have been right all along. How could she face Karen? Lisa knew she had to put an end to this sometime. She decided she would take Scott up on his offer, but not just yet.

Again, no one was in the temple. Had everyone fled Atlantis? Would she ever see Sylor again? Jenielle had to be lurking about somewhere.

She entered Sylor's room and looked around. This is where she would live. She smiled, and walked over to the huge bed. She took hold of the covers and inhaled. Sylor's scent was evident. She closed her eyes and took it all in, knowing this was where she belonged. This was her home.

She went over to the altar, opened the jade box, and held the crystal. It would be so easy to just take it with her. She shuddered with that thought, and then relaxed knowing she would have some kind of proof soon. The thought of that made her shudder even more. Her stomach felt sick from the thought that this all could be over soon, because it was nothing more than her imagination. She was not ready to handle that.

She wandered into the Records room and wondered if she should take the chance of using the disks on her own again. What would Jenielle do if she found her again? She decided she would take the chance, and took hold of Hollina's disk.

The glow of a new day was upon her, as she stood at the shore watching the sun rise. It would be the day of her new birth. A gentle breeze blew, and her sheer, white dress felt like a second skin adhering to her slim body. Lisa realized what was happening. She knew Sylor would be following. She began shouting to Hollina to go back, that Sylor doesn't want her to make transition. She kept trying to will her. Damn, it was so frustrating. She hated the fact she had no control over Hollina's mind.

Hollina was sitting in the chair outside the cave. She wanted nothing more than for Sylor to stop her. She felt she had nothing to live for, and she knew this was not a sufficient reason to make transition. She knew she had almost as much pride as Sylor, but was determined to go through with this anyway.

A soft humming sound developed, along with a misty form.

"Dreedon!" Hollina said, startled.

"You have lost your vision, my One. Feel the love you have for Sylor. Feel the love you have for yourself. Without Sylor, you may still go on to the far away lands."

"No Dreedon, I can not." Lisa felt pressure in Hollina's chest area. Her pride was the wall that kept her emotions in check.

"You need not take this action. Let your eyes invoke a new vision. See what can be!"

"I could not bear to go on in life without him, and I can no longer envision him as the man he once was. If I were to remain here, he would only look upon me with repugnance. I am sorry, Dreedon. I will make transition."

"Thy will be done," Dreedon said as he faded away.

Hollina did not have the strength inside herself to see a new vision. She wanted to give up. She stood and took one last look around. This is how she wanted to remember the land she loved; unlike the day of that horrible vision.

"Don't do it. Don't do it, please!" Lisa kept yelling at Hollina. She felt like a ghost trying to get someone's attention, and the other not being able to hear or see her. It was no use. Lisa couldn't stand the feelings of helplessness.

Hollina walked deep into the cave having no fear, only sadness. She came to an open area lit with crystals everywhere. It nearly took Lisa's breath away seeing the room filled with radiant iridescence. There was a waterfall that Lisa could have sworn was made of light, as it poured into a large pool of water.

Hollina disrobed without hesitation, and made her way into the brilliant water. Lisa wasn't sure what color the water was, or even if it had any color. The reflection of the jeweled light bounced off of it, giving it a mesmerizing effect.

She elegantly glided into the water which gave a tingling sensation as if one was immersed in champagne. She dove and swam with grace while focusing on the Source. She made her way over to the other side of the pool and stood under the waterfall, which to Lisa's amazement really *was* light.

A tall and beardless man, robed in white, was waiting for her as she emerged from the pool. She stood naked before him. As he placed his hand on her forehead, she instantly became clothed in a robe of light. She knelt before him, and he placed a crown of diamonds on her head. She stood, and he took her hand, and they began to walk deep within the cave to the chamber where she would transform to spirit and prepare for a new incarnation. Lisa felt anxious for Hollina, but was also curious to know how this would all come about. It didn't matter. The next thing she knew, the head-piece was being ripped from her by a very angry Jenielle.

"How dare you? How dare you again misuse the law? Have you no respect?"

This was the first time Lisa ever became afraid of Jenielle as she heard the murderous tone in her voice. Jenielle must not have realized Lisa was using Hollina's disk, and not another's.

"Jenielle it was Hollina's…"

"Silence!"

"Where's Sylor?" Lisa nervously backed away from her.

"Sylor is away on assignment. When he will return is unknown. I order you to leave now, and *never* return to Atlantis again! Those who have no respect for the laws do not deserve to live in Atlantis. If you return, I promise you, sorrow will be your reward."

Panic stricken, Lisa fled the room. She was angry at herself for being afraid of Jenielle, and even angrier for letting Jenielle see that she was afraid.

"So what are you going to do, Leese? Are you going to go back?" Scott asked as they sat on Lisa's deck on a hot late August afternoon.

"Scott, I really believe my home is in Atlantis. Nothing and no one, especially Jenielle, is going to stop me from being with the man I love if that's what I choose to do."

"But she's threatening you."

"I know, and that does make me feel uneasy."

"From what you've told me, it sounds like she never did like you."

"I think she was jealous of Hollina, and I being the incarnation of Hollina, well...I'll just have to take my chances."

"I don't know if I like this. My hunch is that she is not kidding."

Lisa wondered if she should tell Scott that Karen is the incarnation of Jenielle. That was the one thing she had left out. She had never even told Karen. For some reason she never wanted to make it an issue, as she thought it may cause more problems in their already delicate friendship.

"I don't know. She did sound like she meant what she said. Maybe I'm naïve, but Hollina loved Jenielle very much, and it's hard for me to believe that Jenielle could hate her own sister so much to want to cause me harm in any way."

"Just be careful." Scott put his hand over Lisa's. "And remember, if you want me as your 'proof,' the offer still holds."

"I know. I've been thinking about it, and I'm going to take you up on your offer. I'm not sure when I'm going back yet. I'm nervous about it now. I think I'll wait another week...maybe the following weekend?"

"No, that would be the holiday weekend. I'm meeting my buddy Matt at the Vineyard. We've been meeting there every Labor Day weekend for the last four years. Before that, Matt used to go by himself. It's something I look forward to. I don't see Matt all that much so..."

"Will Karen be joining you?"

"Nope, it's just the guys."

"Oh, that's nice." Lisa said, happy to hear that Karen would not be going.

"Getting back to your situation here; I will have a day off the end of that week. How about then?"

She nervously let out a deep breath. She placed her hands to her stomach.

"Okay…I'm…"

"Are you all right?"

"I'm not sure what I'm more nervous about; facing Jenielle again, or the fact that this will be judgment day, and I may be setting myself up for a bout at a mental institution. If this turns out to be nothing more than my imagination, I don't know if I could handle it."

"Leese, my gut tells me it's not your imagination."

"If that's the case, and it is real, then my mind is made up. When the time comes, my decision will be to stay in Atlantis. I know I will have to deal with Jenielle and, of course, the destruction. I know time will be short, but it will be worth it to be with Sylor. I've found my true love, and I will be with him. I never should have left him the first time."

Lisa saw the look of sorrow on Scott's face. She got the feeling that she meant as much to him, as he did to her.

Scott stopped by Lisa's a couple days after he had come home from Martha's Vineyard. She was greeted with a big hug.

"How was your weekend?" Lisa asked, happy to see him since he had stopped by unexpectedly.

"It would have been better if Matt hadn't been such a drip. Matt's musician friend Henry was supposed to join us, but he ended up having a gig at the last minute. I so wish he could have come. Henry thinks Matt is going through a mid-life crisis," Scott said, with a slight chuckle.

"So, what happened with Matt?"

"Oh, he's brooding more than ever. It was tough to be around him at times. As long as I've known him, he's been a deep, introspective guy, and that's fine, but...he and his girlfriend split up earlier this year. He said he was never really in love with her, but it was the fact that she left him. He's had a hard time with that. They had been together quite a few years."

"Didn't you say he had planned to move here?"

"Yeah, but that may change. He's thinking of going to Arizona for a while. He has some family there. He's not sure if he's going to move there, or keep his apartment, and just try it out for a few months or so. Not to change the subject, but are you ready for tomorrow?"

"No." Lisa picked up a blank piece of paper that was lying on the table, rolled it up, and squeezed it into a ball.

"Second thoughts?"

"No. I have to do this. That's it."

"How about if I come by in the morning, say about eleven?"

"That's as good a time as any I guess. It's funny huh? By this time tomorrow, I'll know if I'm going to be packing for Atlantis, or packing for the nut house." Tears formed as she glanced over at Scott, who was gazing down at the floor with a somber look on his face.

Lisa tossed the paper ball up in the air several times, catching it each time. "Tell me everything is going to be okay, Scott." She tossed the paper ball across the kitchen, where it landed directly into the trash bin. "Two points!"

Scott did thumbs up, and nodded with a smile.

Where was Scott? Lisa paced back and forth. She kept wiping her sweaty palms on her jeans. It was almost 11:30, and no sign of Scott. This wasn't like him. Maybe something happened to him. She tuned into her intuition as best she could with the way she was feeling, and felt that he was all right.

11:45…no Scott. She tried calling him at home, and on his cell phone…no answer. At ten minutes past noon she said, "That's it, I can't take this anymore." Her head felt like it was ready to explode. "I will get my proof one way or another." She marched upstairs, leaving the back door unlocked in case Scott did show.

Lisa held onto the lion's mane as they walked to the bath area. She felt like she could pass out at any minute. She had never felt so nervous in her entire life. Her heart was pounding, her stomach was churning, and her legs felt like they were ready to give out. What was she thinking?

There was no one in the bath area. They walked to the Records room. She saw the head-piece, and then eyed the wall with the disks. No way! They walked down the long hall. The deadly silence was unnerving. They proceeded to Sylor's room.

Yelling! There was yelling. She found the strength to walk faster. The voices she heard were Sylor's and Jenielle's. She put a hand to her head. It hurt so badly. She was becoming dizzy. She stopped at the door for a second to balance herself before entering the room. She began having chest pains. She took a very deep breath and entered the room.

"How dare you return?" Jenielle shouted.

Lisa was having the ultimate anxiety attack, and the vile look on Jenielle's face made her want to throw up.

"Silence!" Sylor commanded as he turned to Jenielle. "You have spoken enough."

Jenielle walked over to the altar and took the crystal out of the jade box. Lisa stared at the crystal Jenielle held in her hand. The room began to spin, and she felt like she didn't know where she was or what she was doing. She watched, almost becoming hypnotized by the crystal, as Jenielle waved it in the air. Sylor made an attempt to grab the crystal, but Jenielle was quick, and the lion moved in near Sylor.

"Have you taken ill?" Jenielle smirked, not taking her eyes off of Lisa.

"The crystal is my proof," Lisa mumbled. "It's the only thing I... I'm all alone...Scott didn't come; Karen doesn't believe...this is a dream, isn't it? This is all a dream. This can't really be happening."

The horrified look on Sylor's face made her step back. "You don't understand, Sylor, you don't...I need the crystal. It's the only way...I need..."

"No! You can not! Hollina you can not do...He watched in horror as Jenielle slowly moved toward Lisa, ready to give her the crystal. Lisa's eyes were riveted to it, and then she suddenly backed away.

"No, Jenielle I can't, I can't take it with me. I'll never be able to come back."

"You can. You *will* take it." Jenielle continued moving towards Lisa. Sylor tried to move but the lion kept him in his place.

Lisa began to feel a sharp pain in her head, and then she began to see a ghostly image. "What are...who...Oh God, Hollina?"

"Who does she speak to?" said Sylor, turning to Jenielle.

"Ha! She speaks to no one. She has lost her head."

Lisa looked into the eyes of herself; Hollina. Lisa suddenly remembered Hollina's words to Sylor, when she vowed she would not be a witness to the end of Atlantis. The ghostly image disappeared. Still in a daze, Lisa turned to Jenielle, and held out her hand. Jenielle placed the crystal in her hand.

"No! What have you done?" Sylor tried to get to Lisa, but the lion pushed him down. He quickly got back up. Lisa saw the look of shock on his face, and tears filled her eyes.

"I'm sorry, I don't...I'm so sorry..."

"Go! You fool, go now...now!" Jenielle demanded.

"No! Hollina do not, do not." Sylor turned to Jenielle and said viciously. "You will pay for this! You will pay!"

Lisa walked slowly to Sylor. She held the crystal behind her back with one hand, as she leaned forward to touch his face with the other. The lion roared before she could. She then backed away, taking in the traumatized look on Sylor's face. A look she was sure she would never forget.

"I love you, Sylor. I will *always* love you." She had an ache in her heart such as she had never known. She couldn't cry. She wouldn't. She knew she would break. She turned, and never looked back.

Lisa opened her eyes to see Scott hovering over her beaming, and with tears running down his face. "Leese, you did it! You did it! I'm sorry I was late. I was in an accident. But I saw you. I was looking all over the house for you. Then it hit me. I came back up here, and I saw the crystal on the bed, and I waited, and I heard the humming noise, and saw light, and I couldn't believe what was happening. You materialized out of thin air right before my eyes. You really did it!"

Lisa held her breath as she lay there, remembering. She didn't want to remember. She looked up at Scott's bruised and bandaged face. "Are you all right? Were you badly hurt?"

"I'm fine. Never mind. Leese, don't you get it? You really did it." Scott saw the look on Lisa's face. "Leese, what's wrong. Why do you look so upset?"

She sat up slowly, holding on tight to what was in her hand. She looked deeply at Scott while her other hand searched the bed. She found it. She placed the two crystals together to make one single crystal ball.

"Leese, oh no, what did you do! What happened?"

"I may just as well have stuck a knife through his heart. I will never, ever forget the look on his face." She wouldn't let herself cry. If she did, then she would have to face it. She couldn't face it. "I have to try to go back."

"What? Leese you can't, you..." He watched her desperate attempts for the next half hour trying to do what they both knew she couldn't do.

He cried watching her. "Leese, please, no more. Don't put yourself through this."

He sat on the bed next to her, holding her, rocking her as she cried. "Why? Why? Why did I do it? I can't believe what I've done. I love him so much Scott and I've hurt him again. Oh God, what's going to happen to him?

"Leese, it's been three days, you have to eat something, come on," Scott said as he rubbed Lisa's shoulder.

"I can't. I still feel too sick to eat, my stomach..." Tears came, and she put her head down on the kitchen table. "I just want to sleep."

"Lisa, why don't you put the crystals down for awhile?" Karen said as she placed a slice of toast and a cup of coffee in front of her.

Lisa sat up a little, and pushed the plate away. She brought the two crystals together. "It wasn't supposed to end like this. It's not over. *It can't be over*. Two embodiments connected by one soul, one heart, can not forever be separated. Sylor said those words to me." Lisa suddenly felt goose bumps all over and sat up straight. "He's out there. Karen, I know you said it was unlikely we could incarnate at the same time, but he's out there. I can feel it."

"I know that's what you want to believe but, again, I'm sorry, but I don't think so."

"You're wrong, Karen. But if Sylor and I are ever going to come together in this life, I know what I have to do. I don't want to do it, but it's the only way."

"What are going to do, Leese?"

"The day Sylor and Hollina met as children was the day they would part. Dreedon gave them the crystals and said, 'With your love you must release each other to find each other, and always trust your heart.' They let each other go, not only physically, but mentally and emotionally. Of course they never forgot each other, but they always trusted their heart. They always knew that when the time was right they would reunite.

"Then, what does this mean?" Karen asked.

"It means I'm going to trust what my heart has told me all along. That *he is* here in the present. The only way we are ever going to find each other is by my releasing the crystal that holds my essence or, *Hollina's* essence. I have to release the crystal to the ocean, and somehow it will find its way to him. That's the only way. Both of us must have the crystal in order to find each other."

Karen let out a breath, depicting annoyance. "Well, good luck. I've got to get back to the shop. Mum hates filling in. Are you staying, Scott?"

"Yeah, I'm going to try to get some food into this one."

"She seems aggravated," Lisa said as soon as Karen walked out the door.

"She's having a very hard time with all this. She still doesn't quite believe it."

"Even though you witnessed it?"

"Yip. I hate to even think this, but she almost sounds...I don't know..."

"Jealous?" Lisa added.

"Yeah." Scott nodded. "Do you think?"

"I'm beginning to." Lisa was really starting to see the connection between Jenielle and Karen. She wondered what had taken her so long.

Lisa picked up the two crystals, and placed them together, bringing them to her chest. Just the idea of having both, having Sylor and I as one whole...I'm going to hate to part with it. I look at the inclusions in the crystals, at all the spots and specks, and I think they represent all the lives we've lived, all the battles, and all the love we've both experienced. Some areas are perfectly clear, and others have these beautiful rainbow specks. Maybe those are the lives that we did something good. God help me, I never want to do another Atlantis."

Ten days later, Lisa felt it was time. She had gotten her strength back, and felt a little better emotionally. It was now time to give herself back to Sylor. She didn't know when or how they would meet. She just knew one day they would. Would he have forgiven her?

She walked down to the water. It was a cool, dull day. Rain had been in the forecast. She had on a thick hooded sweatshirt. She wasn't sure if she was shivering from the cold, or because of what she was about to do. She sat in the sand, and prayed for reassurance that what she was about to do was the right thing.

A mist forming above the water caught her attention. Warmth radiated throughout her entire body when she saw and felt the presence of Dreedon.

"My One, though your will is free, you know what is written. It is up to *you*."

"I know. I know what I must do. Dreedon, when will Sylor and I reunite?"

"When it matters, no longer."

"What?" She could hardly conceive of that. Sylor would *always* matter. She blinked away the tears.

"If you think on what you fear, that is what will be."

She knew Dreedon was right. In the back of her mind, there was the fear that they would never find each other, and she might focus on that without even realizing it. She knew she would have to become more aware of her thinking process. Hollina's life in Atlantis should have already taught her that. Never focus on what you fear. Instead, *forgive* what you fear.

"Remember forgiveness. True forgiveness heals all time…true forgiveness changes everything. Look upon your enemy as they *really* are. It is all an illusion anyway; my One…life is nothing but a dream."

"Thank you, Dreedon"

"My One, the future changes the past which changes the future. Your mission has just begun. Remember the visions and understand. Some mistakes *are* life's music. Remember the visions, and remember we are all given a second chance, maybe more. Remember the knowledge you have gained when you return to the place you call home."

Dreedon faded away as Lisa's jaw dropped. This could not be what she was thinking. She held the crystal tightly. She couldn't believe she was having second thoughts about letting the crystal go. If she kept the crystal then...

She sat down in the damp sand. She felt like she couldn't breath, as her heart pounded. She played Dreedon's words over and over in her mind. She jumped when she felt a hand on her shoulder.

"You like sitting out here in the rain?" Scott sat down next to her. He noticed her tightly clenched fist. "Still can't give it up yet?"

"Scott, you are not going to believe this!" She told him what had just transpired.

"Is that what you think? You're supposed to go back to Atlantis?"

"Yes. Having the knowledge of everything that's happened we can go back...a second chance. Hollina was given two visions, it was a test, and she focused on the fear, as did everyone else. Now we have to focus on the positive vision. We have to see and believe in a beautiful and harmonious Atlantis...the second vision. And we have to forgive those who choose differently.

"Don't you see, Scott? The future changes the past which changes the future. What that means is now that we have seen the future; we have the knowledge of what led to this future. Having seen the future from the perspective of Atlantis, we can now go back and change the past by how we think, and what we focus on to create another future, a different future, a *positive* one."

"So what you're saying is that you could go back to Atlantis with the knowledge you now have about what led to its demise, and change its fate so that Atlantis was never destroyed?"

"Sounds so simple, huh?"

"Are you willing to do this?" Scott asked in shock.

"I still have the crystal. The only way this will happen is if Sylor and I find each other, even though I don't think that's going to happen anytime soon. The psychic said the mission was something we would have to do together. If I keep the crystal then it will never happen, at least not in this lifetime."

"What are you going to do?"

"I have to do what needs to be done. If I don't, it will haunt me for the rest of my life. I would never have any peace. And I'll never have Sylor. Which future do I pick? A future where I go back into the past to create a new future? Or stay in the present and live a miserable existence? And even that could be changed by replacing that belief with a new, more positive one. It's all in our mind. And I have to admit I don't completely understand it."

"That's all a lot to take in…wow!"

"Think on it, you'll get it. We'll all get it…someday."

Lisa walked over to the water's edge. She wiped a few tears, and then released the crystal high into the air. "Come back to me, Sylor" she whispered. After a moment of looking out at the ocean she sat down again.

"You okay?"

"I wasn't meant to stay in Atlantis under the circumstances as they were. I realize that now. I was just meant to learn." She reached for Scott's hand. "Yeah, I'm okay."

"It's funny how you saw Hollina before you left. You told me that Hollina had vowed to Sylor that she would not witness the end of Atlantis. She kept that vow. Well at least you'll be around for a while, unlike Matt."

"Is Matt definitely moving to Arizona?"

"He left yesterday. He's got a friend staying at his apartment. He said he'd like to try it out for a year before he makes a decision to give up his place. Who knows? Maybe he'll be back and hopefully in a better state of mind. He would have liked you. He was interested in all that stuff, ancient civilizations, the pyramids, even reincarnation. I wish you two could have met."

"Another life maybe," Lisa joked, and hugged Scott. "But right now I've got to get on with this life here. I know some way; somehow, I will end up back in Atlantis. Me and Sylor, or whatever his name will be. Now, I just have to wait and trust, and forgive both Sylor and Jenielle. But most of all I need to forgive myself. And then wait until the day comes when we will meet. And like the song by the Moody Blues...I know he's out there somewhere, somewhere, somewhere..." she sang.

"He is, Leese. He is."

Lisa stood, reached for Scott's hand, and pulled him up.

"Come on, let's go." She laughed. "We have a life to live."

"What do you mean? What are we doing?"

"You...are going home. And I..." She smiled thoughtfully. "And I have a book to write."

Chapter 12

―――――

16 Months Later

"**B**ut it's only a *novel!*" Henry said, throwing up his hands. "How in the world could you be connected with it?"

Matt flung the hardcover book on to the desk. The book knocked over a paperweight, which sent papers flying to the floor. He walked over to the front window of his apartment, and stared into the street where people busily crossed coming from Sunday mass. Light snow was falling, and the wind was picking up. Everyone was pulling up their collars and tightening their scarves. It would not be a warm day in Boston.

Matt walked back to the desk and held up the book. He tapped his forefinger on the back cover. "Look at her!"

Henry raised his brow. "Hey, not bad, hope the book was as good as she looks."

"You don't understand. I've seen her. I've seen her in my dreams."

"Hey, I'd like to dream about her…and then some."

Matt shook his head. "You don't get it. I've seen this woman in dreams for the last two years or so."

"Keeping secrets, huh?"

"I thought she represented what Jung called the anima, you know, the feminine expression of the male…never mind," Matt said in a condescending tone. "Obviously, you haven't read this novel."

"Nope…too busy reading self help. And I know what the anima is."

"There is a character named Sylor, and I can relate to him. I understand him. I understand him so well it's eerie. I feel like I *am* him, and I am one stubborn bastard."

"I won't touch that one," Henry said as he picked up the paperweight and tossed it from hand to hand.

"I read the book twice. This whole time-travel thing, I keep wondering if...maybe it's not fiction. Maybe this is the author's actual experience. There has to be an explanation. But like you said, it's only a novel. Damn it, I feel like I *lived* this story!"

"Hey maybe you did, or something like it. You said you believed in past lives, the afterlife and whatever else," Henry said still tossing the paperweight.

Matt walked back to the front window. "She lives on the Cape."

"Ah, and it just so happens that you are in the process of moving there. On what part of the Cape does she live?"

"I don't know," Matt said with a superior tone.

"Why don't you ask your buddy, what's his name, Scott? He may have heard of her."

"He doesn't even know I'm back from Arizona."

"You've been back for months! Didn't you meet him at Martha's Vineyard Labor Day weekend?"

"No. I had just gotten back here. I went to the Vineyard alone. I wanted to be alone. I still do."

"Man, what's wrong with you? You're worse than ever. For once in your life, *talk about it!*"

"I'm restless. I don't know what I'm doing, or why. Why am I here?"

"In Boston?" Henry smirked knowing full well what Matt meant.

"No! I mean what is my purpose in my life? What's real?"

"Whoa, okay, the man is opening up."

Matt wondered if he *should* open up. He could never let himself before. He walked over to the desk, opened the bottom right hand drawer, and took something out wrapped in white tissue paper.

"I'm going to show you something." He un-wrapped the object and held it in the palm of his hand.

"What the hell's that?" Henry put down the paperweight. He reached to touch the object, but Matt pulled it away.

"I found it at the beach…at the Vineyard. It's just like the crystal described in the book. The one the character Lia threw into the ocean near the end of the story. Anyone could have picked this up. It was right there in the open with dozens of people around. "Why *me?*"

"Do do do do, do do do do…" Henry mockingly hummed the first bars of *The Twilight Zone* theme, then said, "Maybe it's fate."

"Shut up!" Matt shook his head.

"Hey, why don't you just Google her to get some info…maybe she has a blog or something, or make some calls and go pay her a visit."

"Are you out of your mind?"

Henry shrugged. "Hey, I know; why don't you go see the psychic I met last week, ask her some questions about this."

"Sorry, I don't trust psychics that call themselves Madam. Matt placed the crystal on the end table near the sofa. He went back to the desk and picked up the book again. He stared at the author's picture. She was the woman that dug at his soul.

"To hell with it." Matt flung the book back on the desk, sending more papers flying. "I'll get over it. Let's get some breakfast."

They walked into the crowded coffee shop. "Hey, I'll grab a paper while we wait," Henry said.

Matt nervously tapped his fingers on the counter near the register. He couldn't get her out of his mind. Obsessed? Why did he have these feelings about a woman he had never met? The attraction to her was all too consuming. He wanted to devour her, and yet at the same time he wanted to hate her.

A few minutes later, a server with long and stringy, dark hair, tapped Matt on the shoulder, releasing him from a self imposed trance. Henry had to be unglued from the obituary section as they followed her to be seated. She left them menus, and said she'd be back in a moment.

"Hey, this woman was one hundred and four," Henry said still reading the obituaries. "I'm telling you, we're living longer and longer. I've read we may even see one hundred twenty years in our lifetime."

Before Matt could retort, the server, whose hair was now tied back, came to take their order.

"Coffee?" she said, slightly quivering.

"No coffee. I'll have tea," Matt said, his eyes fixed on the menu. "Also, I'll have two eggs scrambled, home fries, and toast with peanut butter."

"I'm sorry sir," she said as her hands shook slightly, "We don't have peanut butter."

Matt turned and looked directly at the woman. "This, I don't understand. They can put butter and jelly into those little tubs, why not peanut butter? Must I bring my own?"

She looked at him meekly, and said nothing. One side of Matt's mouth curled up as he looked back at her, then he broke into a full smile. "I'll have butter with my toast please."

Henry finally took his nose out of the newspaper, and turned to the server. He gazed at her for a few seconds before giving his order. She left, and Henry leaned over to Matt. "I bet she's new. Her hands were shaking. And hey, could that girl use a new 'do' or what?"

The server came back quickly with the breakfast drinks. Henry checked her out again, and then went back to the paper. He turned the page and picked up his coffee, only to put the cup back down before it reached his mouth. "Hey, you're not going to believe this. That writer you were just talking about, her picture's right here. That book is on the best sellers list. She'll be here next weekend to do a two day book signing."

Matt slowly brought down his tea cup. He didn't lift his head or show any emotion. Henry shoved the paper at Matt. "Look!"

Matt coolly glanced over. "Oh yeah," And then took a sip of tea.

"What do you mean, 'oh yeah?' You can meet her, have her sign your book, talk to her."

"Maybe."

"Maybe? What's with you man?" Henry rolled his eyes and shook his head. "I haven't seen you in over a year. You've always been intense, but this is...what's happening to you man?"

"Nothing."

"Are you still living like a hermit? Ever since Diana left...two years is too long, man. You need a date. Actually, you need more than a date. You need to get.."

"Your eggs, sir." The server placed the plate in front of Matt, along with two tubs of jelly. He pushed the jelly away and looked at her.

"I'm sorry, sir." She nervously placed the jelly near Henry.

"Thank you, ma'am." Henry smiled, and watched her walk away. "She's cute, but definitely needs a new 'do.' There *is* potential. So, what are you going to do?" he asked as he bit into his toast.

"Do? About what?"

Henry let out a sigh. "The dream girl…the book, are you going to meet her?"

"Maybe."

Matt heard Henry mumble something under his breath. He put his fork down, sat back, and raked his dark blonde hair with both his hands.

"Ah, the professor does have something on his mind," Henry quipped.

"Don't call me professor. Being a professor implies that you know something. Right now, I feel like I don't know a *damn* thing! People, the world, everything is crazy, and I feel like I can't do anything about it. I want to believe there's more to life than acquiring possessions, getting to the top, and having meaningless sex. Sometimes I feel dead inside, and..."

"Not good," Henry said with his mouth full.

"There's something that's eating me up inside, and I just can't grasp it. I know I didn't love Diana, and I don't think she was really in love with me. I cared about her, but I couldn't give her what she needed. She said I was aloof. After all those years she left. I didn't blame her. I should have ended it myself, but it was too comfortable. It was comfortable because I wasn't in love with her."

"Ever see her?"

"Last October, before she moved to Colorado. We talked, made our peace. I didn't feel a damn thing. I lived with the woman for six years, and felt nothing. Why is that?"

"You're scared, man, it happens all the time. People love, get hurt, and then build a wall...makes it hard to love again, and to be loved. You've got to knock down that wall, my friend. It seems like it's been there all of your life. Besides, what good is living if you can't love? Love is what it's all about."

"Like the song says, love stinks."

"You've got to change your attitude...got to release the old baggage, man." Henry flicked his finger against Matt's head. "I've been hurt. That's not about to stop me from finding love again. There's someone out there. Smarten up; she's probably waiting for you."

Matt forced a smile, and picked up his fork again. He thought about the novel, *Return to Atlantis*, it was called. He still felt it was *not* fiction. Even the character's name; Lia, was similar to the name Lisa. He thought about Sylor, who had been dumped twice by the woman he loved. Okay, the guy had been a jerk, a *real* jerk, but he loved Hollina deeply. Deep down, Matt knew there was that kind of love inside himself. Could he ever allow himself to experience it? Could he ever surrender to it?

He didn't like the way the story ended. You never knew if they got together in the present. It was left for you to assume they did. He wondered if there would be a sequel.

He took a bite of toast, and started thinking about having a new relationship. The fear rushed in; *no, no way, out of the question. It would never work.* Every woman in his life had left him, starting with his own mother.

He hadn't thought about his mother in a long time. He didn't want to. It still hurt, watching her die. And then there was the promise that she made to him on her deathbed. The promise she never came through on. Yet, the six year old in him, that watched his mother die, was still waiting.

Matt's mother had always believed in an afterlife. She had made a promise to Matt that she would communicate with him somehow. She told him that on the other side there would be beautiful flower gardens, and she would somehow confirm this; 'You will know this through your truest love. I promise this, but you must remember *your* promise.' This is what his dying mother said to him. He still didn't understand it, and he never told a soul.

"So Matt, my man, you quit teaching and now the move to the beach. What's up with that?"

"Time for a change. I need change. I need something. I can't seem to grasp that something, whatever it is. I thought moving to Arizona would help, to see my cousins and the uncle that raised me. It was nice, but I couldn't live there. I came back in August. It felt good to be back. I was looking forward to getting out to the Vineyard for Labor Day, but I just wanted to do it alone. I didn't want to have to talk to anyone. I found the crystal, and now the book…I feel like my life is more confused than ever." Matt toyed with his eggs. "I've always wanted to live at the beach. I started driving down to the Falmouth area, two, three times a week. The closing on the house should be sometime next month if all goes right. It's a great house. Not too far from Scott. It's about time I call him."

"Now you can write your book."

"Yeah." Matt glanced over at the newspaper. Henry had folded it so that the author's picture was face up.

Henry noticed Matt's expression. "She's really getting to you, huh? What made you read that book in the first place?"

"I was in the bookstore, and it was right there in front of me. Atlantis in the title had caught my eye. I was in a hurry, and didn't have time to skim through it, but I just had the feeling to pick it up. I'm almost sorry I read it. Now I can't get any of this out of my head. I know I'm connected to her, the dreams, the story, and...I don't think I like it."

Henry pushed his empty plate away and looked at Matt. "I think you've got it bad. I don't know who she is, but I have a feeling she's wiser than you professor. Maybe you should pay attention. I wish I could stick around for the outcome of this, but I'll be high tailing it back to Cali by the end of the week."

Matt quietly tucked the paper under his coat as he watched Henry flirt with their server at the register. He waited for Henry outside, in the snow, which was now falling steady.

"I've got me a date tonight," Henry said proudly. "Her name is Jennifer, and she likes to be called Jenna, and she loves the Blues. I'm going to sweep her off her feet and take her to Cali with me. Then I'm going to marry her, and we'll live happily ever after."

"Knowing you Henry, that's exactly what will happen."

"Hey, if you don't write your own script, life will have a way of writing it *for you.*"

"Maybe the script was *already* written." Matt said, gazing at the steeple as the church bells were ringing.

Matt threw down the newspaper on the kitchen table as he walked into his apartment. He changed into his sweats, and plunked himself down in front of the tube. He mindlessly flipped through the channels, not even realizing that he settled for an infomercial peddling cookware. He hated infomercials. He couldn't see anything but her.

He could fantasize about her all he wanted when she was just a phantom, but now she was real. How could this be? What should he do about it? She would be at the mall bookstore next weekend. Should he go? Maybe take a quick peak? Maybe he could mingle with the other guests, and check her out. She wouldn't know him after all, even if the description of Sylor's features were similar to his own, blue eyes and all.

In the dreams he'd had of her, she didn't say or do anything. She just looked back at him, beautiful, warm, and especially loving. He even knew then he could fall in love with her. It was safe. He firmly denied the notion that he already had, especially since a voice inside told him not to. No, he would not go to the book signing, which would be asking for trouble. He laughed out loud nervously, feeling the butterflies in his stomach.

He sat through two more infomercials for exercise equipment and diet food, and then went into the kitchen. He broke open a beer, and made himself a peanut butter and banana sandwich. He grabbed a bag of cheese popcorn, and started to head back to the sofa. He eyed the newspaper and grabbed that too.

Her picture entranced him. It was a different picture than the one on the book jacket, but she was just as beautiful. He fought back all the feelings that were welling up in his chest, and threw the paper aside.

A chill ran through him. What if he *was* Sylor? How could he have been that stubborn, that arrogant? Was he himself that arrogant, he pondered. No, not professor Matt Fields! What about Hollina? Of course, she was right about the scientists. Why didn't she just go on to Egypt without him instead of choosing to die? Was Sylor really worth it? Matt thought not.

He wondered what happened to Sylor after Lia had left with the crystal, abandoning him yet again. He must have gone down with

Atlantis. He would probably never know. Did he want to know? He glanced over at the crystal then shook himself out of his delusion. "What the hell is the matter with me? None of this is real!"

And if none of it was real, what would be the harm of going to the book signing? There was nothing to worry about, he confirmed. He would go to the book signing, his mind was made up. And once professor Matt Fields made up his mind there was no changing it.

"What a day!" Karen said, as she locked the door after the last of the customers left. "I'm exhausted." She then sat on the floor and placed herself into a cross legged position.

"How do you think I feel? I've got writer's cramp." Lisa shook out her hand. "I can't believe this many people turned out, even with the rain. Your sales must have been fantastic."

"Yes. You'll have to do a book signing more often."

"Next week it's Boston. I have a weird feeling about it. I can't put my finger on it. There's something…"

Both women jumped when someone knocked loudly on the glass paned door. Karen quickly opened it.

"How are my girls?" Scott said, as he gave Lisa a peck on the cheek, and Karen a lover's kiss. "You two look worn."

"It was non-stop all day. But I wouldn't have it any other way," Karen said.

"Good going." Scott put his arm around Karen. "Did you give any thought to my proposal?"

"You asked her to marry you?" Lisa turned to Karen. "And you didn't tell me?"

"No, no, no." Karen laughed. "Scott wants us to go into business together. His idea is to combine a health food store and the bookstore, maybe even throw in a few tables and serve herbal tea and natural baked goods."

"That's a great idea. Are you going to do it?"

"I'm going to think about it," Karen said, smiling at Scott.

"Sweetheart, you know it's a good idea."

"It sure is," Lisa said, and hugged them both. Then she suddenly backed away. She had gotten a feeling that was loud and clear; the partnership would not take place. She didn't like what she was feeling. She forced herself to smile as Scott talked about it.

"I wish this place was big enough to do it here," Karen said, "We'll have to move, and that will mean higher rent and…"

"Hey babe, I live at home for next to nothing. I drive an economical car, and live in jeans and t-shirts. I've put every single dime I could into my savings. I knew one day I might invest it in something worthwhile. I just didn't know what, until now. It will be good."

Lisa wondered why she had those feelings. Maybe Scott and Karen would break up. She knew Karen cared very much for Scott, but was not truly in love with him. Scott was a great guy, and much in love with Karen. Lisa hoped Karen appreciated him.

Lisa was happy that the weather cleared for the drive to Boston on Saturday morning. She drove her Corvette, the one she was sick of people telling her she should put away for the winter. She took good care of it, and it was transportation, not a trophy car, she would argue. She turned up the volume on the radio to hear a song she hadn't heard in quite some time. It was a song by The Moody Blues that had become meaningful. A strange feeling permeated around her heart. "Yes, Sylor," she whispered in a trance. "I know you're out there somewhere, and the promise that we made each other haunts me too."

It hadn't taken her long to write the book, and she had made up her mind to put Sylor *out* of her mind after she had finished writing it. She had done a pretty good job of it too. A part of her wanted to forget, and she needed a rest.

It had been well over a year since she released the crystal and… nothing. That was okay; she still trusted one day it would happen. She never dwelled on it. Every once in a while she would ask Scott if he really had told her the truth, and that it wasn't her imagination.

After all, she no longer had the crystal as her *proof*. It did take her awhile in the beginning, but she did come to realized she would be happy if Sylor came into her life, *or not*. She did think about him occasionally, but she finally had gotten to the place where it *didn't* matter anymore.

Writing the book had been a catharsis. She felt all the negative karma that had been incurred from that lifetime had been dissolved, or so she hoped. She had felt at peace with her life. She was doing volunteer work at the homeless shelter, and had even started writing again. She was happy, really happy, for the first time in a very long time.

Matt was getting dressed when he turned on the radio, and heard the same song. He started to sing it, and then stopped when he remembered she used part of the lyrics in her book. "Oh, too much," he said, annoyed as his stomach fluttered. "Get over it." He tucked his dark blue, long sleeved, Henley shirt into his jeans and buckled the belt.

He brushed his hair back just right, or so he thought. A piece kept falling onto his forehead. He refused to use hair spray. He refused to cut his hair. He considered wearing cologne, then reminded himself this was not a date, something he hadn't had in two years. He was just going there to watch…to observe her from afar. She would never even know he was there.

Matt tried to ignore his nervous stomach. He began singing again, but his throat felt tight, and he was starting to feel angry. He didn't want to hear that 'love eternal will not be denied.' Why was he becoming angry?

Maybe, he thought, he shouldn't do this after all.

Chapter 13

———

There was quite a crowd, as Matt slowly inched his way into the bookstore. He made a turn down a magazine aisle and hung back. All he wanted was a glimpse of her, but it was too crowded even for that.

He haphazardly picked up a copy of a hunting magazine. He frowned, and traded it for a health magazine. He pretended to read as he watched for any kind of hole in the crowd. He would not allow himself to get any closer.

Finally, a man with a big coat moved out of the way. Matt caught a glimpse, and stuffed the magazine back in the wrong spot. He could not take his eyes off of her. Her thick, golden hair hung just right over her shoulders against the emerald green, satiny scoop neck blouse. She was wearing a gold pendant, something circular, but he couldn't make it out.

He watched her smile, sign, and thank each person. He was in awe of her. Without thinking, he moved closer. She began to converse with a tall, good looking man. Matt didn't like what he was beginning to feel. Twinges of jealousy stung his heart. He moved closer. He almost came into her sight, when a couple of people moved, creating a gap. That was too close. He moved behind a DVD rack.

For the next fifteen minutes, he stood in hiding, observing, wanting. Yes, wanting. He took a deep breath. If this story was not fiction, and he was the reincarnated Sylor, then she was the woman who was his true love…the woman with whom he must reunite. On that realization, he took one long last look at her, and then hurried out of the store.

He didn't care what the Gods had to say about it. Matt would never allow himself to get hurt like that again. He would never again put himself in that position. And to go back to a place where he had screwed up big time? No way!

Late the next morning, Lisa stood in front of the bathroom mirror in the hotel brushing up her hair. She was glad she had chosen to stay over. She thought of the day before and how nice it all was. The people were nice, the hotel staff treated her like royalty, and she was very appreciative. But there was something…

She remembered the feeling she had the week before. It was a feeling of expectation, and it hadn't been fulfilled. Maybe it was her imagination. Either way, she was looking forward to another day of signing.

Matt stood, as he looked out the front window of his apartment. The sun was shining, the snow was melting, and everyone had their coats open. He loved days like this after there had been a big storm. There was no excuse not to go out. Should he go for a walk, a run? He hated himself for wanting to go back to the bookstore.

The little sleep he had the night before was suffused with dreams of her. He had dreamt that instead of hiding like a fool behind the shelves, he walked over to her and she knew who he was. They embraced, and made their commitment to each other. It was as if he had seen a parallel reality, the one he was supposed to have chosen. Matt had always wondered about the choices we make in our lives, and what the outcome would have been, and where we would now be if we had done something different.

The bookstore wasn't as crowded as the day before, but there was enough of a crowd to hide him. A chill of goose bumps shook him when he caught sight of her. He did not want to be attracted to her, but her smile…it drew his heart from his chest. Henry was right.

He had it bad. She was the one he had waited for all his life. She was the thing he couldn't grasp. And he wouldn't, a voice inside told him. He would not!

As he watched her, again behind a shelf, he felt like two people. One that wanted to let out his anger and shake her, the other wanting to go to her and tell her that he loved her. What? No, he couldn't face that. He didn't want to feel that particular emotion did he? He knew he loved her deeply, and at the same time was scared to death of her.

He collected himself, and made his way closer. There were still enough people around to blend in. Some others were coming through, and he had to move out of the way. That put him five feet away from her. There were several people in front of him, and though he was still hidden, he got a clear look at her.

Her elegance radiated, with her hair swept upward and with a mass of curls caressing her neck. She wore small, gold, dangling earrings and a light pink, silk suit with a low cut, but lady-like, neckline. She took his breath away. How could he get this close to her without wanting to let down his guard, scoop her up into his arms, and bring her into himself?

His gaze wandered to the pendant she was wearing. He shivered upon recognizing it. It was the symbol of Atlantis, the one that adorned the cover of her book. Then the unthinkable happened.

As if by fate, the crowd around her dispersed. He stood alone, unguarded, totally exposed. Naked! Her emerald eyes met his blue ones. The color drained from her face as she searched for her breath. He sensed a light coming from all around her that reached out and wrapped itself around him. He felt an unseen light coming from himself intertwining with hers. He felt every particle of the love she held for him, or was it the love he held for her?

Every instinct told him to go to her, embrace her, and pour out his heart and his eternal love to her, as they engaged in this emotional orgasm. But there was the voice. The voice that said let it go. Let *her* go!

Her pen dropped to the floor as she slowly stood up.

"Sylor," she whispered, with their eyes still locked.

Yes. He had heard it. It came from her mouth. He had seen her lips move as she said it, as if in slow motion. She had said *his* name.

He thought of the dream, the parallel reality. He knew he now had to make a choice. He heard the inner voice again. She would hurt him, she would leave him, it would all be a disaster, and history would repeat itself. Matt took one last look into Lisa's eyes, knowing he was looking into himself. He decreed right then and there that she would never know how much he loved her. No one would ever know. On that, he turned and fled, vowing he would never see her again.

Lisa stood shocked, not believing what had just occurred. Her heart had just been ripped from her chest. When she found the strength, she moved to go after him. She was behind a table, and there were books, chairs, and suddenly, people in the way. She searched the mall to no avail. The back of him would be forever etched in her mind, the long black wool coat, and the hair that hung well below the collar.

She didn't remember the drive home. She still couldn't comprehend what had happened. She couldn't believe they had found each other. What was worse is that she couldn't believe he had run *away* from her. She remembered the feeling as they connected. He had to have felt it, she thought, he had to. Why did he run away? If he had read the book as she thought he had, then he would know they were meant to be together. If he had read the book, he would also know how much she had hurt him.

"He holds all the cards," Lisa told Scott the next morning at the health food store. "I have no way of finding him. He can find me if he wanted to, but...I don't even know his name. God, I called him Sylor." She tried to hold back the tears.

Scott gave her a hug, and his handkerchief. "I'm sorry it turned out like this for you. But remember, you had been right all along. He is alive, here and now. Maybe he'll come around eventually. He'd be a fool if he didn't." He hugged her again.

"Well, well, aren't we all cozy," Karen said upon entering the store.

"Lighten up. Lisa's not feeling well."

"How did the book signing go?" Karen asked as she read a label on the back of a jar of natural peanut butter.

"Let's go for breakfast and I'll tell you about it," Lisa said reluctantly, knowing what would come when she told her.

"It wasn't him Lisa, I don't believe this."

Lisa rolled her eyes expecting this very reaction. "It was him. I would know him anywhere."

"It was probably someone that looked like him, maybe even someone playing a joke."

"Karen," Lisa said, trying to control her temper. "We connected. Something happened while we were looking at each other. It was as if our auras had reached out and meshed. It was incredible, it was..." Lisa was glad she had Scott's handkerchief.

"Then why did he run?"

"All I can think of is that he had to have recognized himself in the story. Look, when I was in Atla..." Lisa lowered her voice. "When I was in Atlantis, I saw how devastated Sylor was when Hollina made transition...I felt it. God only knows how he reacted when I...Hollina left him a second time. He never wanted to hear that I may never stay in Atlantis. He couldn't deal with it."

"None of this means it was him."

"The book could have triggered all the pain he felt, and then when he saw me it hit him, and it scared him. He loves me, I know it, I felt it, and I would bet my life on it."

"You sure about that?"

Matt had stayed up most of that Sunday night. He sat on the sofa, and, in the dark, stared out at the street light. He kept telling himself he would get over it. He clenched the book over his chest, but he'd get over it, he affirmed.

He eventually turned on the lamp that was on the end-table next to him. He ran his fingers over her picture like a lovesick fifteen year-old. He would forever remember the look on her face when she saw him.

He recalled the love he felt coming from her. He didn't believe someone could ever love him that much. That hadn't been part of his life experience, and he felt he wasn't worth it anyway.

He opened the book and started skimming through it. He came to a part where Sylor was raising his voice to Hollina. Matt could feel the intense vibration behind the words. He felt the same vibration from that inner voice, Sylor's voice, he confirmed, as he amazingly realized that Sylor was a part of him. What would he do now, see a shrink? He thought not.

He felt compelled to pick up the crystal that was still sitting on the end-table. He resisted. He thought of how he messed up in Atlantis. Why couldn't he have listened to Hollina? He had been given a second chance to listen when Lia told him what would happen. Hollina had told him that she would prove to him that Atlantis would fall. She did prove it through Lia, and he still wouldn't hear of it.

Matt felt he didn't deserve happiness. How could he? He resigned himself to the fact that this is the way his life would be. This reminded him of a poem he had written after Diana had left him.

I woke up in the morning to look outside and see, that there were no more people, what did God do to me?

Empty space, nothing to replace, everything's been taken. Why me I ask, why me oh lord, why have I been forsaken?

Is this the end or is it all a dream, God I feel so helpless, it must be a devil's scheme.

I walk back in the bedroom, see my body on the bed, I try to pinch myself and can't, my God I must be dead.

This was his karma. He was to live his life alone in misery. He would be dead to everyone and everything. He would not allow himself to feel anything. He denied the fact that he was being given another chance to change things.

He impulsively picked up the crystal. He was in awe of the fact that he had held the piece 12,000 years before. He closed his eyes, suddenly feeling sleepy. A mist began to form in his mind's eye. He was shocked to see a vision of a bearded man in a white robe.

"My One, open your eyes to a new vision. Your power is never lost. You have just forgotten. Use it, and use it wisely."

Matt's eyes flew open. He clearly remembered those words. He rushed through the pages to find them. Here he was being told again. He knew he had the power to change things, but he didn't want to.

He decided he had had enough of all this. He wrapped the crystal again, and put it back in the desk drawer. He would decide what to do with it at another time. As far as the book, he walked over to the trash bin, but he couldn't bring himself to throw away a book. He placed it on a shelf with some other books that he planned to donate to the library.

He sat up all night staring out of the window. He watched the night change to a pinkish glow on the horizon. Never in his life had he watched the sun rise. Now he knew why. It would bring back the memory of Hollina's death. Matt shut the blinds and went to bed.

It was the third week of February. The snow was finally melting from the big storm that occurred a week and a half before. Karen was away on a buying trip, and Lisa was filling in at the store. She was in the back room, going through some used books, when she heard the door open.

She sighed, being that it was nearly closing time, and she did not want to deal with any more customers. She put on a happy face, and trudged out to the front room to be greeted by someone holding a bouquet of flowers in front of their face.

"Those better be for me," she wisecracked, knowing full well who it was.

"Ah, the beautiful lady has had a tough day. I knew that." Scott put the flowers down on the counter, and gave Lisa a hug. "I know how crazy Saturdays can be here, and with how you've been feeling since Boston, well...you've got a friennnnd," he sang.

Lisa burst out laughing. She knew she could always count on Scott to lighten her mood.

"My lady, I would love to take you out for dinner. Would you accept my humble offer?"

"If it includes pizza and a beer or two, I'll go anywhere with you dear one."

"Pineapple pizza, Scott?" Lisa said a little while later at the pizza shop. "I thought you were doing that food combining thing."

"I am, but I'm in the mood to eat anything. I'll run it off in the morning. Oh, by the way, remember my buddy Matt Fields, the professor?"

"Yeah," Lisa said with caution, remembering Karen's lust for the guy.

"He called me yesterday. He's been back from Arizona for six months."

"And he just called you now?" Lisa frowned and shook her head.

"Yeah, and I let him know about it too. That's Matt. I had hoped he changed some, but he still seems troubled, and he didn't want to go into it. There is some good news though. He's going to be moving here after all. In fact, he's going to be your neighbor."

"Wonderful. The guy you wanted to fix me up with that hates women."

"He doesn't hate women, and he is a good guy. He takes things seriously. He takes life seriously. I know you're waiting for your beloved, but in the meantime...I think you'd be good for him, just as a friend. He's planning to write a book and..."

"No. No way. I love you Scott, but I don't think I want to be his friend, or anything else."

"Why? Leese, this doesn't sound like you."

"I know. I just..., I don't know, I can't explain it." Lisa was really wondering how Matt's moving there was going to affect the relationship between Karen and Scott. As far as she was concerned, the less Matt Fields was around, the better.

"Since Boston you've been so depressed, I just thought maybe meeting Matt..."

"I appreciate that, but before Boston I was really happy. I wrote the novel, and somehow I was able to put it all behind me. I knew I could be happy even if Sylor never came into my life, though I knew he would someday. I just didn't worry about it. Now, everything is upside down again. I can't believe I'm saying this, but it's worse knowing that he's alive. When he ran away like that, it did some-thing to me. It's been a month. If he really wanted to get in touch with me, I'm sure he would have by now. And brace yourself, I'm thinking of moving to Florida."

"What? You love it here!"

"Yeah, I do. I've never wanted to live anywhere else. All my family is in Florida, and maybe it's time for a change, start a new life, I don't know. You guys can come down and visit."

"I don't want you to leave, but if that's how you feel..."

"I don't *know* how I feel, Scott. Right now it's just a thought. Oh, you said Matt was going to be my neighbor. How is that?"

"He said he bought a house on Point beach; the Morrison house or something.

"The Morrison property; that's been for sale for a long time. It's about a quarter mile from me. I've been in that house. When I first moved here, I used to walk down that way a lot. Mrs. Morrison was always outside and we got to know each other. She died a few years ago, and her son took it over."

"Well, that's one way of getting you to meet Matt. He loves to walk the beach. And if you don't meet him that way, it will be arranged." Scott smiled devilishly.

"When is he moving here?"

"End of March, I think."

"Great. I still have time to make my escape to Florida!"

"I'm going to bring you two together somehow. I will."

"These angel tee shirts are great," Lisa said as she and Karen were putting the shirts on hangers.

"Scott told me you two went out for dinner Saturday night."

"Yeah, we had a nice time. He knows how depressed I've been, and you were away so…"

"So when the cat's away, the mice…"

"Oh God, I don't believe you said that."

Karen said nothing, and went into the back room. Lisa had noticed Karen didn't seem to like the relationship she and Scott had, even though they were like brother and sister. Lisa went into the back room a few minutes later. "Scott told me his friend Matt is going to be my neighbor." Lisa watched Karen's face closely, looking for a reaction.

"Aren't you lucky," Karen said, never taking her eyes off the book she was flipping through. "Scott wants to get you two together, but you don't want any part of it. Why?"

"Sounds like a bad risk. And now that I know Sylor…"

"Oh please. I can't believe you're still insisting it was him that day."

"Karen, I'm going to ask you something, and I hope you'll be honest with me."

"I'm always honest with you. Fire away."

"How do you feel about Matt moving here?"

"I thought you weren't interested in Matt Fields."

"I'm not. Are you?"

"If I saw Matt again, I know I would still be attracted to him. I haven't forgotten about him. Look, I care for Scott, and I love being with him, but if there was a chance with Matt, I'm not sure if I could pass it up." Karen was still fixed on the book. "I don't know what's going to happen with Scott. I won't pursue Matt as long as Scott and I are together. I won't cheat on him. I don't even know if I could let Scott go. I know he loves me, and I can depend on him. But if Scott and I break up, well..."

"I don't believe this. You've got the greatest guy in the world."

"You asked me to be honest with you. Scott knows how I feel about him. He knows our situation. I've always been honest with him."

"Really? Then you must have told him how you feel about Matt, right?"

"No. How can I?"

"I see what you're doing."

"What do you mean?" Karen put the book down.

"You plan on testing the water, so to speak. You won't let Scott go unless you know Matt's a sure thing."

"That's not true."

"Yes, it is."

"So are you going to go blab this to Scott?"

"Karen we're not in junior high. Besides, if Matt is as good a guy as Scott says he is, he wouldn't go after his friend's girlfriend, would he?"

Lisa felt sick to her stomach on the drive home. She hated the thought of Karen hurting Scott, which could very well happen. She remembered the feeling she had that day at the store when they talked about combining the bookstore with a health food store. She knew then that it wouldn't happen. Now, she thought she knew why. Why couldn't Matt Fields stay in Boston where he belonged?

Chapter 14

———

"I can't believe it's the first day of spring," Scott commented as he and Lisa walked along the beach. "Time is moving so fast," he added sadly.

"Yeah, I know," Lisa said, half listening.

"I can't wait to get out every day and run in the fresh air. I'm sick of the treadmill and going to the track. I did manage to get out a couple of times this week, now that the snow is melting. It's been a weird winter, but I love the freedom of the road."

"The roads are still pretty icy." Lisa stopped and looked out at the ocean.

"Some are. You okay?"

"Yeah, I'm fine," she scowled.

"Lisa?"

"All right, I'm not so fine."

"Still depressed, huh?"

"It will be two years this week. I was out here walking on a day just like this. That's when I found the crystal and started having the dreams. I felt like my life was such a mess at the time. My marriage ended, I had writer's block...Karen came back, and had me questioning what I really wanted in my life. That was good. I had it planned out. I would write a best seller and find my twin soul."

"And you did!"

"And I did." She looked content for a moment. "I wrote a best seller, and found my twin soul. I found him in the past, I found him in the present. It's getting harder to trust that we'll be together in the future. Some days I'm optimistic and feel in my heart it will happen. Then other days, I think it's hopeless. I have to just trust and believe…have faith."

Lisa stopped suddenly. "This is the Morrison property. When is Matt moving in?"

"I think, not until the end of next week. I'm going to help him move. I'm just waiting for the call."

Lisa began thinking about Karen. "Have you and Karen given any more thought to your idea?"

Scott looked down at the sand and let out a heavy breath. Lisa saw him in a way she had never seen him before; dispirited. In fact, he was not his usual upbeat self at all.

"She blows it off whenever I mention it. She was enthusiastic in the beginning, but now…she's been distant."

Lisa probably knew why and didn't have the heart to say anything. "Everything seems to be changing," she said. I don't know what it is. I feel so much sadness. It's not just Sylor, I don't know, it's something else. I can't put my finger on it. It makes me want to cry, and I don't know why. I don't like this feeling, it scares me." She wiped away a few tears.

"Karen says you haven't been around much."

"Nope…I've just been wallowing in my misery." Though this was partly true, Lisa couldn't tell Scott that it was better if she didn't see Karen for awhile.

Scott stopped and looked around. "You ever come out here at night?"

"Dave and I did a couple of times."

"I mean alone. I think it would be great some night to walk out here alone, sort of like a meditation."

"No thanks. I would never come out here alone at night."

"I'm going to do that some night. When there's a full moon. Yeah, I've got to do it. You should try it. Make it an adventure."

"I've had enough adventure. I went to Atlantis, remember?"

"Ah, try it anyway."

Later, Lisa walked Scott to his car. He gave her a long hug, and then studied her face. "Don't worry; everything's going to be fine. You're going to have everything you want."

She was concerned by the tone of his voice. There was something different about it, and she had never seen him so serious. "Scott, you sound...funny. I don't..."

"You know, I have two sisters, and I've never been as close to them as I have been to you. I love you, Lisa Burke. We've only known each other what, a little over a year and a half? You've been the best friend I've ever had. I'm sure we were friends long, long ago."

"We were. I'm sure of it, too. But Scott, why..."

Scott opened the car door and jumped in. He rolled down the window. He smiled softly, his eyes were wet. "You're going to be happy. I don't know how I know, but I do."

Lisa stared into his eyes, bewildered. He started to roll up the window.

"Scott, wait!" She paused, "I love you, too."

In tears, she watched him drive down the road until she couldn't see him anymore. She went into the house and cried, though she wasn't sure why. Yes, they had only known each other a little more than a year and a half, but she too, felt that he was the best friend she had ever had.

A week later, Lisa decided to put her negative feelings aside, and pay Karen a visit at the shop. "How does Scott seem to you?" she asked Karen.

"What do you mean?"

"We took a walk on the beach last week, and he was so...I don't know...melancholy. He wasn't his usual happy self. I know every-one has his or her day, but not Scott. This was a first. I haven't talked to him since, and I've been thinking about him all morning. I can't get him out of my head. I tried calling his cell phone, and at the store, but he wasn't in, and I called his house, but…"

"Scott's taking a few days off from work. He's helped Matt move in, and he wanted to take a couple of days for himself. I didn't see him at all yesterday, but I did talk to him this morning. He was going to go for a run, and then drop by here later.

"Oh, good!" Lisa felt relieved.

"He and Matt had a bit of a tiff, but they're okay now."

"What happened?"

"Apparently, Scott was trying to pick Matt's brain. He's sick of Matt always being in a mood. They're so different; Scott being the free spirit, and Matt wrestling with his role in life. I don't think…"

The phone rang. While Karen answered it, Lisa picked up a book. Before she could look through it, she heard Karen's cry; "No, no, don't tell me this, this can't be!"

Lisa stood paralyzed, while she watched Karen's face turn pale with tears streaming down it. Lisa held her breath, while Karen listened to what was being said on the other end. When she hung up, she couldn't speak.

Lisa braced herself for bad news, and walked slowly to the counter. "Karen, what is it? Is it your mother?"

Still not being able to speak, she shook her head no.

"Karen…what?" Lisa held on to the counter.

"It's…it's Scott." It would be another thirty seconds before Karen could go on.

"What's…what do you mean, it's Scott? Karen, what?" Lisa's stomach was beginning to hurt.

"When he was out running this morning, a driver lost control of his car on a patch of ice. Scott never saw him coming, according to a witness."

"He's going to be all right, right?" Lisa asked, not wanting to face what she already knew. "Please say he's going to be all right."

"He died at the scene, he didn't...Karen couldn't continue, and ran into the back room.

Pain settled in Lisa's throat. She wanted to scream, but it felt like her throat was closed. She held her stomach, and backed up against a wall. She slid down to the floor, and stared into a tiny dust ball that had attached itself to the carpet.

"Oh God, not Scott," she managed to mumble. "Not Scott."

Her throat opened, and she sobbed. She sat there for quite awhile listening to Karen's sobs, which only made her cry more. Karen finally came out from the back room with a box of tissues, and sat on the floor next to Lisa.

"He knew Karen, he *knew*. That's why he seemed so different. He talked to me in a way that one would if they might not see that person again. I didn't know where he was coming from."

"I had been putting him off so much lately, I can't believe I've..." Karen wiped her eyes.

"Now, I think back to the night we met him at that stupid club I didn't want to go to. He was so likeable. I wasn't sure if he was for real. Then, the next day at the market, I can still see him holding up that bunch of organic carrots." She wiped a few tears, and laughed nervously, savoring the memory. "There was something about him. He pulled at my heart."

"I did love him, Lisa. I only wish I had loved him enough to want to spend the rest of my life with him. He deserved better."

"He can't be gone. He *can't* be. I can't imagine him not being in our lives. I'm sure it's too soon, but there haven't been any arrangements made yet, right?"

"All I know is that he wanted to be cremated, and his family will be planning some kind of service."

"Who called you? I can't believe no one came to tell you in person."

"That was his sister, Kate. I guess Scott never told you that his sisters and I didn't get along entirely well. They seemed jealous and over-protective." Karen stood up and looked down at Lisa. "They loved *you*, though." Karen left to get her coat.

Lisa couldn't believe the sarcasm in Karen's voice, and leaned back against the wall. "God, Karen, not now," she whispered.

"I'm closing. I want to go home and be alone."

"Are you sure? I can go with you."

Karen shook her head. Lisa stood up and put her arms around Karen, who reluctantly accepted the embrace.

"I'm so sorry, Karen."

"I am, too."

That night, Lisa spent some time with Scott's family. She learned some things about him she never knew. When he was ten years old, he had gotten hit by a car. He had run into the street, chasing a ball when he slipped and fell. He only ended up being bruised, and proudly told everyone it didn't hurt. She also learned he was a foster parent to a child in another country.

Lisa couldn't believe he was gone from her life. She wasn't sad for him. She knew he was absolutely fine. She was sad for herself, and for everyone that loved him, but she felt especially sad for Karen. Now, Lisa only hoped she could make it through the service that would be held two days later.

Lisa was to meet Karen in the church basement before the service. Everything was a blur that morning as she got ready. Except for her aunt, no one she loved had died. She still had her parents, her brother. Two of her grandparents had died before she was born, and the other two grandparents when she was too young to remember. Maybe it was better that way. This hurt too damn much, she told herself.

On the drive to the church, she realized she would probably meet the infamous Matt Fields. She broke into a smile. She knew Scott would have loved this. As much as she hated to admit it at a time like this, she *did* want to know what Karen saw in this person.

Lisa headed for the basement, and made her way down the stairs and through a set of doors. She entered the hall, and stopped right where she was, and held her breath. About twenty-five feet away she saw the back of a man standing in a long, black wool coat with dark blonde hair long enough to put in a tail. He was talking to Karen.

"That's impossible," she mumbled. "It can't be...it can't."

She proceeded slowly. Karen hadn't noticed her yet. She seemed to be in a deep conversation with this man. Lisa was now just a few feet behind him. She didn't want to see his face just yet.

"Lisa, come here." Karen motioned to her. "This is Matt Fields. Matt turned, and he and Lisa came face to face again. They both stood motionless for a few seconds, not believing they were seeing the other. This time Matt couldn't run, at least not at the moment. Karen caught the strange encounter, and broke the silence. "Matt, this is my friend Lisa, who was also a friend of Scott's."

He managed a somber smile. It was all that Lisa could do not to put her arms around him. Instead, she purposely offered her hand so she could touch him. He took it, and she held it long as their eyes locked. He didn't pull his hand away like she thought he would.

They felt the electricity between them. He smiled at her sadly, the same sad smile as when she met Sylor for the first time. Lisa felt like they were in a world of their own, almost forgetting where she was. She did not want the moment to end.

Karen stood dumbfounded, as she watched their hands still held together tightly. She motioned for everyone to start going upstairs. Matt quickly pulled his hand and sped away, leaving Lisa and Karen to watch him.

"What the hell was that?" Karen asked, as they were walking upstairs.

"Karen, you would not believe."

Scott's sister interrupted, and told them where they could sit. Matt was already seated, and Lisa managed to get a seat in the row behind him off to the side, about four feet away from him. He sensed someone's eyes on him, and he turned. They made eye contact. Lisa smiled. Matt returned a hint of a smile.

Throughout the service, Lisa stared at her beloved. She loved his hair, and wanted to run her fingers through it and grab it up into a tail. She could hardly believe that Sylor and Matt Fields were one and the same. She suddenly remembered he didn't live too far from her. This made her heart want to burst.

She berated herself for feeling like this during the service for Scott. She laughed inside. Scott was probably right there beside her orchestrating the whole thing.

Matt couldn't believe this was happening. This was the woman he loved, and the woman he swore he would never see again. What were the Gods doing to him? He did not want to feel what he was feeling. He knew he had to get out of there as soon as it was reasonably possible.

One of the children on the little league team Scott coached, said some words about him that brought everyone to tears. Lisa wept softly, not wanting anyone to hear, but Matt did. His resistance gave out and he turned to her. She saw the tears in his eyes. There was so much she wanted to say to him, and it was all he could do to not jump over the row of chairs and hold her, comfort her. But he couldn't. He wouldn't.

Matt was a few feet ahead of Lisa when everyone was leaving the church area. Everyone was going downstairs for the breakfast. Matt headed in the opposite direction, toward the exit. Karen was stuck in back of several people as she watched Matt, just as Lisa was doing.

Lisa was able to break free of the crowd, and rushed to Matt just as he was about to walk out the door. Karen hung back and watched.

"Matt, please don't leave. We have to talk."

"I can't." He started to open the door.

"Matt, there is a lot we have to talk about."

"I can't. Not now," he said. *Not ever*, he thought.

"Scott told me about you, only I didn't know. I didn't know who you were. He'd mentioned Matt Fields. I had no idea." She felt like a blabbering idiot.

"I have to go."

"Matt, we live on the same beach. We're only a quarter mile away from each other. I know you bought the Morrison house."

Matt remembered Scott saying he had a friend up the beach that he wanted to introduce, but he never said her name.

"Please, Matt. You know who and what we are to each other. I know you do." She touched his face. He refrained from putting his hand over hers like he wanted to do. He looked into her eyes with longing, and remembered how he had felt that day they 'connected' at the bookstore.

"I'm sorry," he said, and sped out the door.

"It's okay Matt. I know where to find you," Lisa whispered, thinking she was alone.

"What the *hell* is going on?"

Lisa nearly jumped out of her skin.

"Do you know him?" Karen demanded.

"You could say that. But now is not the time to talk about it."

"I think it is. Why don't you…"

Scott's mother came upstairs, looking for Karen and Lisa.

"Karen, come by my house later and I'll tell you."

"I don't believe for one minute that Matt is Sylor. I think you've really lost it. I don't know who the hell you saw that day in Boston, but it wasn't Matt, and even if it was Matt, he's *not* Sylor!"

"It was Matt." Lisa raised her voice. "And he knows who he is, and who I am." Her voiced cracked. "God, I never thought I'd see him again. I can't believe he's the same person you and Scott talked about."

"That's because he isn't! What's the matter with you?"

"If you don't believe me, ask him."

"Why does he run away?"

"I told you before, I think he's afraid."

"Of what…you?"

"Of what happened in the past. I know I hurt him."

"I think you flatter yourself. I'm going to talk to Matt. I don't know when, but I will."

Lisa knew, now with Scott gone, Matt would be Karen's target. Even though she knew Matt loved her, Lisa knew Karen would worm her way into his life. That made her nervous, especially if Matt didn't want to face his feelings.

Karen put on her coat and walked to the door. Lisa followed. "Lisa, you know I've wanted Matt for a long time."

"Karen, I love him."

"He's fair game." Karen slammed the door on her way out.

"Don't fool with destiny Karen. You may get hurt."

A quarter mile down the beach, with Pink Floyd's 'Comfortably Numb' playing in the background, Matt sat in the dark, crossed legged on the floor, in the middle of his living room. It wasn't that he didn't have the electric hooked up; it was his state of mind.

His friend was gone. A friend he was looking forward to having good times with, a part of what was to be his new change in life. It was over before it began. Then, there was the love of his life; the love of *all* lives. Two of the hardest things he had to deal with in his life, and they both had to happen on the same day. He felt like a part of him was dying, but another part was waiting to be born, and he wasn't yet ready to give birth to it. This reminded him of the Death card in the tarot.

He hated how he felt. He knew sooner or later he would have to come out of it. Scott was a happy-go-lucky guy whose life was taken too soon. What right did Matt have not to live, not to love? Like Henry had said, what good is living if you can't love? It didn't mean it was Lisa he had to love, he affirmed in his denial.

Lisa cried in her pillow that night. It had been the worst day of her life, and the best. Matt was in her life now, whether he wanted to be or not. They should be comforting each other at this time, she thought. She still had Karen to contend with, and this made her cry even more. This was her childhood best friend, and nothing had been the same since Karen's return. But underneath all the crap, all the bickering and the pain, Lisa still loved her like a sister.

She turned on Beethoven's Moonlight Sonata, and listened to it over and over. She envisioned herself and Matt making love to it. That's what that piece was for, to make love to. She and Sylor were never able to make love in Atlantis. They would in this life, she affirmed.

Matt had just stepped out of the shower the next morning, when he heard a knock at the door. He cringed when he realized it couldn't be Scott. Maybe it was Lisa. He thought about not answering. There was a second knock, and a quick third. He threw his jeans on and left the towel draped around his neck.

He opened the door, and to his disappointment, and relief, there stood Karen. He noticed how her gaze moved up and down his nearly bare chest. He should have felt complimented, but he didn't.

"Is it all right if I come in?"

He said nothing, and motioned for her to step in.

"This is a great house."

"You can have a seat if you'd like. As you can see I don't have things quite organized yet."

"Matt, I'm...not even sure why I'm here. I'm happy you came to the service. Scott thought a lot of you and…"

"We should have had more time." Matt couldn't shake the guilt he had of ignoring his friend the last few months. He should have called him as soon as he got back from Arizona.

"I know. It's not fair. He was one of the good guys."

"Excuse me; I'll be back in a minute." Matt went to his bedroom for a tee shirt. He was pulling it over his head as he walked back into the living room. Again he caught Karen checking him out, and felt uneasy. He knew he didn't care for Karen right from the first time they met, yet, he felt there was no reasoning behind it.

"Matt, there is something I'd like to ask you about Lisa."

He held his breath and said nothing. He didn't want to talk about Lisa, especially to Karen, but he didn't know why. He looked forcefully at Karen, waiting to see what she had to say.

"I'm not sure how to put this...okay, Lisa insists she saw you at her book signing in Boston, back in January. She says you ran away. I feel foolish saying this, but she thinks you ran away because you had read her book. She's under this delusion that you are the reincarnation of a character in the book, and his name is Sylor."

Matt just stared at her and wondered what kind of friend Karen really was to Lisa. He could hear the tone in her voice, and it was not one of caring. It was more a tone of deception. His first thought was to deny that he was there, but he felt that somehow she would use it against Lisa. He suddenly felt the need to protect her.

"I was there. I saw her, but we never spoke."

"Oh, uh, well...did you read her book?"

"Yes. It was very good." He knew these were not the answers Karen expected to hear.

"Did you run away, like she said?"

"I wasn't feeling well, and I left."

"Do you believe you're the reincarnation of Sylor?"

"Who said I believed in reincarnation?" Matt let out a breath of impatience.

Karen nervously played with the handle on her purse. "How do you feel about Lisa?"

"We've barely spoken. How could I feel anything about her?"

Matt stood up, hoping Karen would get the hint. She got up, and her keys fell to the floor. Reflex made them both squat down to pick up the keys. Their hands touched, and they looked into each others eyes. She had very pretty eyes he found. They both slowly stood up holding their gaze. In a drawn out effort, she took the keys from his hand. Her touch lingered a bit too long for his liking, and he pulled away.

"Look, if you ever need to talk, I..." She took out a business card. "I'll write my home number on the back, and my cell. Come by the store anytime. It will be nice to see you. Maybe we could share some stories about Scott."

He knew where she was coming from, and now realized he had felt it the first time they met. It was the way she looked at him, and talked to him. She was a good looking woman. Any man would want her. But he wasn't any man, and she wasn't Lisa.

He thanked her for the card and opened the door. He commented how nice a day it was, and that he would later go for a walk.

The temperature reached the mid-fifties. It was a bright, sunny day, and Lisa decided she would take advantage of it by taking a walk on the beach. Thoughts of Scott haunted her. She missed him so much already. Who would she talk to? She could always talk to Scott about anything.

Her first thought was to walk up towards Matt's house, maybe 'accidently' bump into him if he was outside or out walking himself, but she knew it was too soon, and that he probably needed some space. Instead, she headed in the opposite direction and nestled into her private little hideaway at the rocks on the east side. Of course, she couldn't stop thinking about Matt. She knew he would never come to her. She would have to go to him. She just didn't know when.

She sat for twenty minutes, relaxing with her eyes closed, listening to the ocean sounds while thinking about her life. She spontaneously opened her eyes. She couldn't believe it. Faded jeans, running shoes, and Matt obviously didn't see her up on the rocks as he continued to walk at a leisurely pace.

She scrambled down the rocks. "Matt!"

Startled, he turned quickly and froze for a few seconds upon seeing her. He fought with himself on whether to go to her or walk away. He chose the latter.

She ran up behind him, grabbed his arm and swung him around to face her, as she had once done to Sylor. Matt held the same stunned expression.

"You can't keep running like this. We have to talk."

She stared at his face. He hadn't shaved, and he looked incredibly sexy. She had to hold herself back from touching him.

She stumbled on her words. "Matt...I...we have to talk, please."

"Okay," he mumbled, looking down. He was afraid to look at her. He was afraid of what he might do.

"It's kind of chilly standing here. My place, your place, or up there?" She pointed to the rocks where she had been sitting. "It will shield us from the wind."

Matt didn't know what to do. He looked up at the rocks. The cave like appearance made him break out in a cold sweat. There was something about caves he was deathly afraid of. It had been that way all of his life. If they went back to either of their houses, again he was afraid of what he might do; surrender.

He nodded toward the rocks. What the hell was he doing? Why hadn't he stayed in Boston?

There was hardly enough room for two people in this little nook. They couldn't help but touch each other as they sat. He knew it was going to be extremely hard to separate himself from her on all levels. But he would. He had to fight the urge to put his arm around her, and bring her closer.

She turned to him. "You read my book."

He nodded, not looking at her.

"Then you know who we are and what we are to each other."

Matt closed his eyes wearily, and then opened them. "Yes."

"You had to have found the crystal. You know we are destined to be together. Why are you running away from me?"

He blinked his eyes several times as he looked out at the ocean, and then finding the courage, he turned to her. He searched her face, gazing at every facet, settling on the mouth he wanted so much to kiss.

"I found the crystal last Labor Day at the Vineyard. It was sitting in the middle of an area of the beach where there were a lot of people. It seemed no one saw it but me. I didn't know why I picked it up, but when I held it I knew it was mine, like it was meant for me in some way. I was fascinated with it. But it also reminded me of something, something painful, and I didn't know what. I wrapped it up and threw it in a drawer."

"What made you read my book?"

"It was around Christmas when I picked it up. I had always been interested in ancient civilizations, especially Atlantis. I was in a big hurry when I bought it, so I didn't get to look through it. I hardly even read fiction anymore."

"But now you know it's not fiction."

"I didn't know what was going on with this. It really messed with my head. But I felt like I had lived it, and I knew I lived it with the woman who wrote it. I saw you in dreams long before I bought your book."

Lisa turned closer to him and pushed back some hair that had fallen into his eye.

"I know what you want," he said, looking into her eyes. "And I know we're supposed to go back to Atlantis, as crazy as that sounds, but I can't do it, and I can't be with you."

Her heart sank. "Matt, you can't mean that. This is our destiny. I know we have free will, but if we don't do this now, it could be many, many lifetimes before we get another chance, and it may be even harder to do."

He shook his head firmly. "No, I won't do it."

"Even if we chose not to go back, we can still be together. We belong together."

"No. Like you said, we have free will."

"How can you say no? That day at the bookstore, you know what we both felt! I *know* you felt it. You *know* what we have together."

He turned away. His remembering that feeling made him want to make love to her right then and there.

"What we *had* was a long time ago, in another life."

"What we had is right here, and right now, and it's not going to go away. I knew you were alive in the present. Even when I was going to Atlantis, I knew you were here, somewhere. Karen tried to convince me otherwise. Karen is the reincarnation of Jenielle. I didn't include that in the novel.

Sylor and Jenielle didn't get along, Matt thought. That explained why he had mixed feelings about Karen. But why was she coming on to him now? He had no intention of telling Lisa that Karen had come by to see him.

"Matt, it's no accident that we met. It's no accident we practically live next door to each other. I've waited so long for you."

He looked down, shook his head, and said firmly, "It won't work. It didn't work then. It won't work now."

She took his hands in hers. He made no effort to pull away. He wanted to feel a part of her. He turned to her again, and saw the tears in her eyes as she looked back at him. As much as he tried, he could not look away.

"Matt, I love you."

He closed his eyes and took a breath. He pulled his hands away and looked out to the water. Her face was covered with tears when he looked back at her. He gently wiped her face with his fingers. He hated what he was doing to her. He hated what he was doing to himself. Her pain was his pain.

"I'm sorry, Lisa." He made his way down the rocks.

She watched him walk away. How could he do this? He was hurting her as much now as he did in Atlantis.

He couldn't believe he had walked away, leaving her like that. She told him she loved him, and he couldn't handle it. Why couldn't he just tell her he loved her more than life? Because he would lose it if she ever left him again. The pain of living without her couldn't compare with the pain if she left him again. He didn't believe in that 'it was better to have loved and lost' crap.

He was relieved they had stayed on the beach. He knew what would have happened had they gone anywhere else. Then he would have been in over his head. He would have made the commitment, and there would have been no going back.

When Lisa arrived home, she noticed an envelope had been slipped under her front door. Inside there was a note and another envelope. The note explained that this was a letter from Scott, and it was to be given to Lisa sometime after the service.

Lisa sat down to catch her breath. She began to cry. She wasn't sure if she could read it. She pulled herself together and opened the envelope. The letter read:

My beautiful lady,

If you are reading this letter, then you know where I have traveled to, and I could be with you right at this very moment! I want to tell you how much fun, laughter, and joy you brought into my life from the moment we met, as well as the experience of seeing someone materialize right before my eyes. One does not look at life the same when they have been a part of what you have experienced.

By now, I'm sure you have met the professor. I must have known all along who he was, which would explain my insistence on hooking up the two of you. I figured it out when I was help-ing him unpack. I found a small box without a cover, and inside

there was a couple of things wrapped in tissue paper. One of the things was partially unwrapped; it was your novel.

When I picked up the box, Matt anxiously took it out of my hands, saying he would take care of 'that one' and took it into another room. When Matt stepped outside for a minute, I checked out the box. I could not believe what I had found with the book. It was the crystal! It all made sense when he put on the long black wool coat, and his hair hung below the collar like you said. He looked just like the Sylor you described, unfortunately with the same stubborn attitude. I didn't tell him what I knew.

Matt is not going to make it easy. He is a very conflicted soul. Atlantis did a number on him. You somehow survived it better than he did, I think because you are willing to face things and deal with them. He has not forgiven himself for his mistakes. It may help him to know that you forgive him, but ultimately, he must forgive himself. And the only way he can do it is to take that step, and do what he came here to do!

I ask that you do not give up on him. He loves you more than you could ever imagine. I know this. He needs to know how much you love him. Keep telling him, and don't let your pride stand in the way. That's easier said than done, I know. Don't let obstacles deter you. Again, please do not give up on him.

As I sit writing, I can sense many things. I feel like I'm already one step in that other world. I don't know how or when, but I feel it is very soon. I am not afraid of death, having had the experience I told you about, so I am ready. I will miss you, and that saddens me at this moment. That is what you felt our last time together. I knew then I had to let go of you, just like in Atlantis. You may have guessed I was Sylor's brother, Matua.

Time is short, and I have another letter to write. I will always love you, and I will try to give you as much help as I possibly can from my end. May we all be together one day, in a resurrected Atlantis!

Love,
Scott

P.S. One day you will give Matt a piece of information that will surprise the both of you!

When Lisa finally stopped sobbing, she wondered if Matt had gotten a letter too. She was grateful for Scott's letter. She was amazed at how Scott knew of his impending death and how he took it so gracefully. She hadn't guessed that Scott was Matua, Sylor's brother. It did make her feel better knowing she may be reunited with Scott if she ever did get back to Atlantis.

In his letter, Scott asked her not to give up on Matt. That hit home with Lisa, because that's exactly what Hollina had done with Sylor. Hollina's stubborn pride kept her from going to Egypt. Had she gone to Egypt, Sylor may have eventually followed. Even if Atlantis had been destroyed, they would have been together, and probably things would be different between them now.

"Okay Scott, I won't give up on him. How can I?" That would be giving up on herself. She decided she would give it a few days and pay her beloved a visit.

Chapter 15

————

Lisa decided to put her pride aside, and stopped in to see Karen at the shop. "How are you doing?" She asked.

"I'm alright, but it's weird. I keep expecting Scott to pop in anytime. I miss him."

"I know. I have to keep resisting the urge to go to the health food store. I don't know if I can ever set foot in that place again."

"I was there yesterday. I wish the one in our area hadn't closed. It's going to be hard to keep shopping there."

"Scott may be gone, but he did have a good idea. Maybe you should go ahead with it."

"I don't know if I could do it. He was so knowledgeable about health and natural food…"

"You've always been a quick learner. God, I remember that when we were kids in school. I'd be struggling, and you'd pick it up in an instant."

"Did that bother you?"

"No, I thought it was great. Why do you think I always asked you for help with schoolwork?"

"Right." Karen cleared her throat. "Have you seen Matt at all?"

"Yeah, I have. It was the day after the service. We met on the beach that afternoon. We talked."

"And?"

Lisa was already starting to get agitated by Karen's tone. "We talked, that's it!"

"It doesn't sound like I'm hearing wedding bells."

Lisa bit the inside of her mouth. "Not yet!"

"I take it he didn't tell you I had gone to see him the morning of that same day. It looked like he had just gotten out of the shower. All he had on was a pair of jeans and a towel around his neck."

Lisa tried not to show any emotion. It was the first time in her life she had ever been jealous of Karen. What had happened all those years ago, the big secret Lisa wasn't supposed to know about, didn't touch this as far as Lisa was concerned.

"Did you ask him what you wanted to?" Lisa asked, trying not to let her voice crack.

"He admitted to being at the bookstore that day. He left because he wasn't feeling well. He also said he read your book and he thought it was good." Karen smirked. "I foolishly asked him if he thought he was the reincarnation of Sylor. His exact words were, 'Who said I believed in reincarnation?' And he gave me a strange look."

"So he didn't admit he could be Sylor?"

"Nope." Karen smirked again.

Lisa smiled inwardly. He had admitted it to her. That's all that mattered. Lisa figured Matt wouldn't trust Karen anyway.

"I gave him my business card and my numbers. I don't think he's your Sylor, Lisa. And I told you twin flames rarely incarnate together."

"There are exceptions." Lisa smiled confidently.

"Of course, just not in this case."

Lisa decided to let things go at that, and not reveal any of the conversation with Matt, or Scott's letter.

It had been well over a week since she had talked to Matt that day on the beach. She toyed with the idea of going to see him. It made her blood boil that Karen had gone to see him that day, and to talk about her no less. She wasn't used to feeling insecure like this. Maybe because it was the first time in her life she had ever been truly in love. It was time to go see him, she decided.

When Matt answered the door, she noticed a sparkle in his eyes, which made her heart beat faster than it already was.

"Matt, I would really like to talk to you. Is it all right if I come in?"

He gave a meager smile and held open the door.

"I've always liked this house. It has been years since I've been inside."

"Have a seat if you'd like."

She was surprised he was cordial, she half-expected him to turn her away. Maybe she was making progress.

"I came here on the spur of the moment. I don't even know if...I just needed to see you. That day, the way you just walked away, it hurt....a lot."

He put his head down, and let out a deep breath. "I'm sorry. I never should have walked away like that."

"Then why did you?"

"I can't be what you want. You'd end up hating me. It's better this way. I'm sorry."

"I could never hate you." She moved over to the sofa and sat next to him.

"Lisa, I hate what I did in Atlantis. I hate what I did to you, and I hate what you did to me. I feel him inside me. I don't even know who I am. Near the end of the story, when you left with the crystal, I couldn't read anymore. I did eventually, but I felt the pain; Sylor's pain."

"Do you have any memories of what happened to you...Sylor, after I had left with the crystal? I've always wondered what happened to him, if he...you had left Atlantis or..."

Matt felt a swelling in his chest and throat. Whatever happened to him after was *not* good. This he was sure of.

"No. All I know is the pain. And it's raw, like a wound that's been re-opened. As I read the part when you left, I also felt anger, anger that was so overwhelming. I hated you."

"Please don't say that. It never was suppose to happen that way. Never! I wanted to stay with you. You don't know. I was such a mess. I thought I was losing my sanity. Sane people do not teleport or time travel to Atlantis, or anywhere! Just like you're feeling now...not knowing who you are, I felt the same way. I didn't know what reality was anymore. Jenielle was edging me on, and then there was the vision of Hollina...I..."

"It does not matter! *Again* you had abandoned me! You took the crystal. I could not bring you back again. And I had *nothing* left of you!"

At first, Lisa backed away. She knew she wasn't dealing with Matt at that moment. The voice she heard was Sylor's.

"I'm sorry. I am so sorry." She held his face in her hands. She saw the tears in his eyes. When he calmed, she took his hand. "You have to realize it wasn't meant for me to stay in Atlantis, not under those circumstances. And Hollina vowed she would not witness the end. It wasn't me that ran away with the crystal, I wouldn't have done that. God, to never see Sylor again...no, I would have risked everything to be with him. I would have died with him. When I realized I couldn't get back to Atlantis, I *wanted* to die.

"Matt, if I had stayed there, you would be here and I wouldn't. Where would that leave us? Or maybe if I had stayed there neither one of us would be here, who knows. But we are both here now because we know how we screwed up our lives, and the lives of others. It is our responsibility to go back and fix it. This is a gift. We have the knowledge. We can do it."

"No. I won't go back there. I won't." He raised his voice. "*It's over,* Lisa. There is no going back. I'm sorry."

"If you won't go back, then give us a chance here and now."

"I told you, it won't work."

He stood up, walked over to the door, and opened it. "Please leave me alone. Forget about me."

She followed him to the door. She turned to him and touched his face. "Forget about you? Matt, I want to love you in any and every way possible. I want to give to you, and give to your life. I want to give you everything that I am. We are one. One soul, one heart."

"I'm not worth it."

"What do you mean? I *say* you're worth it. You are everything to me. I love you!"

"Why are you doing this to yourself? Why are you still here?"

"If I thought for one second that you didn't love me, I wouldn't be here."

"I *don't* want to be with you," Matt said in a hostile voice he knew wasn't his own.

"Knock knock? Oh, I'm sorry if I interrupted," Karen said smiling.

Lisa turned white, knowing Karen must have heard what Matt had just said.

"Should I come back?"

Lisa looked at Matt waiting for his answer.

"No. Come in. Lisa was on her way out."

Before Matt could close the door, Lisa reached for the knob and slammed it shut.

Lisa's stomping up the back stairs made Charcoal clear the deck. "That's right Charcoal, I'm pissed!" She slammed the back door and tore off her jacket. She threw Beethoven's Ninth into the CD player, set it to the second movement, and then jumped on the treadmill.

"Okay, Matt, like you said, it's over! If you can't get over it then just forget it! You're right, you're not worth it! Be with Karen. She doesn't love you. Maybe that's all your worth!"

She ran the entire movement, and then collapsed on the sofa. As she listened to the slower, softer, third movement, she thought of Scott's letter. "I'm sorry, Scott. I don't know if I can do it, not when he treats me like that. I can't get through to him. He won't allow himself to love me, or to let me love him."

She could picture Scott sitting next to her, frowning and shaking his head, but telling her to hang in there. She quickly shut off the music as it started the fourth movement. The last thing she wanted to hear at the moment was 'Ode to Joy.' She decided she would pamper herself in a hot bath with rose oil, then head to the mall.

"You can have a seat." Matt told Karen as he went into the bedroom to change. A few minutes later, he came out wearing jeans and a dark green Henley shirt.

"Is there a problem between you and Lisa?" Karen fiddled with the handle on her purse.

Matt grabbed his jacket that was hung over the desk chair.

"I'm sorry, but I have some errands to run," he lied.

"Oh. Oh, I'm sorry. I did come at a bad time. Look...would you like to go out for dinner sometime?"

"Karen," he paused impatiently, "I don't want to date anyone right now. I've got too much to think about. I just moved, my good friend just died, and I'm not sure what I'm going to do with my life, since the book I had planned to write does not hold any interest for me right now."

"It doesn't have to be a date. Come on, Matt. You don't know anyone else around here. I'm sure you could use a night out."

"Right now, no. Give me some time, okay?" He couldn't believe he said that last part. It almost implied her would go out with her eventually!

Matt drove around for awhile, wanting to familiarize himself more with the area. Two beautiful women banging down his door, he thought, and he's sending them away. *What an idiot!* And what kind of friend was Karen to hurt Lisa in that way? Lisa!

He suddenly remembered everything she had said to him back at the house. He broke out in a sweat, and pulled over to the side of the road. She had said all those beautiful things to him, and he had pretty much thrown her out the door. Matt thought he was many things, but being cruel was not one of them, until now.

All those things she had said to him were things he could very well say to her. But he would never say them. Never! Even though she had taken the risk and bared her soul, he would not. He could never trust her with his feelings.

He knew he couldn't let this go as it was. He couldn't be with her, but he loved her too much to let her hate him. He would have to apologize. If only for a moment, he would let his guard down and go see her, if she didn't slam the door in his face.

He drove slowly down her road, with his stomach in knots. He wasn't sure which house it was. His only indication would be a name on a mailbox. He came to a house with a green Corvette in the driveway. Matt smiled. It had to be her place, that car suited her. The name on the mailbox confirmed it.

Lisa had just stepped out of the bath. She dried off and slipped on a pair of white satin panties. She combed her wet hair back and dabbed on some perfume. She had begun searching for a bra when she heard a knock at the side door.

"It must be Karen, damn it," she whispered. She probably wanted to rub in what had happened earlier. Lisa reached for the closest thing at hand to throw on; a pink, mid thigh length satin robe. *What if it's not Karen?* It had to be. She was the only one who ever used the side door. There was another knock. *It's got to be her.* She quickly tied the belt around her waist and ran down to the door, gearing up for some heavy conversation!

She thought her heart would stop when she saw Matt through the glass. He thought *his* heart would stop when he saw the way she was dressed!

She opened the door, and tried to contain the joy she was feeling upon seeing him. Maybe he had a change of heart. Matt consciously made a point of not looking below her face. His peripheral vision gave him a definitive outline of her breasts against the soft material.

"I had to...I want..." Matt hated himself for feeling like a tongue-tied schoolboy. "I want to apologize for what I said and did earlier."

Trying to keep her cool, she gave the barest of a smile. "Come in." Charcoal found his way in with Matt.

Matt followed her into the kitchen, and she motioned for him to sit at the table. As he walked passed her, he got a subtle whiff of her perfume. She sat across from him and looked directly into his eyes with no expression. With her wet hair combed back, and wearing no make-up, he saw that she was a natural beauty. He wanted to kick himself for thinking how easy it would be to untie her robe.

"I'm sorry about this morning. I never should have treated you that way. You, of all people, didn't deserve that. Those things you said to me, no one has ever said anything like that to me before."

"I meant every word Matt. I love you…I always will."

She felt Charcoal rubbing his nose against her leg. "Oh, hi sweetie." She picked him up. When she did her robe opened slightly and Matt caught a glimpse of a breast. He felt the flow of blood penetrating his face, as well as another area. He hoped to God she couldn't read his mind.

"This is Charcoal." She scratched around the cat's ears.

"Do you think he would mind if I held him? I love cats."

She walked around the table and placed Charcoal in his arms. Matt got another hint of her perfume. It was becoming more than what he could handle, and tried to concentrate on the cat.

"He's usually pretty friendly. He seems to like you." Charcoal rubbed his face against Matt's. "You don't have any animals, do you?"

"No, I don't."

"If you like cats, you can pick one up at the no-kill shelter. I used to volunteer there. It was so sad with all the abandoned kittens we used to pick up. If you're interested, the shelter's at the south end of Elm Street."

"No, I don't want one."

"Oh, they're so easy."

"It's not that, I..." He wasn't sure if he should open up. "I had a cat once. I was six, and lived in the country. Then my mother died, and I had to go live with my uncle who lived in the city. About a month after the move, the cat was hit by a car. I never wanted another pet."

"You were six when you lost your mother? That's awful."

"Yeah...that's life. Sometimes you lose..." He put Charcoal down and stood up. "I have to be going."

"Matt, you don't have to leave." She walked over to him and rested her hands around his neck.

He closed his eyes feeling the intoxicating effect her warm hands had on his flesh. Against Sylor's will, he brought his hands up to her face. Slowly, he slid his hands down the sides of her neck and slipped them under the pink satin grasping her shoulders. He drew her closer.

Entranced, he took a deep breath. With his right hand, he made one long stroke up her neck to her face. He cradled the back of her neck with the other hand. He looked into her magnetic eyes, and his mouth found its way to hers. He kissed her slowly, deliberately, forgetting...forgetting the past, forgetting his vow.

With their bodies pressed together, and their tongues intertwined, her hands held his flushed face. For a moment, they were not of this world as they found themselves falling into each other.

She slowly pulled away, sucking his lower lip in her mouth. "Matt, I love you."

He quickly pulled away. "What the hell am I doing? This wasn't supposed to happen. I can't do this. I'm sorry."

"Matt!"

He ran out the door.

"Matt!"

She stood in the middle of the kitchen, smiling. She ran her fingers over her lips. She had gotten a little piece of him, and it was wonderful. It would happen. It *would* happen, she told herself as she envisioned them making love on the moonlit beach.

She thought of when she and Sylor almost made love on the table, and he backed off. She laughed out loud. "Is there any other man that could have that kind of self-control?" Matt had learned it in Atlantis.

At home, Matt was not laughing. He couldn't believe what he had done. He hadn't made love to anyone for over two years, and he had never wanted anyone more in his life, but he could not make love to her without committing to her. And he was not about to go back and relive the nightmare of Atlantis.

Something suddenly came to Matt. He realized every time she told him she loved him it would push his buttons, and he would want to get away from her. He remembered that, in the book, 'I love you' were the last words she had said to him. Those were also the last words of his dying mother. When someone told him they loved him that meant they were going to leave him.

In the three weeks that followed, and as difficult as it was, Lisa made no attempt to see Matt. Matt, on the other hand, kept expecting her to show up at his door anytime, and they both wondered if they would run into each other as they took their daily walks on the beach.

Lisa had not seen or talked to Karen in those three weeks. It was the first week of May; time to go collect a rent check. She got a big surprise when she walked into the store.

"Lisa, hey, how are you?"

"Dave, hi!" She gave her ex a big hug. "You look great. When you said you were going to Hawaii for six months, I never expected to see you again; I know how much you loved it there before."

"Like the saying goes, great place to visit but...I have to admit, I miss good old New England, specifically Cape Cod. And congratulations on your new novel, I see it's doing very well."

"Thanks. It's been quite an experience."

"Maybe we can get together. I offered Karen dinner Saturday night. Would you like to join us?"

Lisa glanced over at Karen, who did *not* give a welcoming look. "I'd love to, but I can't. Can we get together another time?"

"Will do. I've got to go. Karen, I'll give you a call on Saturday. Lisa, it was great seeing you. We'll talk soon."

"How are you doing?" Lisa asked sincerely.

"Not bad. How about you?"

"I'm okay." Lisa hated the tension between them. "Dave looks good, huh?"

"Dave looks fantastic! With that tan, and his hair much longer, he reminds me of when we were eighteen. I'm glad he asked me out for dinner. It's so good to see him."

"You sound interested."

"Would that bother you?"

"No, not at all. I think he'd be good for you."

"And Matt wouldn't? I have no intention of giving up on him. That day, when we were both at Matt's, I asked him out. He said he wasn't ready to date anyone, and wanted me to give him time. And I'll be honest with you, I heard him say that he didn't want to be with you."

"Well, he came to my house that afternoon and apologized," Lisa retorted with a sly smile.

"He did? Have you seen him since?"

"No. Have you?" Lisa hated the déjà vu feeling. It was like being back in high school when they both liked Jimmy Rogers. Some things never change, and they were getting too old for this!

"No. He said to give him some time. So I will. Then, when the time is right..."

"Karen, he doesn't love you. He never will."

"Like the song says, what's love got to do with it?"

Lisa shook her head. "Then why are you doing this? What is the purpose? You know how much I love him!"

"What I know is that you love someone that doesn't exist, and I have wanted to sleep with Matt since the day I met him. And I will. You don't have to love someone to go to bed with them."

"I do. Maybe it's time you should know Matt admitted…"

Karen wasn't listening. "You of all people should talk about going to bed with someone they didn't love. You *married* someone you didn't love!"

Lisa knew Karen was right on that one. "That was well over twenty years ago, and I was wrong, but I cared very much for Dave, just like you cared for Scott."

"I didn't marry Scott."

"Maybe it's no excuse, but I was twenty, and Dave had given me an ultimatum. I didn't want to lose him."

"Why? Huh? Why? You didn't love him! You *did not* love him. But there was someone who did! Me! I loved him! And if you think that's a shocker I'll tell you something else. I slept with him!"

Lisa kept a blank expression and let Karen go on.

"I slept with Dave shortly before you two married. He kept asking you to marry him, and the little princess kept putting him off. One night you had a big fight about it and you broke up. He got drunk and called me to talk. We didn't do too much talking, but we did have a lot of sex. And I'm going to tell you something else…I got pregnant that night. I was going to have Dave's baby."

"I know," Lisa said with no emotion.

"What?"

"I knew you had sex that night. Dave confessed to me the very next day. And I'll tell *you* something that's going to knock your socks off. A month later, when you announced to Dave you were pregnant, he gave me an ultimatum. Either I marry him, or he was going to marry you. I didn't want to lose him. Before I gave him an answer, I asked him if he loved you. He said he *did not*. He would only marry you because of the baby, and would eventually divorce you. Had he told me that he loved you, or could grow to love you, I would have let him go."

"I can't believe this!"

"Karen, I knew that was the real reason you moved down to South Carolina. I knew about the miscarriage, the breakdown, the psych ward. And whether you believe me or not, I felt horrible about it all. And I hated the fact that I couldn't console you, because I wasn't even supposed to know anything. I admit I *should* have done things differently, and I am so sorry I didn't. I am *very sorry* I didn't."

"Dave was going to marry me? How could you have done that to me?"

"He didn't love you. He repeatedly told me it wouldn't have worked out. You would have been even more hurt in the end."

"But *you* didn't love him."

"No, not in that way, but I wish to God I had, because I've paid for it by missing out on *real* love, being with someone you are so deeply in love with, someone you love more than life. I ache for that. But I had made a commitment and I stuck to it. Maybe that makes me a martyr; maybe it just makes me stupid. I realize now why I stuck to it; because in Atlantis I didn't. What goes around comes around; otherwise known as karma. You know the term. And you know something; I'm still paying for it. I've found my true love, the man who shares my soul, and he won't have me, if that makes you feel any better."

"Well, for the first time in her life the little princess doesn't get what she wants. Don't expect me to feel sorry for you."

"What are you talking about?"

"All of our lives, it was *you* that got everything. I was fat and ugly, you were petite and pretty. Everyone loved Lisa. All the boys, all the girls, everyone wanted to be *your* friend. Boys would call me up asking for your phone number. Your parents were supportive;

I had to do everything my father said. I hated nursing; you got your first book published when you were twenty. You got the beach house you always wanted, the Corvette, the…"

"My God, I didn't realize you…I didn't know you felt that way."

"You mean your intuition never picked up on it? I would have loved to have one out-of-body experience, and you get to time-travel to Atlantis. But there is one thing that you are *not* going to get, and that's Matt. Even if I have just one night with him, I'll have something of him you *never* will! And you don't know the whole story about the baby. I didn't…Oh, just get the hell out of here; I'll put your check in the mail."

Chapter 16

———

Lisa tried not to cry as she drove home. This obviously had been festering in Karen for a very long time, and she didn't understand it. Did Karen feel this way when they were kids? Did this all stem from Hollina and Jenielle's relationship? Why did Karen want Matt so much when in Atlantis she seemed to despise him?

She knew Karen wanted Matt since she met him. Did she want him in Atlantis? A deep chill ran through her. Yes! Jenielle wanted Sylor, and he must have rejected her because of his love for Hollina. This must have been the tension that had existed between Sylor and Jenielle. No wonder Jenielle didn't want her there, no wonder she had treated her the way she did. It all made sense now.

Jenielle was determined to have a man that was with someone else, but she never said who that man was. Lisa knew in her heart it was Sylor, and now it seemed Karen wanted him even more just to spite her. Like Jenielle, Karen was determined to have him, and deep down Lisa was afraid she might, even if it was just one time.

Lisa longed to go over to Matt's house, but pride wouldn't let her. He would have to come to her, she affirmed, even though she began walking the beach twice a day hoping to run into him. If she didn't meet him on the beach, she knew it would be a long wait before he came to her, *if* he came to her.

Karen was less determined to wait. It had been over a month since her visit with him. It was time. She took a step back when a strange man answered the door. "Who are you?"

"I'm Henry Robertson Smith. And you are...besides beautiful?"

"I'm Karen. Where's Matt?" She poked her head in and looked around.

"I'm so sorry. I'm forgetting my manners. Please come in. Matt just stepped in the shower."

Karen kept her eye on Henry as she moved passed him, until she caught sight of a copy of *Return to Atlantis*.

"I haven't had the chance to read that one yet," Henry quipped. "I mostly read self-help. Hey, aren't you the lady with the bookstore?"

"Yes, how did you know?"

"There was a book I was looking for and Matt mentioned your name. I was hoping to have time to go by your place before we left for California, but I don't think I'll get there."

"California? Who's we?"

"Me and my best man, Matt. In three weeks I'll be marrying my soul mate."

"When are you leaving?"

"Tonight."

"So Matt will be gone for three weeks?"

"No, mid August is the plan. Says he needs to get away. I *thought* he was getting away when he moved *here*. I'll never figure that dude out."

"Mid August?" Karen sighed and unconsciously picked up the book.

"You must know all about that reincarnation stuff, right?"

"Uh huh, why?"

"I don't know what it is with that book. He still has it hanging around, but he doesn't want to talk about it."

"What do you mean?"

"Oh, he talked some nonsense about being the reincarnation of some dude in the story, and having some connection to the author.

If you ask me, I think he has it bad for her, but he won't say. He's so tight."

"When? When did he first mention this?"

"Oh, it was..." Henry cocked his head and put his finger to his chin. "It was just after Christmas. Yeah, I had just come back for a visit. How can I forget? That was the day we went to the coffee shop and I found my soul mate. I told him to go to the book signing. He had it bad. The man is a stubborn one. Then he pulled out this silly crystal. Said it was like the one in the book. He found it on the Vineyard.

Karen's eyes widened, and her jaw dropped. "Please tell Matt I stopped by, and that I'll see him when he gets back."

"Sure thing. Now why doesn't Matt go out with a nice lady like you? It was my pleasure to meet you."

"My pleasure too, Henry, and congratulations."

Lisa spent the next two weeks working on a new novel. Her heart was not in it. Nothing could compare with 'Return to Atlantis,' but she needed something to take her mind off Matt. It wasn't working, and her resistance wore down.

She berated herself as she walked to his place. What was she doing? Talk about a glutton for punishment. Idiot! She almost turned around, but noticed all the blinds were closed. Maybe he was still sleeping. She continued walking passed his place, then turned around, and decided to just go home. It was just as well. At least her pride was saved.

The next two days brought the same results. Now, she was beginning to worry. She knocked on his door, then looked through the garage window and saw the black Jag. Either he was away or... she didn't want to think of the alternative. Intuitively, she felt he was fine. Where did he go? Somehow, she had a feeling Karen might know. She did not want to see Karen. Again, she would have to put her pride aside.

"I didn't expect to see you for a long time," Karen said dryly, hardly taking her eyes off the book she was reading.

"I feel very bad about what happened last time, and I am truly sorry you feel the way you do, but I'm not here to make nice. Have you seen Matt? I've gone by his place the last three days and…"

"He's in California. A friend of his is getting married. He won't be home until mid-August. Matt never told you?" she said with a smirk.

"No," Lisa said softly, putting her head down, hating to admit it, and trying not to show that she was hurt. "I had lunch with Dave last week. He told me you have been seeing quite a bit of each other."

"Just dinners and movies. Nothing romantic," Karen snapped.

Lisa felt depressed and lonely most of the summer. She hated the way things were with Karen, whom she saw little of. When Lisa did visit it, was mostly small talk, and Karen no longer asked for Lisa's help at the store. Lisa had frequent dinners with Dave, as did Karen.

She thought two weeks in Florida with her family would help. It didn't. Granted, she did have some fun, but the hole in her heart only grew bigger. As much as she loved her family, the longing for Matt never ceased. She almost felt like she did two years before, when she longed for Sylor.

Every attempt at writing was a half-hearted effort. She wondered if she could ever write again. She didn't seem to care anymore. Not knowing what happened to Sylor after she left with the crystal still haunted her. Maybe Matt would be open to a past-life regression. She remembered the business card Scott had given her the night they met. She found it in her wallet, and read it for the first time. How she wished Scott was here with her.

The third week of August was approaching. Intuitively, she felt Matt was home. It took her a few days to work up the nerve. On this ninety degree day, she felt she looked good wearing a pink, silk tank top tucked into a pair of white very short shorts, with a to-die-for tan. She needed all the confidence she could get, as she nervously walked over to his place.

Her heart skipped a beat when she saw all the blinds open, and the Jag in the driveway. She knocked twice, and almost gave up when he opened the door dressed only in a pair of cut-off jean shorts and a towel around his neck. Traces of shaving cream dotted his face. His nearly hairless chest took her breath away. She remembered she was the one that was scantily clad on their last meeting.

She thought his smile showed that he seemed happy to see her. He wiped the rest of his face. "Come in."

She sat on the edge of the recliner. "How was California?"

"Very nice." He sat on the sofa.

"I've missed you. I wish you would have told me you were leaving. I was worried, I didn't know what happened, and then Karen told me."

"Yeah, Henry said she had stopped by. I'm sorry. I should have said something. I tried to. I walked out that door many times to go see you. After what had happened the last time, I..."

"Are you sorry that it happened?" She held her breath.

After a long pause, one side of his mouth curled up, "No," he took in a deep breath, "which is why this has to end. If I had rented this house instead of owning it, I would have already moved. I'm even considering selling it. Lisa, I don't want to hurt you, but I ask that you don't come here anymore. You and I are never going to be. I want you to accept that. Please. Accept it so we can both get on with our lives."

Lisa's heart sank as she tried fighting back the tears. For the first time, she felt that it was final. It really was over. There was something in his voice.

"Matt, it's not like we're never going to see each other. We both love to walk the beach. We're bound to run into each other."

"We'll take that as it comes, if it comes."

"You don't understand. It will kill me to see you."

"I'm sorry Lisa, but this is the way it has to be." He couldn't tell her that it would kill him, too, to see her.

Lisa walked over to the door. Matt followed. She took something out of her pocket. "This is a business card Scott gave me two years ago. I'm glad I kept it. The man is a psychologist and does hypnotherapy. He specializes in past-life regression. If you decide, well, maybe you'll know whatever happened to Sylor." She put the card in his hand. "But you're right. It's time to get on with our lives. I can't live like this anymore."

She turned to him and touched his face. "I love you, Matt. I won't bother you again."

"Lisa, I'm sor…"

She put her fingers to his lips. She couldn't stand to hear him say 'I'm sorry' one more time. She lightly kissed his mouth, and walked out the door.

He watched her walk up the beach until he could no longer see her. It was for the best he kept telling himself, as a few tears trickled down his face. When he got his bearings, he walked over to the desk and pulled an envelope out of a drawer. He took the letter out and read some of it:

Allow happiness into your life. Do not let what happened in the past waste this life. You have already paid for your mistakes. Stop taking on more than what you need to. There is no one on earth that will love you more than she does. It's your call. Take the risk. Do what you came here to do. No one can cause you more pain than you cause yourself. I love you buddy. May we all be together again one day.

Love,
Scott

Matt wished he could believe Scott. He put the letter down and took a look at the card Lisa had given him. Part of him was afraid to know what had happened after Lisa left. He had a strong feeling it wasn't good, but there was still an urge to know.

When Lisa got home, she pulled out Scott's letter and reread it. She felt like a failure...again. "I'm sorry Scott; I can't do what you've asked. I can't make him want to be with me, and I won't lower myself anymore."

She stuck the letter back in the envelope and picked up the phone. "Hi Dave, I'm sorry to bother you, but I'd like to take you out to dinner Friday night to discuss something with you. I need your help. I'm moving to Florida."

Matt didn't expect to get an appointment so soon with Dr. Clark. It was for Thursday, just two days away. No matter what he learned from the regression, he told himself, he and Lisa would not be together.

Matt was happy that his appointment was first thing in the morning. Had he been forced to wait until later in the day, he was sure he would have canceled it.

He explained his situation to Dr. Clark, and what he wanted to learn. Matt slipped under hypnosis easily. The doctor took him to the point in time where Lisa had fled with the crystal.

"What have you done? What have...how could you? You placed the crystal in her hand! How could..."

"She does not care for you. How could she? She did not believe. I only placed the crystal in her hand. It was her choice to flee."

"She will never be able to return, it is because of you!"

Sylor stood motionless, looking through Jenielle. He clenched his fist as his face became flushed.

"She chose to never return. It is I who cares for you. We may now be together."

Sylor watched, as Jenielle slowly removed her gown, never taking her eyes off his. She walked over to him and stood before him, naked. The anger that burned inside him was overwhelming. With his fist still clenched, he eyed her up and down. He knew what she wanted, and he hated himself for what he wanted to do. His life was over, and he needed to lash out at someone, something. He didn't see her as a woman, a person, or a human being. He only saw her as a focus for his anger.

He grabbed her by the shoulders and threw her down on the bed. He pushed his mouth down hard on hers, as he held her arms above her head. He wanted her to fight him. He was waiting for her to fight him.

"I have longed for this day," Jenielle broke the hold Sylor had on her, and she violently shoved his face between her breasts. She threw her head back and laughed. "If only Hollina could witness you at this moment."

Sylor stopped. Those words cut through his soul. He could never bear for Hollina to see him in this state.

"Get out!" He threw her from the bed. "Get out! You will not rob my soul. Hollina is the only woman I will give myself to in any way. You are not fit to love."

"I have waited much time for us to be together. You wanted me."

"Don't insult me! Get out!"

He watched, as she gathered her clothes with tears streaming down her face. Sylor learned she had left Atlantis that very day. He never saw her again.

Dr. Clark moved him forward in time. Sylor has been imprisoned by the other scientists in a cave up on a mountain. He is in an ill and weakened state. The scientists have tortured him because he refuses to reveal the codes in the journals. Every day one of the scientists would come and offer him food in exchange for the codes. Sylor will not reveal the codes, ever.

As he lay dying in the cave, he begins to hallucinate, seeing Hollina. "Hollina, I am so alone. I am cold, I am hungry, and there is no love. They torture me daily, and yet I still live. They will not kill me.

How I wish they would. One day they will decipher the codes. They will receive no help from me. I will take it to my death. You were correct. You knew. For this, how can I both love you and hate you?" Hollina fades from his sight. "Yes Hollina, abandon me once more. You have become quite adept at this. Never again will I allow you to control my heart! Never! Never!"

Matt's face is reddened, and he is sweating as he is brought back up. The doctor would like him to come back for another session to deal with the anger he feels towards Hollina. Matt didn't think he would. He would work it out on his own, he lied to himself.

At home, Matt took a shower and put on shorts and a t-shirt. He turned up the air conditioner and plunked himself on the sofa, feeling drained from the session. He was relieved that he had never revealed the codes. At least he knew he did one good thing. He thought of Jenielle and sat straight up. How could he have been so cruel? She had been a lost soul looking for someone to love her. He now felt the compassion he should have felt then.

He thought of Hollina and sat back. He didn't want to be angry with her. Deep down he knew the only one he could be angry with was himself, but it didn't change his feelings. It didn't change anything. He and Lisa would not be together. End of story.

He pulled out Scott's letter and reread it. **'Do what you came here to do'** stood out in his mind. How could he be so in love with Lisa? He would give his life *for* her, but he wouldn't give it *to* her. But then whose thinking was this; Matt's or Sylor's?

Matt was drifting off to sleep when he heard someone knocking. Part of him hoped it would be Lisa, but how could that be? She was done with him now, he was sure of it. How much more of his rejection could she take?

"Hi Matt, how was California?"

"Good." He motioned for Karen to come in.

"Are you okay? You look tired."

"I'm fine."

"It's been a while since we last talked. I was wondering if...well, would you like go to dinner tomorrow night?"

At first Matt wanted to say no. He remembered the regression, and his feelings softened as the guilt kicked in. What would be the harm? It was only dinner. He would go.

Matt wondered if he had done the right thing. He felt tense, and ordered a second glass of wine while he and Karen waited in the lounge. It wasn't until they were seated and had placed their orders, did he finally relax. He noticed Karen seemed nervous, as she kept checking her watch and looking at the door.

Suddenly, Karen placed her hand on Matt's and leaned closer to him. "I'm glad you accepted my invitation, it means a lot to me. I've been attracted to you since I first met you."

Matt could only smile, and again he thought back to the regression, and how Jenielle wanted him. She surprised him by moving in even closer. She began to kiss him on the lips. He wasn't sure what to do. He didn't want to hurt or embarrass her, so he allowed the kiss.

When Karen finished, Matt cleared his throat, wanting to say something. He sensed a presence near him. His stomach flipped and the blood drained from his face when he looked upon a goddess standing before him. Her creamed colored, silk tank dress stood out against her bronzed skin. Her hair was worn up in a twist, while tendrils hung, teasing her cheeks. But the goddess wasn't smiling, and who was that guy she was with?

Karen quickly introduced Matt to Dave. Before anything else could be said, Lisa forcefully communicated that the hostess was waiting to seat them. Matt sat on the edge of his chair. He wasn't sure whether or not to run into the other room, where he was grateful Lisa had been seated, and explain to her what she had just witnessed. It didn't matter, he thought. She obviously had gotten over him real quick. She was already with someone else. Tension was pulling his chest, and he felt a lump in his throat. He felt like he was back in high school.

"Who was that?" Matt asked, trying to remain calm and composed.

"Oh, Dave? He's her ex."

"Are they getting back together?"

"No. They're most likely here to discuss the move."

"What move? What are you talking about?" Matt felt anxious.

"Oh, you didn't know?"

"Know what?" Matt said impatiently.

"Lisa's moving to Florida. She plans on selling the house, so Dave's going to take care of it for her."

Matt felt a sense of panic. "When? When is she moving?"

"In about two weeks, I think."

He sat back and relaxed. It would be for the best, he tried to convince himself. He gulped down his third glass of wine, and ordered another. "I hope you don't mind driving."

"I've never driven a Jag before. I love it." She pulled into her driveway, and shut off the engine. She turned to Matt, who was staring out the window in the opposite direction. He felt so far away. What the hell was his life about?

"Hel...lo," she said softly.

He turned to her, and smiled slightly. She reached for him and began to kiss him deeply. He didn't pull away, but he didn't put anything into it either.

"Come on, let's go in," she whispered.

"I don't think I'm in any condition to meet your mother."

"Mother is over-nighting it with a slot machine in Connecticut."

Karen poured herself a glass of wine, while Matt opted for bottled water. She took his hand, and walked him upstairs to her bedroom. He felt like he was in another world. She lit some candles, while he toyed with some of the crystals she had on her dresser.

She walked up in back of him, and placed her arms around him. He turned to her and gazed at her face. She was very pretty. Any man would want her, he thought. Right here, right now. And he was a man, and it had been a long time since Diana.

She guided him to the edge of the bed where they sat. She put her arms around his neck and began kissing him. She lay back on the bed, taking him with her.

He placed himself on top of her. He was sure she could feel the natural reflex any man would have being in his position. He kissed her long and deep, but in his mind it *was not* Karen he was kissing. In his mind he saw the hurt look on Lisa's face at the restaurant. If she didn't hate him already, she would now.

As he kissed Karen, he wanted Lisa more than ever, but none of it mattered. Lisa was moving, it was done. If she wrote the sequel to *Return to Atlantis* the readers would hate this, he was sure.

This wasn't right, he thought. This wasn't fair. This would be the meaningless sex he thought so little of. But would he be crazy not to? It had been so long. He felt as if he had an angel on one shoulder and a devil on the other. What should he do?

Karen's hand made its way down the side of his leg and up around his inner thigh. She moved her hand very slowly, teasingly. He made his decision.

"I can't do this!" He pulled himself from her clutches.

"What?" She turned on the light. She was red faced and teary eyed. "Why, Matt? I have wanted you from the very first day I met you."

"I'm sorry, Karen." He turned away.

"Don't you look away from me! Tell me why!"

He still couldn't look at her.

"It's Lisa, isn't it? I saw your reaction at the restaurant. It is because of her, isn't it? Damn it, answer me!"

He turned and looked right into her eyes. "Yes. I love her." There, he had said it; for the first time, out loud, and to another person.

"She's moving to Florida, Matt. Or are you going to try and stop her?"

"No."

"Then make love to me. I know you wanted me." She started to unbutton her blouse.

"Karen, you're a beautiful woman, and looking at you right now, any man would want you. But I'm not any man. I don't know if I can ever make love to anyone else again."

"That's crazy!"

"I'm sorry I hurt you. I've got to go."

A sense of relief had come over him when he turned on the engine and started down the road. He had done the right thing. His conscience was clear. He didn't have sex, but he had a clear conscience. He started to laugh; as if he could run to Lisa and say, 'Look what I didn't do.' Needles picked at his heart. He didn't know what to do with his feelings. He was being eaten up inside. What would he do with his life? He could get serious about writing the book. He had put some notes away. No, he wasn't ready. He didn't know what he wanted. He didn't know anything.

Matt pulled over to the side of the road. He hugged the steering wheel, and cried like he never had before.

Lisa, too, cried as she lay in bed listening to Beethoven's Moonlight Sonata. After Dave brought her home, she jumped in her car and drove by Karen's. She saw Matt's car in the driveway, and the glow of candlelight in Karen's bedroom window. She decided she would not wait two weeks to go to Florida. She would leave the day after tomorrow.

Matt lay in bed thinking how stupid he had been to accept Karen's invitation. But then, he never would have found out about Lisa moving. He had driven her to it, he just knew it. Could he really let her walk out of his life again?

He had a choice. Yes, he had free will. He could pour out his heart, and beg her to stay. Or he could just say good-bye. He had to see her one last time and say good-bye. If…he could bring himself to do it. Either way, he had two weeks to get his thoughts together.

Chapter 17

———

Lisa inhaled the rose scented oil she had poured into her bath. She settled back and relaxed from a long day of packing. Since there was so little room in the 'vette', Dave would send the rest of her things as she requested. As far as the furniture, she decided it could be part of the sale of the house, or Dave could take whatever he wanted.

She took a sip of wine and blinked back the tears. There was a part of her that wanted to die. She knew she was running away again, and she could understand why Hollina did what she had, even if it wasn't in her best interest. Oh, the joy of free will, or was it? At least this time she was just going to a 'far away land.' If Matt ever changed his mind, at least he could find her, assuming Karen tells him.

Even if he did change his mind, what he had done with Karen would always be there. As much as she loved him, she now saw him in a different light.

She raised her glass. "You did it, Karen. You got what you wanted. Congratulations!" She gulped down the rest of the wine, wishing she had bought champagne instead. That one would keep for Florida, where she would celebrate her new life.

It had been the hottest day so far that summer, and the gentle ocean breeze felt good against Matt's bare arms. He felt the need to get out and walk. And think. He appreciated the beauty of the full moon reflecting off the water as he made his way to the east side. He could understand why Lisa liked it there so much. He felt protected in the nook that surrounded him. He no longer feared its cave-like appearance.

He leaned back against the cool stone, and began thinking about Scott. He missed him so much. "All right Scott, what's happens now? I love her. You know that. And I still can't bring myself to tell her. I still can't bring myself to do what I supposedly came here to do. Aren't there any guarantees? The thought of going back and doing it all over...to possibly make the same mistakes...to lose her again...I can't do it. I will never again let another person have that kind of emotional control over me.

Okay, Scott. I still have almost two weeks to say good-bye, if it is to be good-bye. Give me a sign, Scott. Please give some kind of sign that Lisa and I should be together, and that we can do what we came together to do. Please give a sign."

Matt waited for a while. Did he really expect Scott to appear before him; or for the ocean to part? He laid his head back to ponder a little longer.

The scent of the rose oil had permeated her skin and the air around her. She dried her hair and walked over to the window. She felt it was such a beautiful night, with the full moon and all. She was sad she hadn't taken a walk that day. She had been so busy she hadn't even thought about it. It was too late now.

She lay on her bed, bathing in the rays of the moon coming through the skylights above her. She began to think of Scott. She remembered the day she and Scott took a walk on the beach, the last time she would ever see him, and how he said he would love to take a walk out there on the night of a full moon. He never had the chance.

The hair on her arms stood up. A warm loving feeling brushed through her. "Scott, it's you, I can feel it. Oh God, I can feel you!" She stood up, wiped the tears, and walked over to the window again. "I'm scared, Scott, but I know you are with me. I will take that walk. I will take it for *you*. I love you, Scott."

All her clothes were packed away. Only a few dresses remained which she had no intention of taking. She remembered a dress she had bought about three years before, and then ran to the closet. At the time she had no idea why she had bought it. She thought it was pretty, but it wasn't her style.

She pulled it out. The tags were still on it. A chill ran through her. She had purchased it subconsciously. The dress was similar to the one Hollina wore the morning she entered the cave. It was made of layers of sheer white material with long sleeves and a flowing skirt, only it had pearly white buttons running down the center. She slipped it on. Though she had never tried it on before, it fit perfectly.

She apprehensively made her way down to the beach, but she trusted she would be safe. As she stood at the ocean's edge under the full moon, she found it very easy to envision that she was in another time and place. She could imagine it. She could feel Atlantis within her, and how she missed the great land.

Matt emerged from the rocks minus the sign he had hoped to receive. The cool air was now giving him goose bumps, and he proceeded with a jog to warm himself. His jog became a slow walk when he thought he saw someone up ahead. "What the hell?" He stopped completely when he came closer.

In the brilliance of the moonlight a figure in a long dress, flowing with the direction of the wind, took his breath. This was too familiar. He had seen this very image before. It flashed in his mind with the feeling of longing and despair. He began to feel light-headed as he questioned whether he had traveled through a time warp. It all came back to him. He was Sylor, watching Hollina the morning of her transition. Except for the full moon and the lack of mountains, the scene was the same, and now he had remembered it in the novel.

He raked his hands through his hair. Was he imagining this, or...was this ghostly image of Hollina a sign from Scott? He began walking again, following. As he was getting closer he started walking faster. He saw the long blonde hair, and she was beginning to look pretty solid. He moved in closer. She quickly turned around.

"Matt! Oh my God, thank God it's you. I thought..." She nearly put her hand through her chest trying to catch her breath. "What are you doing out here at this time?"

"*Me*? What are *you* doing out here?"

"I wanted to come out here one last time. You must have heard I'm moving to Florida."

"I did, but that isn't for a couple of weeks."

"No. I'm leaving tomorrow."

Matt stopped breathing. It was the last thing he expected to hear. "Why tomorrow?"

"The sooner, the better." She firmly told herself she would maintain control of her emotions. He would never see a tear. She rubbed her arms. "It's getting chilly out here. I'll be on my way. Look I...I didn't expect to see you before I left. I'm sorry for both of us things didn't turn out the way they were supposed to, but there will be other lives."

"I'm sorry, too. Lisa, I am really sorry."

She moved in closer to him, and smiled. "You know, Matt, nothing can really separate us. We truly are connected. 'Two embodiments connected by one soul, one heart, cannot forever be separated.' Sylor said those words, remember?"

Matt nodded with a sad smile.

She touched his face. "I love you. Good-bye, Matt." She turned quickly so he wouldn't see the tears that were beginning to form.

He said nothing and watched her walk away. So many thoughts, so many voices flooded his mind. He knew if he ever changed his mind he could find her. But would she have a whole new life by then with someone else? She may have loved him like no other, but she was still human. There would always be room to love another, even if he felt he could not.

He stood paralyzed. He felt Sylor clearly was stopping him from going after her. The vision of the morning she entered the cave appeared over and over. Could he again let her walk out of his life? He remembered Dreedon's words to go to her before it was too late.

"No...No." He broke free of Sylor, the voice he had listened to all along, and listened to his heart. "Lisa, no!" He ran up behind her. She turned around. He placed his hands firmly on her shoulders, looking at her tear streaked face, "Please don't go. I can't lose you again."

She didn't believe what she was hearing. This couldn't be. She turned and proceeded to walk away. She didn't want to be played with.

This time it was Matt that grabbed her arm and swung her around to him. "Please don't leave me. Lisa, I love you. I don't ever want to lose you again. I want to spend my life with you. Here or Atlantis. I don't care. I love you."

Her mouth quivered, tears spilled, and her whole body shook as he held her face. "Matt, I know you slept with Karen last night. How can you expect…"

"No! I didn't! Nothing happened!"

"Matt, I'm not an idiot. I drove by her house last night. Your car was there, I saw the candlelight glow from her bedroom window. I *know* what that means."

"Yes, I was there, she lit candles, but nothing happened. I wouldn't let it. All I could think about was making love to *you*. I couldn't do it because I love *you*, and I told her that."

"You told Karen you love me?"

"Yes. I love you, Lisa. I have all along. I fought it right from the beginning. I knew I loved you before I saw you at the book signing. I couldn't face it."

She threw her arms around him and they held each other for a moment. He then pulled back and ran his hands through her hair, finally cupping her face. He tenderly brought his lips to hers, kissing her with a gentle passion. She let herself go into it, hugging his body, swallowing him.

They inched their way to the ground. He lightly kissed her hair, her face, and her neck. He unfastened the top button of her dress, and continued with the rest of the buttons kissing each area as it became unveiled.

Her body trembled in anticipation of what was to come. She was ready and willing to receive any and all of what he was willing to give. He delicately opened up both sides of her dress exposing her. She rejoiced as he moved his mouth over every inch of her.

She opened her eyes and looked at his face and the beautiful soul behind it, knowing too that she was looking into herself. Her body reached up so to kiss his mouth, savoring, devouring, taking in his energy, giving her life as she gave him life.

When she was ready he eased his way into her, and she reached to receive him. They moved into each other until they were breathing as one. The pregnant moon took them, engulfed them, and bore them new life. The silvery orb took them over and over again. She swore she could hear the strains of Beethoven. That vision was later realized when they bathed in the moonlit rays over her bed, making love to Moonlight Sonata.

They both knew they would never be the same again. With accepting and receiving her love, Matt knew he could go back to Atlantis.

It was after 4:00 a.m. They took a walk on the beach, heading to the rocks on the east side. For the first time in his life Matt wanted to see the sunrise. They watched silently, meditating, wrapped in each others arms. They stayed that way for a long while, each afraid to move, to break the connection, though they both knew the connection could never be broken.

He kissed her hair. She looked up at him and saw how different he looked. Calm, serene, the sadness in his eyes was gone. He was smiling, really smiling.

"How do you feel?" she asked.

He searched her eyes seeing something beyond the both of them, and let out a sigh. "Reborn. Last night, when I told you I loved you and committed to you, it felt like the dark cloud that has been hanging over me my entire life had dissolved. I feel as if this light is coming into my body and filling me up. What about you? How do you feel?"

"Like singing, 'Ode to Joy,'" she laughed.

Matt laughed too. "I love you."

"You have no idea what it means to me to hear you say those words."

"I think I do." He kissed her, "How about if I make us some breakfast?"

"Oh wonderful, a man who cooks."

"I'm going to use your phone. I've got to call Dave. He was supposed to come by and see me off this morning."

Matt put his arms around her. "Then you are not leaving? I just need to hear it."

She smiled and made her call. "I will never leave you again… ever." She kissed him with the intent of some further satisfaction. He picked her up and carried her into his bedroom.

When she woke up it was almost 12:30 P.M. It was wonderful to feel a warm body wrapped around hers. She moved her arm and the next thing she felt was a mouth on her neck. She turned to face him, "So much for breakfast."

"I promised you breakfast, you'll get breakfast."

"God Matt, how can you eat that stuff? It even smells gross."

"Didn't you ever eat it when you were a kid?" he asked, taking a bite out of his toasted peanut butter and banana sandwich.

"Yeah, once! But I will say this is the best damn omelet I've ever had."

"Enjoy it now. When we're back in Atlantis it may be nothing but fruits and flowers." Matt chuckled.

"Oh yes, fruits and flowers. There's no place like home. Which reminds me, I suppose we'll get some kind of sign on what we're to do and when. I have a strong feeling Dreedon will make his presence known to us with some kind of instruction."

"This is making me nervous already. What if we can't cut it? What if we fail Atlantis again?"

"We won't. We didn't go through everything we have in order to fail. We have to envision it and believe. We'll see it when we believe it. Not the other way around. But first, and most we have to forgive ourselves for what we think we did or didn't do. True forgiveness heals all time. Forgiveness is the key to all healing.

We have to forgive every negative thing we encounter. We have to look at the people of the north and forgive them. If we create our own reality on some level; then we created them...we made them up, even if we don't understand why. We are all connected by Source including them. We have to see them for what they really are; spirit...whole and innocent. Underneath our ego, that is what we *all* are. I'm not saying it's easy; it's just what it is. I'm sure we'll understand it better once we go back."

"Do you mind if I look through these?" Lisa asked, finding a small box of photographs which Matt hadn't gotten around to organizing.

"Sure. Some of them are ghastly. I had weird hair."

Lisa dug in and pulled out a handful, and gasped seeing the picture that was directly on top of the pile.

"Oh my God, Matt, who is this woman?"

Sadly, he said, "My mother, why, what's the matter?"

She flipped through more of the pictures coming to another that made the blood drain from her face. "This little boy...it's you, isn't it?"

"I was probably four or five at the time. That was my mother's favorite picture of me. What's going on?"

Lisa held on to the two pictures and threw the rest back in the box. She grabbed Matt's hand. "Come on, we're going back to my house. I have to show you something. You're not going to believe this."

He followed her upstairs, and watched in amusement as she tore apart the hall closet. She took out a big old scrapbook.

"I think you better sit down." They went into the bedroom, and sat on the bed. "Before I show you this I should tell you something. When I was about four or five I started making up stories. I knew I wanted to be a writer. The very first character I made up was a little boy. I saw him very clearly in my mind. He had blonde hair and sad blue eyes. I named him Jeff. I loved him so much."

Matt put his arm around her and toyed with her hair as he listened.

"Sometimes I would draw pictures to go with the stories, and one day I decided I would draw a picture of this boy. I was only five, and became very frustrated that I couldn't draw this picture the way I saw him in my mind. I had given up and was crying when all of a sudden a light filled the room and there was a woman standing there. She came over behind me and put her hand over mine, and together we drew Jeff. Then she disappeared." Lisa wiped her eyes. "Matt, as God as my witness, that woman was your mother."

Matt gave Lisa a doubting look at first. She opened up the scrapbook. Matt's jaw dropped when he saw the drawing, and even more so upon recognizing his mother's initials; K.F.

"Matt, are you okay?" She rubbed his back.

"My mother was an artist. She signed all her work K.F. She always used her middle name, Katherine. Her first name was Mary."

"I didn't even remember there being any initials on this drawing. My God it really was your mother. Wait! We wrote something on the back. I've never remembered what it was." She turned it over;

Dear Jeff,

If you are reading this, then you remembered your promise and you are where you are supposed to be. Be happy with your new life, and know that anything is possible. And Jeff, the flower gardens are beautiful. I love you.

He put his face in his hands and broke down. Lisa held him, and cried with him, though not fully understanding.

"All these years, I've waited for, I..."

"I don't understand. I know the drawing is of you, but who's Jeff?"

"I am. Jefferson is my first name, Matthew is my middle."

"Jefferson Matthew Fields...Jeff...my God. What is this about flower gardens?"

"My mother believed in an afterlife. She used to talk about there being flower gardens on the other side. On her deathbed she promised she would let me know this...that somehow she would communicate this to me. She said I would know through the one who was my true love. She promised this, but it never happened, and she told me I must remember *my* promise. I never understood any of it. But all these years a part of me has waited for *her* promise. She had kept it."

"Wow, this is unbelievable, but after everything..."

"Lisa, I know this sounds crazy, but I received a letter from Scott after his death. He told me there was no one on earth that would love me as much as you do." Matt wiped his eyes.

"It's not crazy. I got a letter, too. He told me not to give up on you. And I did."

"I drove you to it."

"You didn't make it easy." She laughed, and held up the drawing. "I had this taped to the wall near my bed up until my senior year of high school. Over the years my parents tried many times to make me take it down. I guess it was the equivalent of having an imaginary friend."

"Why did you take it down…a boyfriend?"

"No one could have made me take it down. I wrote many stories throughout the years growing up, and 'Jeff' was in all of them. He had a life of his own. I had him growing up as I was growing up. Then something happened. It all sounds absurd, but he rebelled. I had no control over him, I can't explain it. I didn't know what to do with him, and it hurt. I took it personally, so I gave up and blocked him out, and then found a boyfriend in human form."

"When you were a senior I was a freshman in college. That was around the time I had changed. I had become very rebellious. I had been pressured to go to college. It wasn't that I didn't want to go; I just didn't want to be told I had to go. I started hanging out with a bad crowd, hated authority…no one could tell me what to do. That was when I started using my middle name. It's all fits with 'Jeff's' rebellion."

"Looks like there will be another name change soon, Sylor." She grinned. "Yesterday I thought I was leaving you forever, and now I know I'll *be* with you forever."

"And you think this is a good thing?" Matt snickered.

"Yes," she pointed to the drawing, "because you are all I have ever wanted my whole life."

"Matt, Matt, wake up!"

He jumped up, "What's the matter, did you have a bad dream? Are you all right?"

"It was a good dream. No, actually it wasn't a dream. I was out of my body. Dreedon came to me, and there were all these other beings, men and women, all dressed in white robes. It was beautiful. Everything was all aglow with brilliant white light. They are going to help us. They are going to help us get back to Atlantis."

"How…how are we going to get back there?"

"On the eve of the equinox we are to go down to the beach, that's all I know."

"Christ, this is really going to happen isn't it?" Matt rubbed his forehead.

"Matt, it's okay, we are in good hands. Please trust me on that."

"I want to. I do. This is all just too surreal…like it's all just a big crazy dream. It's not enough that we are going back to Atlantis, and *how* we're going to get back there, but it's just when we do get back there…I'm still afraid history will repeat itself."

"Well, that's the chance we have to take. But we have to try. It's our responsibility, and we have the knowledge."

"But what if we don't do it? What will happen with us *this* time?"

"I honestly don't know. Maybe we will end up right where we are now. Maybe we've done this before, too. Maybe we have to keep doing things over and over, until we get it. We get as many chances as we need. Ever see the movie *Groundhog Day?* But what we need most to remember is that *forgiveness changes the course of everything*."

The next three weeks they spent just loving and enjoying each other. But as time got closer Matt was getting nervous.

"Matt, please calm down. God, you can't even eat."

"We're leaving in three days. How can you be so relaxed?"

"Maybe, because I like a great adventure…kind of like jumping out of a plane. You never know if you're going to make it."

"I think you have a death wish."

She laughed. "And speaking of a death wish, there is something I have to do before we leave."

"Hi, Karen," Lisa said softly as she walked into the store. They had not spoken since the night at the restaurant.

Lisa saw the tears in Karen's eyes.

"I heard you and Matt were together. I've wanted to call you. I was so afraid you would never speak to me again." Karen wiped her eyes. "Lisa I am so sorry for everything. That night when Matt told me he loved you, and that he could never make love to another woman...I...well, everything changed. I was wrong. You and Matt are one soul. You belong together. I read your book. I hadn't read it, you know. I'm Jenielle, aren't I?"

Lisa put her arms around Karen and embraced her, letting the tears flow. "Karen, you will always be my sister. I love you."

"You forgive me?"

"In my eyes you didn't do anything...there's nothing to forgive. We are a part of each other, like soul mates. Besides, in life you have to forgive in order to move on. If you don't, you stay stuck and only hurt yourself...only create more karma to deal with. I've had enough of karma, bad karma that is. It's time for some good karma."

"I wish I could tell Jenielle how wrong she was, and how things might be different if she changed her attitude...got her ego out of the way and how she needs to forgive herself."

"You can. Tell her in a meditation, talk to her...*forgive* her. It may totally change her future...*your* future."

"You're going to be leaving soon, aren't you? You're going back to Atlantis."

"Matt and I leave in a couple of days. Dave is taking Charcoal, believe it or not."

"How will you get back?"

"I'm not entirely sure, but I do have an idea, I...I really can't say."

"I'm never going to see you again."

Lisa wiped Karen's tears. "If Hollina and Sylor accomplish their mission it will change history, it will change everything. Most likely I would not have reincarnated, at least into this life. Actually, I think if Hollina and Sylor do what they're supposed to do, they would never have to come into another physical lifetime, so we would never know each other. You would never know I ever existed, as myself anyway, the person who I am now."

"That's a lot to take in. Before you go I do have some good news. I hope you can be happy for me, for us."

"Us?"

"Dave, and me. All those years ago, when I moved to South Carolina because of the baby, well...I never had a miscarriage. I had the baby and gave it up for adoption."

"Oh my God, I never knew!"

"No one knew, except my aunt, not even my mother who now is so thrilled she is a grandmother. Of course Dave never knew, until now."

"How did he react?"

"He's so happy. We've been trying to find her, and we're close."

"You have a daughter," Lisa said choking up, and then threw her arms around Karen. "I am so happy for you, both of you. I hope you find her."

"Lisa, could you tell Matt how sorry I am about everything. I feel like such a jerk. Please tell him I'm sorry. I really mean it."

"I will, and he'll understand."

"I guess this is goodbye."

Lisa and Karen embraced for the last time.

"This is just too weird for me. Are you sure this is what we're supposed to do?" Matt said as they walked from Lisa's house down to the beach."

"This is what Dreedon instructed in the dream." Lisa and Matt both turned and looked back at the beach house for one last time. "If we do what were supposed to do in Atlantis then none of this will have ever happened. It would be like this had all been a dream."

They held hands and stood near the edge of the water, waiting. Matt turned to Lisa, "When we get back to Atlantis...how is this going to work? Are we going to start out as children again? Will we be the same as we are now, and just somehow…?"

"Wait," Lisa thought for a moment. "I think I know. Yes! We are going to come in at the marriage of Hollina and Sylor. That was when I saw this vortex, and a man and woman whom I felt were part of me. I always wondered what that was about, and who they were. My God, it was us!"

"Oh boy," Matt shook his head. "This is…" Before Matt could finish his sentence it felt like the ground beneath them was starting to shake. About one hundred feet out in the ocean there looked to be a whirlpool forming. They held each other and watched in total awe as a giant pyramid rose out of the water like in the vision Lisa had that one day on the beach.

"My God, look, the apex is glowing! This is so other-worldly. Look at the apex against the night sky, and the stars. It takes your breath away."

Matt again shook his head. "This is too much."

The next thing they saw was a ball of light coming towards them. This light formed a walk-way from the entrance of the pyramid to where they were standing. They stepped on to this walk-way of light. "This can't be possible," Matt said in disbelief.

Lisa laughed. "Matt, if you can't believe this then how do you expect to get back to Atlantis?"

"I'm still dealing with that one. No wonder you thought you were losing your sanity!"

As they walked closer to the entrance they could see what looked to be a huge white flame inside the pyramid. They both stood at the entrance, speechless, and then stepped inside the pyramid and to where they were about twelve feet away from the flame.

"What is this? What's going on?" Matt swallowed hard, eyeing the brilliance of what he still couldn't believe he was seeing.

"*That* is how we are going back to Atlantis." Lisa smiled.

"What do you mean?" Matt dreaded the answer.

"The flame; it's a vortex. We have to jump into it."

"I don't think so." Matt turned around to exit the pyramid only to find there was no opening anymore. "Where's H.G. Wells when you need him?" he mumbled.

"There is only one way out now. There is nothing to fear. The flame will not burn. "Do you feel any heat from it?"

Before Matt could answer they were hearing a low humming sound, and many white robed beings began surrounding them.

"Matt, look at the faces of these beautiful beings. Again, there is nothing to fear."

"My mother, it's my mother. She's one of them."

"Oh my God…my aunt Bella."

"Scott!" They shrieked in unison.

The flame started to spin creating the vortex.

"Is this a dream?" Matt asked.

Lisa sang "Merrily, merrily, merrily, merrily, life is but a dream."

"Are you ready, Matt? This is it. They're waiting."

"We can do this," Matt said with confidence. Lisa turned to Matt and nodded her head, "We can do this."

She then turned to Matt taking his hands. "I love you."

He saw her nervousness for the first time. He held her face and kissed her. "I love you."

"Take my hand, Matt. Are you ready?"

"Ready."

And they jumped....

Epilogue

———

"Dave, I love this land, I love this place," Karen said to her husband, "and the waterfalls are like nothing I have ever seen before in my life! At one point, I thought I had wanted to move to Europe, but now… I'm so sorry we have not vacationed here sooner. This really *is* paradise." Karen lovingly placed her arms around their two young daughters, who were trying to get their parents to come and look at a statue.

"You're the one who kept putting it off," Dave said chuckling. "This museum is fantastic! I think my favorite thing so far is 'The Capsule.' I mean, who wouldn't want to walk into a giant crystal pyramid and travel to other times, or other dimensions. Too bad we can't do that anymore, too bad we screwed up. Although, according to our history books, it could have been a lot worse!" he added, as daughter Kyla ran over to him and began pulling his arm to come over to the statue. Daughter Mari joined in as well, pulling on her mother's arm. No sooner had their parents come upon the statue; the girls were distracted by the next exhibit and ran off.

"*This* is giving me goose bumps," Karen said, as she rubbed her arms. Dave stood behind her, and placed his arms around his wife's waist.

"Eerie isn't it, for some reason," Dave added.

"Yeah, I…I almost feel like I knew them. Like maybe I…well, I've never really believed in past lives, but…" Karen wiped the tear that trickled down her face.

Encased in glass was a life-size statue set high off of the floor on a marble platform. The statue was of a man and woman with the sides of their bodies joined together. They each had an outstretched arm coming together with one hand. The hand was holding a glowing crystal ball.

Karen had no idea why she was starting to cry. "The name-plate says, 'Hollina and Sylor,' and there's an inscription."

The inscription read:

It is said Hollina and Sylor traveled into the future, but would not reveal their findings. Legend has it they helped save Atlantis from a dreadful fate. Those who told the tale have erected this statue in honor and gratitude to the beloved twin flames.

Hail Atlantis!

www.ingramcontent.com/pod-product-compliance
Lightning Source LLC
Chambersburg PA
CBHW050014180626
46810CB00002B/416